MW01593283

X119542744　　　　WITHDRAWN　　BOL

DALLAS PUBLIC LIBRARY

MERIDEN

BOOK THREE OF TINDER & FLINT

By
Matthew Hinsley

Art by
Billy Garretsen

EnvisionARTS

Austin

This is a work of fiction. Names, characters, places, and incidents are the products of the author's imagination, or are used fictitiously. Any resemblance to actual persons, living or dead, is entirely coincidental.

First EnvisionArts Paperback Edition, September 2018

Copyright © 2018 by Matthew Hinsley

Dormarion excerpt Copyright © 2018 by Matthew Hinsley

Art by Billy Garretsen Copyright © 2018 EnvisionArts LLC

All rights reserved. No part of this publication may be reproduced, distributed, or transmitted without the express consent of the author.

Cover Design by Billy Garretsen

Author Photo by Victoria Enders

Artist Photo by John Gibson

Published by EnvisionArts, LLC.

ISBN 978-1-387-91550-7

www.tinderandflintbooks.com

For Miguel

Thank you Joe Williams II and Quentin Lucas, our adventure continues in new and exciting ways! Thank you Joseph Palmer and Nicole Kirksey, let's always be the last to leave. So excited for the new chapter, Travis Marcum and Amelia Devivo, and I'm not just talking about the new arrival in this book! Thank you Glenda Lee, my hero.

My profoundest thanks to my patient, supportive, insightful, and meticulous editors Rebecca Snedden, Robert Knapp, and Glenda Lee.

Billy Garretsen: Yes, yes, yes. Building this thing with you is like a dream come true. Pumped about our big plans, and the road ahead.

Contents

PART ONE

Many more months would pass before Leopold's bony black silhouette slipped past those very same bars leaving behind only frost made by the complete and utter absence of good.

Chapter One
LEOPOLD

---

27 years ago...

It was not the first time his skin had been pierced with a blade.

Even through his drunken stupor and the haze of semi-consciousness he could sense the cowardly nature of the thrust. The tip pushed lamely against his skin at first, like a child testing chill in the water with his toe, before plunging in.

But plunge it did.

Once it entered his abdomen it moved more swiftly through his guts. It bit dully into his spine, before, with a shove, it altered course and found the path of least resistance out his back.

Chapter One

The painful acid warmth mixed and sloshed inside him, chasing the blade's path like hounds on a traitor's trail. The pungent smells of wine and bile engulfed him.

He was dying quickly. His life was dribbling out behind him in spurts. His strength was already leaving him. He had only enough left for one last look.

He wrenched open his left eye.

She was laughing. Candlelight flickered in her eyes as if the flames themselves were burning inside. Bertrand Ingroff, already bent to her will, heaved awkwardly against the hilt of the blade, like it was a shovel that's struck a root in the earth. Carlton lingered warily behind them, jug of wine in hand, with a nervous look as though he would be having a really good time so long as the man on the other end of his brother's blade died quickly and did not make too much of a mess.

A benefit of dying is the deadening of physical sensation. The agony was fading like a moon that has yet to leave the sky though the sun has risen. Leopold's body was convulsing involuntarily, further depleting itself of precious fluids.

But none of that mattered anymore. All that mattered was Estela. The pain wracking his body was nothing next to the flaying of his spirit by her treachery. Her laughter wrapped around the boy's cold steel like snakes of molten ore. Her deceit exploded like white-hot needles inside him, swimming through every inch of him, punishing him mercilessly with the burning wrath of her vengeance.

Leopold's eye shuddered and drooped closed.

He would never breathe again. His heart stopped beating forever.

But the *Southern Sorcerer* did not cease to exist.

The bastards celebrated that night. They celebrated in front of him as only drunken boys and girls will do. And they laughed. She laughed. At him.

There was something he clung to that night. Anyone else would have given in to death completely, would have passed meekly into the shadow. But there was something too important for Leopold to let go. He wanted it fiercely with all his being, and so he desperately flung his magic out into the black void of his extinguishing mind to capture it. And by some miracle, aided by a mysterious flicker of red-hot power, his erratic lines of magic strained and hooked into something solid.

Even as his body cooled, his consciousness clutched his prize like a raft at sea. As Estela and Carlton and Bertrand reveled long into the night, feeding him with the sounds and smells of their ecstasy, he shivered atop it like a rat on debris from a wrecked ship. Ever so slowly it grew in him, and he in it, long after they carried him into the bowels of Ingroff Castle and cast his sunken old body onto the decaying pile of their many other victims.

The thing he held onto was hatred.

Leopold willed himself to subsist on earth for hatred alone.

Several years passed before Leopold had another coherent thought. His flesh had putrefied and sloughed away, feeding the many slithering things that bred in the growing tortured pile made of the Ingroff brothers' tragic conceit.

Hatred echoed faintly in the corpses of the fallen all around him. Hate for the wrongful persecution of their brothers and sisters and parents and children. There were other things too, valor and love and passion and conviction, but these things were of no interest to Leopold's new creeping existence.

His consciousness reawakened and clawed its way out of the black muck of his mind the day Carlton was killed. The death was too swift for the spoiled, deceitful boy who had watched as his brother murdered Leopold in his sleep. In flashes, though, Leopold glimpsed Estela's labors over Carlton's body to reanimate it. He saw her toil, her gagging at the bloated corpse, her hopelessness and despair, and these things fueled flickers of maniacal glee within him.

Then she, her resurrected monster, and the sniveling Bertrand, all died at the hands of the mobs. He dimly registered their deaths, but the extinguishing of their pitiful souls was nothing compared to the glory of the marauding villagers' rage-fueled hysteria.

Every sense was filled at once with the deliciousness of their fury. So much so that Leopold was just barely aware of his own small son, Elias, scrabbling his way desperately through the dungeons, across the pile of death, over Leopold's own bones, to sneak away between the bars of the secret iron grate deep beneath the castle.

Many more months would pass before Leopold's bony black silhouette slipped past those very same bars leaving behind only frost made by the complete and utter absence of good.

"Lay it straight out," Boudreaux said grimly, reaching for his sword.

Chapter Two
AFTERMATH

"It's gonna have to come off," Arden was squinting. Rainwater was streaming from the tip of his nose, and he had to shout to be heard over the storm raging all around them.

Earlier, below ground, they had turned away from X'andria's hellish inferno and left it smoking and hissing behind them. Too weak to walk on his own, Ohlen leaned heavily on Boudreaux for support. They made it just a few paces, though, when he lost consciousness completely and fell. Boudreaux managed to catch him under the arm and was shocked at how little he weighed, like a feather inside a suit of armor.

"Here, take these Arden," Boudreaux had grunted. Struggling to hold Ohlen upright with one hand, he gestured awkwardly with his

Chapter Two

left arm that was also pinning a leather bound book and two rolls of parchment. These Boudreaux had cleared, on Ohlen's orders, from the sickly chamber now smoldering behind them.

"Is he alright?" Gnome appeared instantly at Boudreaux's other side with a dark probing stare, as Arden wordlessly extracted the bloody, sticky items from between Boudreaux's bare arm and naked torso.

"No." Boudreaux replied simply. He meant it. "We need to move."

Arden opened his field satchel and froze momentarily as Ohlen's ivory case glinted dully in the torchlight. He had forgotten he was carrying it. He had forgotten he held the two round horrors that lay within. Arden gingerly laid the book and scrolls atop the case, careful not to disturb it.

They trudged on toward the sewer main, the scene of the earlier battle.

The pool of red slurry that had been Elias had cooled and stopped expanding. The remains of the three mysterious tattooed warriors, the scorpion, the inferno and the seeping acid mound, lay strewn about the broken stone floor.

Gnome walked purposefully toward what appeared to be empty space near the open sewer. He raised his right hand slightly and matter-of-factly pushed it out to the side as though opening an invisible curtain. With this simple gesture the air itself seemed to dissolve as Gnome's perfect illusion dissipated to reveal the sorry scene he had hidden earlier in the evening.

Waif's small thin body was splayed on the stone floor precisely as Boudreaux had left him. The sickly white handless horror that had been Mordimer lay unattended by the edge of the black sludgy sewage. A few feet away Zarina hugged her two daughters close.

They were facing the far wall, and she stared blankly into the middle distance through tangled curtains of brown hair. The girls were catatonic in her embrace.

"I've got the little guy," X'andria's voice was low, all business. "Let's get the hell outta here."

Waif's body rose into the air as though invisible straps about his waist and shoulders had hoisted him gently but quickly from the ground. He hovered reclining in midair, arms and legs limply dangling.

"Right here, Boudreaux," Arden shouted over the pounding rain.

His finger poked firmly into Waif's skinny upper arm, half way between the elbow and shoulder. The rat bite itself was nearer to his wrist. The broken skin and congealed blood had ruptured from the inside with green puss. Virulent red and black diseased lines extended up his arm from the festering wound.

"Lay it straight out," Boudreaux said grimly, reaching for his sword. Waif was blessedly unconscious.

"Let's get help, X'an," Gnome yelled, his huge eyes were wide and glowing as they drank up what little light there was around them. "This way!" and the two of them disappeared like shadows into The Grotto.

Ohlen lay unconscious nearby in what was fast becoming a muddy pool the surface of which danced with piercing raindrops. Zarina and the girls, completely drained of any emotion, stared despondently into the deluge, as the blade traveled through the wet air and cut conclusively with a crack and a thud.

No human concept exists to describe the devastation that occurs in one's soul when the pathetic sniveling weakness of human corruption and failure stands naked before the unfathomable expansive might of absolute good and truth.

Chapter Three
RUPRECHT

The light had blinded him momentarily. After hours stumbling through the trees and underbrush, bumping into trunks and fighting through knobby brambles, the sudden illumination seemed to sear the backs of his straining eyeballs.

Something otherworldly had appeared before him.

Could it be? He thought hungrily. Even in his confusion, Ruprecht began to salivate and the gears of scheming machination whirred swiftly into action. In the absence of sight, he probed the dimly glowing darkness around him with his ears.

"What is it you seek, brother?"

The voice was kind. Human. Ruprecht's disappointment was

immediate and overwhelming. The gentleness was infuriating. It mocked his hunger.

"Brother?" Ruprecht spat out the word, unable to conceal his contempt.

"You want it badly, don't you?" the voice continued.

Oh no, no, no, no! Ruprecht crouched. High alert. *How could he know? There's no way! No one knows!* Ruprecht was paralyzed with suspicion—terrified he might be revealed or, worse, that another might have tasted the glory that was his alone.

"Get away from me," he pleaded anxiously, backing up, staying as small as possible, almost as if he hoped the interloper might lose track of him in the darkness.

Ruprecht's eyes were adjusting now. It appeared to be a man before him, a man who emitted a faint golden glow. Ruprecht's mind began working double time.

"I'm just out hunting," the lie was easy, the tremble in his voice was gone. "Are these your lands?" he added. It seemed like something a polite person would say.

"I've been looking for you," the man advanced slowly, the cloying sweet honesty in his tone made Ruprecht want to jump on top of him like a wild animal and claw the skin off of his face.

He forced down the violent impulse and returned, in a controlled tone, "Because if these are your lands, I will go elsewhere." Then he added more forcefully, "I am traveling in some haste, so if you'll excuse me, I'll be on my way."

Ruprecht turned away from the glow and made to walk into the black, as if he knew where he was going.

"Ohlen nearly died for you," the man's voice cut through the dark fog that enveloped Ruprecht's thoughts and stopped him dead in his tracks.

RUPRECHT

Reality came crashing down all around him.

He had run. He had run from his friends. He had run from himself. He failed in life. He even failed in his feeble attempts at death. He was imprisoned completely by his lust for a power he could hardly even remember. And now, in his first human contact in days, he was instantly consumed by deceit and hunger. Every action, every word was driven by his impulses to hide the darkness of his past while at the same time seek to regain it.

And somehow this stranger knew all about it.

Ruprecht fell to the forest floor and wept.

"Oh god," he sobbed, between heaves. "Oh what have I done?" came over and over again. He saw Boudreaux lying in that alley, he saw flashes of the pathetic and delusional groundskeeper Dortmund he had wasted so much time with, he saw Ohlen, Arden, Gnome and X'andria. His shame was complete.

"Come with me, brother," the man was near him now. He was standing right over Ruprecht. Ruprecht had no fight left in him. The man was kneeling now, was reaching for him, had grasped his upper arm with a warm hand.

And they were gone.

Ruprecht saw himself now from the outside. He was a crumpled dark mass curled up on the ground next to a shining white-gold star.

He felt something he had not felt for a long time. It seemed like a lifetime ago. The agony was indescribable, like his body had been frozen completely and then dumped in boiling oil. The heat invaded him, invaded his soul.

He was in the presence of his deity once more.

It was beyond judgment and shame, beyond embarrassment. No human concept exists to describe the devastation that occurs in

Chapter Three

one's soul when the pathetic sniveling weakness of human corruption and failure stands naked before the unfathomable expansive might of absolute good and truth.

Leopold, too, was free falling. How could he resist?

Chapter Four
THE GORGE

---

18 years ago...

Leopold bled quietly from the bowels of what had once been Ingroff Castle through the ancient and forgotten drain. He slid out through a thicket of overgrown vines that froze and shriveled away from the rusted iron grate like canine lips peeling back in a snarl.

It was a beautiful day, dappled sunlight radiated through a lush canopy of scintillating green and gold leaves. But for Leopold there was no color, only grey. And any light unfortunate enough to venture near him was sucked forever into nonexistence.

A marigold was the first to catch his attention. Standing proudly just beyond the trees, it eagerly drank of the sunlight—

reflecting back color and beauty around it. Fragile roots at once probed the earth for sustenance yet nourished the soil with energy from the wind and sun. The marigold breathed, as do all living things.

And it was loathsome to Leopold. With nothing more than a thought, he found himself drifting toward the brazen beauty. He singled out its tiny golden spirit, wagging like an insulting finger before him, and imagined it instead broken and seeping.

Hovering ever closer, Leopold pitched forward and his skeletal face rushed down to study the unsavory upstart—to experience the life that would soon be his. He particularly enjoyed the faint gasp that rippled through space as the marigold froze, small vessels rupturing within as they crystallized.

Something elsewhere was urgently tugging at his attention. The marigold was dead now—no longer of interest. Though he lingered just long enough to flick the petals lazily with a bony finger and witness the unique slender form obliterate into shards of anonymity. The new distant sensation was deliciously distracting. Rotten black rags streamed behind him as he sailed headlong back into the forest toward whatever mysterious morsel lay in wait.

Grey forms rushed by him as he flew. He sped back past the drain-grate, deeper into the forest, the terrain descending into marshy sponge. Leopold ignored much of his surrounding, though, because the periphery of his vision was edged with a darkness that funneled his focus fully on the object of his flight. The trees and grasses that he did see appeared like bones made of hazy smoke that brayed annoyingly at him with the arrogant air of harmonious life.

The doe's thin black mouth twisted in mute horror beneath two rapidly rolling eyes. Most of the desperate animal had already disappeared within the massive distended brownish-green amphibian maw of an enormous salamander, only the front half of which emerged from the thick muck of the swamp where Leopold now hovered.

Just forelegs and hooves were visible, crammed awkwardly together with the doe's head by the crushing constriction of the salamander's elastic jaw. Ripples along the slimy elongated body showed the internal peristaltic effort to draw the unfortunate animal further and further to its digested death.

Leopold's favorite part was the terror in the doe's eyes. Unable to make noise anymore, unable even to kick, Leopold feasted on the crazed working of its mouth and the black and white and red orbs swiveling madly in their sockets.

A few long moments later the doe had disappeared completely within the massive salamander's mouth. Its form within the enormous slippery predator was an indistinguishable mound that pushed forcefully out against the tightly stretched glistening hide. Full to bursting, the salamander rested motionless, still sticking halfway out of the muck.

Leopold sensed the last vestiges of life leaving the doe. It was suffocating. No air meant no thought, and no thought meant no pain.

Leopold grew bored.

He drifted closer to the ancient swamp fiend. It turned its serpentine eyes ever so slightly in his direction, its mouth an inscrutable thin line, the doe's body slowly being crushed to fit more comfortably within its hulking barrel body. Leopold saw the smoke-bones of a nearby cypress tree rupture and lift high in the air. He imagined the jagged trunk plunging forcefully out of the sky through the wide back and spine of the great salamander, skewering it messily along with the wreck of the half-digested doe now creeping down its long esophagus.

And so it was.

As Leopold floated absent-mindedly away from the swamp in search of new amusement, blood drained from the mouth and nose of the giant amphibian's limp froggy face, the trunk of a cypress tree angling grotesquely upward from someplace beneath the base of the salamander's splintered neck.

To most people Leopold appeared as a night-black shadow moving swiftly across the land as though cast by an enormous bird of prey. Those with pure hearts would be struck with consuming melancholy, those concealing malice would erupt in fits of rage to the shock of anyone nearby. All beings felt chill to the bone.

Weeks passed before Leopold realized he was not completely in control. He was drawn to one curious episode of torment after another. He added to the discomfort whenever possible and gleefully drank up the rewards. But the more familiar he became with his reality, the more he registered that he was actually being led around like a bull by the ring in its nose.

Piloting him was a deep red-hot mysterious power. He was dimly aware that it had created him out of the ashes of his former life. And now it owned him.

Leopold was drawn to pain and fear. But even tastier was pain and fear borne of cruelty, anger or despair. For that reason he quickly abandoned the wilderness in preference for places inhabited by humans. While the forests and fields saw their share of suffering and death, it was the towns and cities that harbored the schemers, bullies, abusers, and sadists. It was a feast for Leopold's senses. Particularly delightful were those instances when his presence actually pushed a weak will to an act of torment or revenge.

Such was very nearly the case one drizzly dawn. The man was passed out drunk in a gutter. The man had lost everything. Leopold had easily incited him to violence the night before and had even assisted slightly as the man beat down the indignant villagers that approached him after he refused to pay for his ale and then wrestled with the barkeep for the coins behind the counter. Without Leopold fanning the flames of his desperation the man would have surrendered far earlier, would likely not have started the fight to begin with. Eventually he was tossed bodily into the rain, after the coins were ripped from his hands and returned to the barkeep.

That was the night before.

This morning a fisher girl hastened toward her father's market stall some minutes' walk away from the nearby sea. She walked quickly to preserve the freshness of the fish wriggling in her woven basket. She walked quickly because she was scared of the near-dark, scared of being alone.

Her fear was glorious.

Leopold prodded the drunk wastrel's polluted brain with a jolt of savage fire, and the pathetic man's bruised and puffy face struggled toward consciousness.

This was going to be good.

The fisher girl's quick steps splashed closer.

But just then the invisible leash about Leopold's neck tugged. It tugged hard.

The drunk was sitting up. His foggy brain was beginning to feed on the dark ideas planted within.

Splish, splish, splish.

But Leopold began drifting away against his own will. *Not now,* he protested. He fought to face the street for as long as he could—saw the girl's wary eyes as she rushed past, saw the stupid drunk pass out again in the absence of encouragement. Straining to fight it, Leopold was finally ripped from the scene.

He was flying quickly from the village by the sea. Smoke-grey fields of tall wavy grain sprung up before him, the stalks cringed in frozen fear as he rushed past leaving a swath of frosty death in his wake. There were people in the fields digging up the earth, scything the tall grasses. The snuffing out of many tiny lives with each whoosh of the long curved blade was vaguely interesting, but Leopold could not tarry.

Mountains loomed before him. A patch of water in a shallow mountain stream froze solid as he sailed past causing the cool rushing liquid behind it to pool and breach the bank. Leopold plunged into thick woods at the base of the mountain and suddenly the terrain began to rise. Shelves of sheer granite, the scaffolding of the mountains themselves, thrust upward out of the vegetation. The higher Leopold rose the more stark and dramatic were the vistas surrounding him.

Leopold slammed into a wall of rock. It towered straight and high over him. Though he hovered above ground, he was unable to gain elevation in flight. All-consuming frustration gripped him with an otherworldly mad fury. It wanted to scream, to destroy. In that same moment, Leopold perceived the unique calling of a far-off deep despair for the first time. It was the object of his flight, and time was running out.

Frantically he raced along the wall looking for a fissure, a navigable grade, anything he might use to gain traction. The red fury grew within him, it felt like his bones would melt from the searing impatience.

A large boulder concealed an opening in the smooth granite face. Melting somehow through the minute crevices around the edges of the boulder, Leopold rushed recklessly into the blackness beyond. He was surprised to find that, a few twists and turns later, he emerged back out into the light of day at the foot of a wide secret staircase cut cleanly out of the solid stone. He raced up the perfect crevice toward the light high above, toward the alluring sadness so consuming he could almost taste it.

There was a long and narrow bridge across a deep chasm. He arrived just in time to see a boy, shy of twenty, cast himself from the center of the bridge into the vast airy expanse. The boy was all bitterness, resentment, and self-loathing, swirling around a quickly growing ball of weakness and fear as the base of the gorge rose to meet his rapid descent.

Leopold, too, was free falling. How could he resist? He dove head-first as if to get as close as possible to the ripples of suicidal grief emanating from the boy. On impact, blood exploded outward from many places, points of broken bones tore through soft tissue. Life was sprinting away from the wet mess on the canyon floor.

Leopold dove onto the body. He thrust skeletal fingers into seeping wounds, he knit shards of bones back together with his thought, he breathed black air into lungs that had caved into sunken sacks of fluid, he read the boy's sad history like a book, he grasped hold tightly of the puzzled and struggling mind and injected it full of a venom most vile.

"I want to be strong," he replied, bubbles cascading from his mouth like visible manifestations of his fervent, desperate desire.

Chapter Five
BOUDREAUX

Rain. It was relentless now and the saturated dirt streets rippled in a lively dance as countless heavy drops pounded into the slow river of brown. After cleaving Waif's diseased left arm from his body, Boudreaux was hunched forward, head down. His exhaustion was so complete that he stayed bent—only barely dragging his blade back away through the mud. Arden scuttled and splashed trying to keep as much of Waif's remaining lifeblood as he could from draining out into the rainwater.

Dawn must not have been far off. Boudreaux was faintly aware that a dim grey glow was beginning to struggle its way through the dense foggy filter that smothered Rockmoor. When his heavy dwarf sword cracked into the small thief's arm, the limb sunk into the mud below the level of the pooling water. Even with the faint light, Boudreaux could not see if the wound bled. He saw only the rain.

Boudreaux had nearly died in the sewer just hours earlier. His mind replayed those frantic moments of sinking uncontrollably beneath that awful sludge. Even now he could feel the stinging in his nostrils and throat where the toxic waste had rushed into the desperate, instinctual gasp that nearly ended him forever.

Water. You beautiful, powerful, cruel thing.

Slumping in a waking dream-state Boudreaux's skin came alive with awareness of the chilly drops driving down onto him from far above. His mind's eye morphed the muddy-bloody puddle around his feet and friends into memory of the undulating sea, the rocky coast of which they had carefully skirted along the night before.

But I am of the water, Boudreaux recalled.

And he dreamt of the restorative pool within the dwarf lair beneath the mountain. And his dreams cast him back further, to the beginning, to *her*.

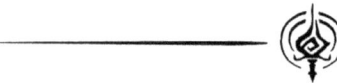

Sun lightly touched the horizon with hazy grey when the skinny boy slithered through the small gap he'd forced between the bottom of the wooden barn door and the packed earth beneath. Jagged, unfinished edges scraped raw streaks in his shoulders and the backs of his calves as he squirmed free into the muggy pre-dawn.

But none of that mattered now to the part-elf slave-boy called Boudreaux.

All that mattered was that the terror of an evening locked in the grain room with those huge hairy spiders was behind him. His master had been angry and this was the punishment. At least this was part of it.

Cowering in the near-darkness he ran trembling hands urgently along his damp skin to be sure no creepy crawlies lurked undetected. He checked the back of his neck a few extra times. His instinct was to run away screaming, to flail his arms and legs and knock free the entire sticky experience, but the horses couldn't be spooked. Spooked horses meant his master stirring to investigate.

The decision to run away had made itself during the night. There was not one single moment when it happened, there was just awareness dawning in his mind, similar to the morning now creeping tentatively over top of the hot, humid night.

He snuck quietly from the grounds, but a boy on foot is no match for a man on a horse. By the time the sky glowed orange Boudreaux heard his master's agitated, threat-laced pursuit. His ensuing frantic flight led Boudreaux into unfamiliar woods with thin branches that slapped his face as if nature itself was taunting him with premonitions of the whipping that was to come.

Then Boudreaux came upon the glistening lake.

The heavens glowed yellow now, but this ethereal water shown from within by its own light. In wonderment the boy stepped gingerly closer to the water's edge, in spite of the cracking limbs and threatening shouts that pierced, ever closer, the still morning air.

It was like this peaceful haven had been plucked from some magical paradise and inserted into the bleak wood, into Boudreaux's miserable childhood of servitude.

It was obvious his master had overrun him, had spotted him through the trees, by the time the boy first saw her floating in the water. She was beautiful, the most beautiful woman Boudreaux had ever seen. Her silken hair flowed gently in an invisible current, and she was shrouded in an undulating glow that danced and flicked all around like thousands of white ribbons in a soft breeze.

With no words and with no motions she beckoned him forth into the glittering pool. Trancelike he entered, the cool water a salve on his blistered and raw skin.

Underwater she was different. Greyish-brown. As soon as his eyes opened beneath the surface, her long tubular face appeared before his in a rush of bubbles. Her marine eyes were huge white orbs with deep black pupils. They probed his own searchingly.

"What is it you desire?" asked the Lady Of The Lake wordlessly, her long webbed fingers cradling the boy's small face. Boudreaux's young soul laid itself bare before her. He had nothing to hide, just sadness, fear, diligence and hope.

"I want to be strong," he replied, bubbles cascading from his mouth like visible manifestations of his fervent, desperate desire.

Moments later Boudreaux magically reappeared on the pebbly shore, dripping and staring defiantly up into his master's arrogant, sadistic leer. His master casually uncoiled the bull whip that hung at his side, as if savoring the moment, and muttered, "It's lesson-learnin' time, boy."

But Boudreaux was different. He had seen something miraculous, he had experienced beauty and kindness, and he felt... strangely powerful.

The flinch came unbidden at the first stinging bite of the whip. Boudreaux caught the second lash in mid-air with his right hand, however, feeling almost as surprised as his master looked when the thong went taut between them.

Instinctively Boudreaux pulled on his end. He pulled hard.

The last time he saw his master, the cruel man was writhing wildly in the water and screaming like his toes were on fire.

"Let's go Boudreaux."

It was X'andria. She lightly touched his arm as her voice probed his consciousness.

Dark forms detached themselves from the shadows around them. One of them was Gnome, who was talking to Zarina in a series of rushed whispers. An enormous man picked up Ohlen's limp body like he was no more than a long sheaf of wheat. Another picked up Waif's lopsided form, dripping water onto Arden who still knelt in vigil.

Boudreaux's sword hilt had slipped from his grasp and disappeared from view. At X'andria's words he stooped dutifully to fish it back out of the muck and then began plodding heavily along behind her and the rest of the sorry procession.

The streets were not deserted. No amount of rain can delay the silent invisible souls along the coast whose lives are intertwined with the ghost-like forms that glide beneath the waves, and the insatiable markets that feed the hungry mouths on land above. But no morning fisherman was accustomed to seeing a gnome leading a gaggle of armed and embattled stragglers including a phenomenally muscular half-elf naked from the waist up, a heavily-laden fighter in full armor with two blades, and an unconscious boy freshly missing an arm. Those they encountered shrunk away with audible gasps, and hurried off quickly, stealing glimpses back over their shoulders.

The sky was a dull grey by the time they passed a large overgrown park in the heart of The Grotto. Boudreaux followed along as the group disappeared within the dark door of a low and wide tenement of caked mud and thatch that faced the messy tangle of trees and vines. Just inside the cramped entrance hall each member of the party stepped left directly into the wall. When it was Boudreaux's turn, he had to duck and squeeze himself through the narrow opening that was, he observed, normally concealed by a panel that had been removed and set to the side. A grim-faced woman dressed all in black—including a scarf wrapped tightly around her head—stood guard as the weary party passed through the secret portal. Her arms were crossed and her eyes darted warily between the haggard face of each visitor and the soaked street beyond.

They were descending a flight of narrow wooden steps set into the earth. Uneven wicks were clamped by thin metal stands and set in shallow dishes containing some kind of yellowish oil dotted with dirt and bugs. Their flames flickered atop shelves of wood and rock that stuck out from either side, propped up precariously by knobby posts at odd angles. The dancing light, the bodies, and the angular protrusions caused shadows to play tricks on Boudreaux's eyes as he numbly followed the stranger who carried Waif before him.

Suddenly the man vanished in front of him, and Boudreaux nearly plowed into X'andria, who stood facing back up the steps with her arm extended, palm out, in a warning gesture.

"Under there, Boudreaux," she said simply, gesturing into murky blackness beneath a rocky ledge. The illuminated wooden steps continued to descend innocuously behind her, but a closer look revealed a multitude of tiny holes in the slatted ceiling that, no doubt, would release razor sharp needles, or some such treachery, upon unsuspecting trespassers who had managed to breach this far into the Thieves' Den, but knew not all its dark and deadly secrets.

Bending low again, Boudreaux trusted his feet to find solid

ground as he maneuvered left into the void. Though in darkness, he could tell the steps beneath his feet were wider now, uniform, and made of solid stone. He risked standing taller and was pleased to find his head did not whack into anything above. The passage twisted gently, but he could easily follow the sounds of the group before him, and was comforted hearing X'andria's light steps behind.

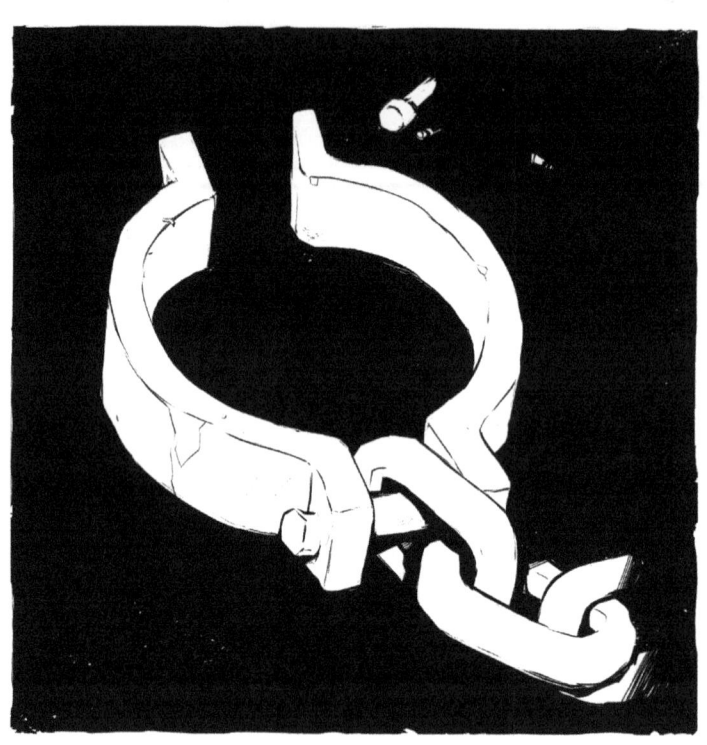

The tether chain extended from its ring in
the wall, but lay limply on the grey stone.

Chapter Six
GNOME

Gnome led the sopping-wet party down the final flight of stone steps into The Den. Upon entering Gnome was shocked to find Rove—the bastard whose gang had ambushed him in the street—chained to the wall with an iron collar around his neck.

In spite of his restraints, and the cracked and bloated welt in the middle of his forehead where Waif's bullet had struck, Rove's skinny angular face stretched into a leering grin as soon as he saw Gnome.

"Well look what scum the rain's flushed in," Rove taunted loudly. "Little pointy-ears's back!"

A few of the thieves loitering nearby giggled and smirked, and looked expectantly at Gnome. Gnome ignored them all and moved purposefully across the room. What he had done and seen, the suffering of the people following him, their pressing need for shelter and care, these things towered over any petty conflict an idiot like Rove was attempting to stir up.

"You look awful little freak, like the river got hold of you after all. Did you run back to The Master for help again, freak?"

The Master himself, coal black hair falling in curls over his face, had, in fact, glided catlike into the room behind Gnome. The smiles of the bystanders vanished, but Rove's hateful glinting eyes obstinately continued to track Gnome across the room.

"Are these all your freak friends?" the voice was thin, grating, tinged with desperation.

"Enough, Rove." The Master's voice echoed with authority.

But the rest of the party had arrived and Rove began to howl with laughter. He pointed and sputtered, his gaunt limbs casting exaggerated angular shadows onto the stone and earth behind him. It was a show, Gnome realized. Rove was putting on a show for all those in attendance. *To what end?* "Wh-what happened to wimpy Waify?" the words exploded out of Rove's mouth in mock concern amid a cascade of manufactured guffaws.

"What did you do to his arm, freak?"

Gnome froze, his face twisted into a mask of contempt. He couldn't believe Rove, or anyone really, would make light of Waif's amputated arm.

"So *now* we see it." Rove addressed the room at large with a crooked, arrogant smile—his audience was assembled. "Now we see how little pointy-ears takes care of his friends..."

But at the word "friends" Rove's needling was cut off in a raspy gag, and he was hoisted straight into the air by his tether-chain. Spittle burbled from his straining lips as he kicked and twisted in the air and clawed at the iron collar clamped around his neck.

The chain seemed to be operating of its own accord—several of its links extended taut into the air toward the ceiling above Rove's head. And soon after Rove was lifted, the chain yanked him by the neck backward and down with such force that his shoulders and head impacted the stone floor before his torso and legs had time to follow.

Rove lay still and silent. The thieves about the perimeter looked shocked and scared. X'andria surreptitiously stowed her gold loop back within her night-blue robes. And Gnome resumed their march forward into the safety and security of The Den's inner chambers, faint satisfaction playing at the corners of his mouth.

Warm, dry furs. The Den's stores were filled with the looted offerings of many years. Amongst the treasures were blankets, rugs and garments of fur and woven hair.

Gnome was exhausted. He sank gratefully, heavily, into a thick black blanket that enveloped him entirely, and he allowed his eyes to close. His body ached from strain and injury, the backs of several ribs were particularly painful where he had been flung against the wall by the scorpion-man during the chaos of the preceding hellish night. The muscles all around his middle were rigidified in an effort to protect those damaged areas. He focused on releasing the tension inch by inch. He focused on the softness of the cocoon in which he was nestled. He tried to relax.

He tried.

But his mind raced with worry. He had asked The Master for help and sanctuary. He had led his friends, outsiders, into The Den, a violation of The Code. He had no idea if Ohlen would survive. Or

Chapter Six

Waif. Retribution from Rove's minions was not a question of if, but when, and his wounded and worn out friends slumbered here, vulnerable, in his house, on his watch.

Adding frustration at the inability to quiet his mind to the list of things weighing down his spirit, Gnome extricated himself from the warmth of the large blanket and stalked from the little storeroom.

I'll just look in on them, he thought. *Then back to sleep.*

The Den was a honeycomb of twists and turns with small chambers almost all of which had hidden passages in the walls or floors or ceilings. Some doors led to solid walls, others led to cozy rooms the first step of which was false and would tip a visitor over to drown and rot in a pool of deep and stale water at the bottom of a long sheer drop. This was a place designed to disorient, frighten and ultimately destroy anyone not meant to be there—and to give maximum advantage to its residents to spy, ambush or flee. As thieves advanced in skill and trustworthiness, The Den's secrets were revealed incrementally. There was no need for locked doors in The Den, as no low-ranking thief would be foolish enough to seek access beyond their station, and no curious stranger would live long enough to tell the tale.

Which was part of the reason why the presence of Ohlen, Arden, Boudreaux, X'andria and Zarina in such a secure part of The Den was so very problematic.

An entire stretch of the floor between his room and the pair of rooms occupied by his friends was paved with one danger after another, so Gnome took to the walls and scuttled, lizard-like, above the network of trigger-steps masquerading as the floor beneath.

Suspended horizontally on the wall, Gnome extended his head beyond the edge of the open archway to peer into the first room. Well below ground, the low-ceilinged stone space had no windows and no natural light. The stub of a candle glowed meekly in the corner giving off just enough light for Gnome's lantern-eyes to discern four furry humps strewn haphazardly on the floor. Placing his feet, one by one, soundlessly on the hard stone, Gnome ventured within and confirmed the two largest lumps were Arden and Boudreaux, deep in sleep. X'andria, also fast asleep, was snoring lightly nearby, as was a swaddled pile of fur containing Ohlen which, Gnome was relieved to note, was rising and falling ever so slightly.

Across the hall was a second identical archway leading to a twin space. Here Gnome found Waif sweating and sticking halfway out of his furs fighting through fever-induced agitation. Zarina was sitting upright and laboriously sucking in heavy shuddering breaths with her head slumped sideways. Her daughters were close, one held in each arm.

Gnome swiveled rapidly in place. His sharp ears had registered the faintest of changes in the atmosphere behind him. A split second later he found himself looking up into the shrouded face of The Master.

"You can't stay here," The Master breathed once they were clear of the room. Gnome noted with alarm that The Master was short of breath and glistened with sweat. "I have traveled within the walls and the clan is speaking," The Master continued. "Some are concerned with The Code, others side with Rove, and a few," and here The Master paused to muster the proper words, "a few whisper of darkness in our midst. Darkness I believe you and your compatriots have meddled in."

Gnome felt like his lungs were being crushed. They were too vulnerable. There was too much to explain, and not enough time.

"Master, we need your help," he began.

"You have until midnight," The Master interrupted. "I take no sides, Gnome, this you know. I guard only The Code. Our very way of life depends upon it. But the presence of your friends in this place shakes us to our very core, and if I survive this at all, it will be not without great struggle."

"Master," Gnome insisted, he had made a decision, "we will leave at midnight but this you must know," he stepped back a pace and gripped The Master's eyes with his own. "The darkness is real. The darkness is beyond my comprehension even though I have witnessed it now more than once. It is coming for us, Master. Not for the thieves, not for Rockmoor, but for the entire world as we know it. You must keep control of The Den of Rockmoor, Master, for I will call upon you someday and, when I do, all we know and love will weigh in the balance."

Gnome's calves were shaking in fear and determination when they heard the shouting in the distance. Like bats in a cave, he and The Master sped toward the commotion. Moments later they tore into the common room, which was lit and abuzz. The tether chain extended from its ring in the wall, but lay limply on the grey stone. Rove had escaped.

Ohlen blinked rapidly to cleanse some of the sandy silt from his eyes and strained to see up into the foggy red.

Chapter Seven
OHLEN

There was a scratching above him. All was dark and he could not see—could not even open his eyes. Whatever covered him was very heavy. He tried to move his arms but found them pinned in place. The only sound was the scratching. *Is it coming closer?* He tried to open his mouth to yell but even that proved difficult and when he managed a slight parting of his lips, the gap was instantly filled with what felt like moist soil. *Have I been buried alive?* Ohlen's mind reeled.

There were things in the earth around him. Moving things. Reaching out, his spirit awakened to a constellation of creeping and foraging beetles and worms, of probing roots that divided web-like into countless wispy fingers, of seemingly eternal living rock far

Chapter Seven

beneath. Ohlen cried out for help with his will.

The scratching approached. *Someone must know I'm here*, he dared to hope. He forced himself to take shallow and controlled breaths. He chose to believe he would be saved, and worked to still the heart hammering wildly in his chest.

It was fingernails, fingernails digging through the dirt to get to him. They uncovered his leg, and Ohlen's first bodily sensation was nails digging deeply into his right thigh. More sour grainy dirt had wedged its way between his lips and into the gaps between his teeth. *Up here*, he wanted to cry out, as the pace of the clawing quickened.

Finally the faintest light began filtering through the thinning and loosening dirt above his face. His torso and his feet were still deeply embedded, and he was unable to move. But perhaps soon he would at least be able to spit out the dirt invading his mouth, be able to breathe normally—be able to see who it was that was here to save him from a slow, solitary death.

The scratching made it to his face. Ohlen scrunched up his cheeks involuntarily and squinted shut his eyes to protect them as the long curved nails raked dirt and bits of skin aside somewhat indiscriminately.

I'm here! I'm here! He sputtered up into the red, smoky light that filled the narrow earthen hole above his face. A gnarled old hand, with dirt falling from yellowy crooked claws slowly lifted up and away. Ohlen blinked rapidly to cleanse some of the sandy silt from his eyes and strained to see up into the foggy red.

A moment later Magda's filthy mop of grey hair pushed into view and the old crone's face came into focus above him. But there was no kindness or wisdom in Magda's visage. There was only hunger. And when she opened her eyes Ohlen's hope drained away rapidly into icy terror. He'd seen these eyes before. Shiny orbs of bottomless black.

Magda's wrinkled and toothless mouth gaped open impossibly wide like she might try to swallow Ohlen, and the earth imprisoning him, within the depthless black that filled the space between her stretching expanding lips.

Then suddenly Ohlen shuddered awake and found himself wrapped in furs, sweating, in an unfamiliar dark stone room, amidst a whispered and hurried commotion.

He shuddered at the memory, but immediately wished he hadn't.

Chapter Eight
ARDEN

Whispery echoes stretched into Arden's slumbering subconscious. He was alone in a small clearing amidst moonlight-silhouetted mature trees. The nearest leaves glowed orange and yellow, illuminated by the playful dance of his cook-fire.

The roast mutton-leg had been magnificent—thick, tender, smoky. His lips and chin were slick with the rich, savory juices that had managed to evade the back of his hand and his hungrily darting tongue. Arden pulled the soft and dark-stained wooden stopper from his round wine skin, took a long drink, and luxuriously swirled the leathery, oaky deliciousness with the lingering aftertaste of his meal.

It was time.

He retrieved his smallest pouch, tied on his waist by its short drawstring, and teased it open. Lifting it to his face he buried his nose and inhaled the resinous, sticky sweet aroma of the precious leaf inside. Mesmerized by the scent, and not ready to extract his nose from the pouch, Arden felt blindly behind him for his pipe.

And that's when his senses jumbled. For the briefest of instances he thought the wind had picked up outside the grove of trees. But soon enough, and in great disappointment, the iron hand of his consciousness recognized the whispers for what they were and wiped the entire bucolic scene—taste, smell and all—clean out of his perception.

Damn, thought Arden. *Damn, damn, damn!*

Arden was bleary-eyed. The fur-lined sleep was a very, very good thing, there had just not been nearly enough of it. Of his many scrapes and bruises, by far the worst pain was around his middle. It felt, at least in his current stillness, like a wide iron belt made of large, bulbous links had been tightened two notches past comfortable around his torso. The memory of the stone giant pounding him in the chest came rushing back, followed by the tattooed scorpion-man who had lifted him from the ground with its freakish claw nearly crushing Arden's ribcage. He shuddered at the memory, but immediately wished he hadn't. Unnecessary movement, Arden realized, was not advisable.

Further souring his reentry into consciousness was the lack of a sole beneath his left big toe. Arden found he could wriggle his toes without any pain at all, and in doing so discovered that his left boot was missing the bottom of its elegant square toe. *Troll-hide soles, they told me*, Arden whined in his mind as he remembered the assurances of the Bridgeton shopkeeper, *can withstand anything,* they said. *Well obviously not anything, obviously not a little step in acid monster juice. When we go back to Bridgeton I'm demanding a new pair!*

The physical pain and sartorial annoyance was ushering in Arden's sharper awareness of the world around him, in spite of himself. The whispers were coming from the hallway—some other more disconcerting noises echoed down the stone passageways from much further away. X'andria was now stirring nearby. The large mound of fur beyond her was definitely Boudreaux, still fast asleep. *Must be nice*, thought Arden jealously.

Beyond Boudreaux was Ohlen. Still, lying on his back, serene. *Ohlen!* Arden suddenly remembered the ivory case containing the two horrid black orbs that Ohlen had entrusted to him in the madness of the previous night. Wincing as he turned over, Arden felt around the floor nearest him, and a few panicked seconds later his hand came upon his old leather field satchel. He willed himself into a sitting position, and drew the bag toward him, careful not to tip it sideways, or do anything that might upset its contents.

It was with great relief that, upon lifting the heavy flap and examining the contents within, Arden spotted the ornate round case, lying innocently amidst his other belongings and betraying nothing of the horror inside.

Oh, my bag is trashed! This day was not starting out well at all. There were several slashes across the front that would never go away no matter how much oiling and polishing he did, the strap itself was beginning to tear, and the whole of it was stained and crusted with blood, dirt, sewage, acid and who knows what else.

X'andria studied the grief-stricken woman for a few moments in silence. She saw hurt and fear, but that was not all she saw. In those eyes she also saw a fierceness, and a resolve. She saw a survivor.

Chapter Nine
ZARINA

Zarina was totally drained of emotion. She felt wrung out. Seeing what remained of Mordimer had left her mired in a vat of numbness.

The last time she had felt hope was weeks earlier, when Mordimer had rushed their captors at the door of their prison cell. *Mordimer, her big, strong, faithful husband. The father of her precious Zordim and Mara. The man who had rescued her from her father's tormenting, from the sea. The man who had shown her kindness and love.*

The hours that followed his departure had crawled by. While she had no idea why they'd been abducted, she had imagined the savages interrogating him—why else would they have taken him from the cell?—and she had imagined him fighting valiantly. She had, of course, been terrified that they would hurt him, or even kill him.

But what ended up happening to her beloved Mordimer was far worse. The thing he became was a soulless shell of the man she had known. A zombified mindless corpse. She had screamed when she saw him and he had stopped. He had *looked* at her. But it was just a fleeting instant, before he had lumbered mindlessly onward.

The whole hellish scene of the night before was incomprehensible. There was so much she could not understand. The she-elf imprisoned next to her, X'andria, seemed to know at least some of the other people. The monster who had formerly been her husband was kicked in the back by a small creature dressed all in black, Mordimer had pitched forward and dropped two small round objects onto a ghastly hairless man in a smoking crimson robe. It was craziness, but all she could focus on was poor Mordimer. When the fight was over, he lay face down, immobile. In a trance Zarina had walked to him, half-expecting him to stir at any moment, to prop himself up on an elbow, to smile that familiar smile. With Zordim and Mara close behind, she had knelt by his side, indifferent to the chatter around them. And then blessedly the group had departed, the chamber grew silent, and they were left alone.

Up close she could see the extent of the damage to his body. The soles of his feet had worn off, there was a massive wound in the back of his right calf, both hands were gone. She had reached out and touched his shoulder and was shocked to find it completely cold. As cold as the stone beneath them.

And that was the moment she had gone completely numb.

"Zarina," the whisper slipped past the veil of her fitful sleep.

"Zarina," this one came with the gentlest of nudges on her shoulder.

She opened her eyes to find the small, dark-clad creature before her. It was like a little man, she now realized, but with enormous eyes that shined luminously even in the darkness.

Mara and Zordim were nestled in each of Zarina's arms. But if they were awake too, they were doing a terrific job of hiding it.

"We are going to need to move soon," the little man informed her in a whisper. Then after a pause he added, "I'm sorry." It was clear from his tone that he was sorry for more than just the fact he had disturbed her sleep.

He was shifting away when Zarina—surprised by the sound of her own voice—said, "Wait, who are you?"

"I'm Gnome," said Gnome, heavily.

"Where are we?" she pried.

"We're in the Thieves' Den. We're not supposed to be here. We need to go." The small man, Gnome, was looking around as he answered, as though worried someone might be listening.

Another now entered the room. Zarina could tell as the dark shape left the glow of the doorway that it was X'andria.

"What's going on?" Zarina pressed Gnome.

"There's trouble with the thieves," Gnome explained. "They don't want us here."

"No," Zarina broke in, louder than she had intended, unwelcome emotion causing her voice to tremble slightly, "I mean *what the hell* is happening...with everything?"

X'andria was now standing next to Gnome, the two of them exchanged the briefest of glances.

"How did we get here?" The frustration of having too many

questions and not enough words or time or energy was overwhelming, "Why did they take us?" Zarina's voice was edged now with the mucousy whine of someone about to burst into tears. "What did they do to Mordimer?" The light filtering in from the now-bustling hallway spilled around the two mute shadows and reflected off of Zarina's runny liquid eyes.

"I'll stay with her, Gnome," X'andria said softly and she knelt before them. Gnome melted wordlessly away like a drop of ink in seawater.

"Zarina," X'andria continued, "we have to go somewhere else now. But I want you to know that you and your girls are safe with us. We will protect you, I promise, and as soon as possible I'll answer all the questions I can. I may even have a few questions of my own."

Zarina's wet stare probed into the dark shadow of X'andria's face as if trying to discern if the elf could really be trusted. X'andria noted how each of her arms, protectively encircling the girls, grew a little tighter.

"It's not over, is it?" Zarina said slowly. She seemed to already know the answer, but her glistening eyes still pleaded for reassurance.

X'andria studied the grief-stricken woman for a few moments in silence. She saw hurt and fear, but that was not all she saw. In those eyes she also saw a fierceness, and a resolve. She saw a survivor.

"No," X'andria finally murmured in response. "It's not over, Zarina. I'm afraid it's just beginning."

*For a long moment those awake just stood
in the dim light staring at one another.*

Chapter Ten
RETURN TO WESTWOOD

Quiet as snowfall, Gnome stole through the cracked door to their Westwood cottage. The familiar smell of their space and belongings filled his nostrils. He was relieved not to detect any foreign scents. Even still, he froze in place and listened for the faintest sound of shifting weight or breath or a heartbeat, anything that might reveal an unwelcome trespasser. Several tense moments later, satisfied that their space had not been infiltrated, Gnome lit a candle. The meager flickering light struggled to fill the narrow gap opening onto the street, which soon widened as Gnome beckoned them all within.

X'andria entered first. She was holding Zordim, whose face was buried defiantly in X'andria's shoulder, leaving visible only her disheveled mop of dark curly hair. Next was Zarina, with Mara fast asleep in her arms. Then Arden brought Waif into the glowing interior, still and silent and wrapped up tightly in a fur blanket. He set Waif down near the space where Arden, himself, usually slept. And last came Boudreaux, carrying a semi-conscious Ohlen, who he laid gingerly on the long wooden table they had all eaten on what seemed ages ago.

For a long moment those awake just stood in the dim light staring at one another. The Master had fed them a hurried simple meal of thin stew and hunks of dark hearty bread before they stole out of the Thieves' Den, but they were all nursing injuries, and no one had slept nearly enough.

"Now what?" Boudreaux croaked. His mind was so foggy it felt like he had forgotten how to make his voice work.

"Security," Gnome willed himself to say. All the anxiety and responsibility of their stay in the Thieves Den weighed heavily upon him, but he knew that no matter what their condition, they had to be mindful of their vulnerability first and foremost, especially with Rove on the loose. "I'll take first watch, you all get some rest."

"No way, Gnome," X'andria crossed over to him and put her hand firmly on his shoulder. "I'm on this, alright? You need to rest, too, and you look like you can hardly keep your eyes open."

Arden and Boudreaux both made unintelligible noises that might have been protests had they evolved past low grunts, but it was clear they were secretly relieved that X'andria was taking first watch.

Gnome looked up at X'andria with a mix of strain and concern before sighing in consent, "weapons out, okay guys?" The big men nodded and began swaying toward their bedding. "X'an I'm going to arm the door with a noisemaker and go to sleep, but I want you to wake me up in no more than three hours. You promise?"

"Four hours, Gnome, I'll wake you in four hours." X'andria replied evenly. Gnome had already pulled a thin filament from his tunic and was retrieving several earthenware vessels to balance outside above the threshold for his alarm.

"I'll stay up with you X'andria," Hovering silently nearby they had almost forgotten Zarina was there. Her voice was strangely soothing. "I can't sleep right now anyway."

"Zordim takes her big sister role very seriously," Zarina said warmly. "She's so patient with Mara. I think she's a better teacher than I am, honestly. It's like they have their own language."

Zarina and X'andria had sat together long into the night, long past the four hours X'andria had promised Gnome. At first they sat silently, watching the solitary candle quietly hissing through its waxy fuel. But after several minutes, once Gnome and the others had safely settled into a muffled chorus of snores and somnolent breaths, Zarina began telling her new friend about her life with Mordimer. X'andria, she found, had an open and calming presence that made her at ease sharing details of her personal life. And it felt good to talk with someone.

Stretching a cupped hand out before her, Zarina continued, "Like the time I was trying to show Mara how to clean and scale fish. Oh what a mess!" She giggled dryly at the memory, "fish guts and juice got all over the floor, and all over Mara. It was a disaster, and we both got frustrated. Then Zordim came back from the docks with Mordimer. She just has this way. She grabbed Mara's hand, put a new fish in it, and gently guided her through the motions. I don't know what I'd do without her."

Zarina's eyes drooped heavily now in reverie. She studied the shadows on the floor. She had shared bits of her childhood on the water, of Mordimer rescuing her from her tyrannical drunken father before they even knew each other's names, of her two greatest blessings in Mara and Zordim.

She had exhausted her options. There was no remaining small talk to be distracted and comforted by.

"I want them to pay, X'andria." Zarina's voice was steely now, and she was staring intently at her companion. The reflection of the solitary candle glowed like burning coals deep in her night-dilated pupils. "I want to know who took us. Who took him away from us." Zarina was becoming more animated now. "You told me it's not over, X'andria. What's not over? Tell me what I need to devote my life to destroying."

A chill rolled over both of them. Distracted by the sudden cold, X'andria was trying to work out where her explanation should begin, when the screaming started and the stillness around them erupted into action.

It was Waif. Rolling and yelling unintelligibly, he was wrapped too tightly in the furs to adequately investigate the space where he used to have a left arm. But, instincts and nerves fueling his terror, he twisted and twitched trying to loosen the blankets and confirm the horrifying truth.

The sudden noise caused Arden, Boudreaux and Gnome to erupt upward in a menacing array of arcing blades. Gnome scuttled spider-like up the nearest wall, dagger clenched between his teeth, Arden and Boudreaux raced awkwardly around the space in search of intruders. X'andria and Zarina were momentarily dazed until both Mara and Zordim lent their cracked and weary shrieks to Waif's agonized howls.

Zarina raced to the girls and settled over them like an eagle landing on eggs in its nest.

"There's nothing here!" shouted Arden, poised near the door, nostrils flaring.

Waif was wriggling loose of his blankets now and his outburst distilled into a series of "no, no, no, no, no…" until finally he was able to reach the stump of his upper left arm with his right hand, and the wailing began all over again.

"Quiet Waif!" barked Boudreaux, the command came out harsher than he'd intended.

"Hey, take it easy, man." Gnome landed on the floor in front of Boudreaux and eyed him accusatorily. "You cut his arm off, Boudreaux, the least you can do is cut him some slack too, now that he knows it!"

Waif settled into a series of heaving whimpers. He was listening.

"C'mon Gnome, ease up." It was Arden shouting now. "I made that call, and we all agreed."

"Will everyone just shut up and calm down?" X'andria, standing, was looking incredulously from Arden to Boudreaux. Waif had grown silent now, and both he and Zarina eyed the four on their feet from their positions on the floor.

"You just never think, Boudreaux!" Gnome flung the accusation bitterly up into the face of the glowering half-elf. "You just say stuff, and hit things…" but that was as far as he got before Boudreaux sunk a swift blow to the side of Gnome's head that sent him skittering like a rag doll off his feet.

Boudreaux was mad.

Chapter Ten

"Anyone else want to take a shot at big stupid Boudreaux?" he shouted. The warrior had arrived. Boudreaux's frightful power strained at the skin barely containing it.

"My friends," the words were pronounced long and slow. "Remember."

It was Ohlen. Upright on the table. The low soothing rumble of his voice had seemed more to emanate from within their ears, than project out of his mouth.

"Remember," his voice demanded again inside their minds.

And X'andria was transported to that calm day with Gnome visiting the bridge of Bridgeton. Arden looked at Boudreaux and the memories of their many sweaty training days—testing each other, helping each other up—flooded back. Gnome, rubbing his temple on the ground, saw in Boudreaux not the man who had just assaulted him, but the fearless fighter who had saved them all battling the stone giant and the tattooed islanders. Boudreaux recalled the touch—the first time X'andria's hand laid gently upon his torn flesh, and he had awoken to meet friends for the first time in his life.

And Leopold, a shadow within shadows hovering just outside, was blasted away by something he had not ever felt before. The glowing strength tore through him, forcing his retreat, denying his creeping emanations of will. Whatever this was, Leopold decided—spinning away out of control—he needed to scrape it from the earth forever.

*Knife in hand, the messy job of slaughtering the first hog still
savagely unfinished, he stood tall, chest puffed out, shoulders
back, trying to look bigger than he really was.*

Chapter Eleven
THE MOUNTAIN

———————

11 years ago...

The twisted red-brown sack of juvenile angst had sputtered back to life at the base of the gorge. Long past the damage any mortal could sustain, the gasp of resurrection had been borne of Leopold's black magic thrust forcefully into the many cracks in both the boy's body and mind.

Leopold's work was finished, and he had drifted slowly upward and away like a spider web blown adrift on the wind. Months and years then passed in a state of semi-consciousness. The gorge became a distant memory. Winds of revenge, deviance, megalomania, and selfishness rippled through space and attracted him from one lazy gray engagement to the next.

Chapter Eleven

The hog was stuck and squealing, but what really brought Leopold from his wanderings into the muddy unkempt farm in the foothills, was the deep-seeded anger of the sticker. The drunk, red-faced man plowed his short hunting knife indiscriminately, cruelly, into various broad parts of the struggling animal while the others pressed against one another on the far side of the pen as if distance might spare them a similar fate.

He didn't want to be here, Leopold perceived. The man felt this dirty work of slaughtering hogs was beneath him. It was hot, sweaty, muddy, bloody, and smelly.

Leopold set down in the glistening urine-soaked pen. The churned wet earth and manure froze on contact and, sensing some new danger, the terrified animals strained even more forcefully against the wooden fencing at the opposite end.

A string of obscenities and threats billowed from the butcher, oblivious to the patch of frozen earth creeping toward him, as wooden fence-beams creaked under the stress of the cowering hogs. The stupid animals were ignoring him. Knife in hand, the messy job of slaughtering the first hog still savagely unfinished, he stood tall, chest puffed out, shoulders back, trying to look bigger than he really was. *It's lesson-learnin' time*, he muttered under his ale-belch breath.

But his first step hit ice. Inebriated and surprised his foot slipped quickly and he hit still-soft mud nearby with a grunt and a squelch.

Now, commanded Leopold. Simple minds were easily influenced, and in a matter of minutes the hogs had so thoroughly trampled their tormentor that it was hard to distinguish his body from the pen's foul earth.

Leopold wasn't able to eat, exactly. He didn't need to anyway, and taste and smell had abandoned his universe along with pity and myriad other human trivialities in the rot beneath Ingroff Castle some time in the forgotten past.

But he ingested the remains of the angry man. He ingested the half-slaughtered hog. He ingested all the others one by one. At first the gnashed goop dripped through his jaw bone and caught in the stretchy sinew crisscrossing his ribcage. But eventually the cavity filled and gravity had its way with the slurry contents and Leopold, seated cross-legged in the muck, began to get buried in a pyramid of digested magic-blackened filth.

It was him, and he was it. Leopold's new meat-body grew indistinguishably out of the pigpen and, with all the hogs long-ago eaten and processed through him, he retreated into the depths of his master's fire-consciousness and fed on the consumed souls of the frightened animals and rage-steeped butcher.

It was about a year before the first goblin pushed, with elbows and claws, through the black mucousy membrane of the tar-skirt mounded around Leopold's inert form. The slick ugly creature moved jauntily at first, but quickly set about delivering the next of its kin, whose head was welling up out of Leopold's soupy mother-form. A dozen or more fiends were pulled wet from the darkness that day, and in weeks Leopold had a small army ranging, hunting, foraging, and fashioning instruments of war.

Seven goblins perished in the effort to separate Leopold from his gestation mound. He had grown into the earth, and it into him, and removal proved tricky. Their stubby fingers froze on contact with him—puny, weak corporeal beings that they were—and they howled with earthly pain. Eventually, though, they successfully cleared and hauled enough to extract him from the gelatinous cocoon he had spent so long creating.

Leopold lost a lot of goblins exterminating the dwarves. He spent months weakening their ranks by corrupting the vain and disenchanted among them. The infighting was satisfying and occasionally deadly, but by and large the dwarves were hard to influence and some among them had psychic defenses he could not penetrate at all.

The onslaught was premature, actually. While Leopold went to work on the spirits of the mountain dwellers, his goblin army tunneled nearby, gathered strength, and developed multiple points of entry from which to ambush the unsuspecting dwarves. But the idiots punched through the dwarf masonry too early. Instead of a stealthy invasion from many places, the dumbfounded goblin miners toppled into a dirty heap in the great hall with a host of alarmed dwarves looking on aghast.

Even so, with Leopold in command, the rear army gathered quickly and overwhelmed the dwarves pushing them from the great hall, slaughtering them in their passageways as they fled, and eventually starving and overtaking the remaining survivors in the throne room deep within the mountain.

THE MOUNTAIN

The dwarves had unearthed an enormous piece of obsidian. Ignoring the aftermath of the battle, leaving the goblins to rebuild and breed and find sustenance in the nearby forests, Leopold found himself compelled toward his next task. Using tools fashioned by the bones of fallen dwarves and goblins, he obsessively chipped and polished the massive black rock for months on end.

It was some time before even he himself understood what he was making. The moment his master's eyes sprung to life within the perfect effigy was the last moment he could bear to look upon it. That briefest instant, seeing the power before him, was the only terror left for Leopold. The ultimate terror. The source of his darkness.

Now rooted in this dimension, his master's voice was clearer. Leopold was needed elsewhere. *Bring me a sentinel to lead the savages*, it commanded. The last Leopold saw beneath the mountain was a gateway to another land being burned out of space itself, by those hateful, glorious eyes.

The forests around the mountain were frustratingly thick. Leopold was pleased to see paths beaten into submission here and there by his goblin progeny. He floated toward a skirmish. A man in a hut was casting mighty forces that were stunning and obliterating goblin assailants on all sides.

Guided by otherworldly knowledge, Leopold dug deep into his own eye-sockets and extracted his two coal-black eyeballs. He drifted into the battle knowing he had located his master's new sentinel, and knowing precisely what it was he needed to do.

"The sun's pretty," he finally mumbled, lamely.

Chapter Twelve
SCARS

"But I really have to pee!" Ruprecht was whining now.

He had tried every manner of protestation since the man who called himself Geoffrey had ushered him onto the barren splintery wood-slat wagon and urged the mule forward into a slow bumpy clop.

The devastating reunion with his deity had left Ruprecht breathless and disoriented, and he had lacked the wherewithal to resist being led through the unfamiliar forest to the waiting transport.

But his wits were returning, and with them came the hunger. He could feel the delicious burn of the orb in that wrecked place in his chest it had once occupied. He fingered the pitted scar surreptitiously and immediately saliva and sweat began to bead in his glands.

"Seriously, I have to go bad," he pouted, lacking the energy to commit to the lie that even he knew was failing to persuade his staunch captor.

"Go off the side, if you must," came Geoffrey's terse reply, "or go on the boards, or in your pants, for all I care. Time is precious, and we mustn't stop, Ruprecht."

"But I shouldn't have to go anywhere with you!" Ruprecht retorted with renewed fervor in a thin, strained shout. "It's not right. And how do you know my name anyway? I never told you my name."

"Ruprecht," the cloaked man said patiently, still facing forward, "I want you to tell me everything you see around us that you think is beautiful. List them to me."

The sweat was flowing now. Ruprecht's armpits were hot and humid pockets emitting trickles of fluid that were sliding and cooling down the insides of his arms and his sides. He was scared. He had lost control.

"What?" Ruprecht guffawed derisively, desperately. "That's got to be the stupidest..."

"DO IT NOW." The command emanated through the back of Geoffrey's hood along with a force that caused air to compress vise-like around Ruprecht's limbs, spin him in place, and pin him squarely in a seated position facing the road behind them.

The overwhelming power and violence of the energy he had just received shook Ruprecht out of the spiral of deceit he had fallen into. It left him speechless.

"I'm waiting," Geoffrey prodded insistently. "I will hear you describe no less than seven things of beauty in the countryside around us."

Several long bumpy, minutes passed while Ruprecht struggled feebly against his invisible bonds.

"The sun's pretty," he finally mumbled, lamely.

"You're not trying very hard, Ruprecht," the hood replied.

Anger soared quickly and unexpectedly past the film of defeat that had settled over him, and Ruprecht yelled, "What do you want from me? Let me go! You don't know me. You don't know what I can do!" The shrill threatening tone hung suspended in the air between them as they jostled along down the skinny dirt road now surrounded by wide and rolling green meadows dotted with shrubs and speckled with birds and the occasional foraging animal.

"The sun is pretty, Ruprecht, you're right," Geoffrey admitted. "Tell me about it."

This was new. It caught Ruprecht off guard. He had, of course, not really been considering the beauty of the sun when he had suggested it as the first of his seven things. He was merely trying to get Geoffrey off his back. But now it appeared Geoffrey was listening to him, taking him at his word. And Geoffrey's request for more information wormed its way into Ruprecht's sour mind before his selfish need could shut it down.

"Well, it's big and bright," the words passed his lips before he had really thought about them. It immediately sounded like a silly thing to say. "I mean, it's not always big and bright, you know? Some days it's dark and gray, and at night it's gone altogether, but today it's clear and strong and warm."

"That is special, isn't it?" Geoffrey's voice floated back to him. "I totally agree."

"It's interesting," Ruprecht was on a roll all of a sudden, "because it makes everything glow. Like that cloud," he pointed up at

Chapter Twelve

a big fluff directly above them not realizing that the iron grip of atmosphere that had previously pinned his arm to his side had evaporated to allow the motion.

"Yes, Ruprecht," his companion said gently.

"And I'm looking out at those two little birds over there, do you see the ones chasing each other? It's like they're playing a game. And I don't know if they do that all the time, but it just seems to me like the sunlight energizes things, you know? Like, have you ever noticed that flowers seem to turn toward the sun? It's like their petals form little faces and those little faces follow the sun across the sky as it moves."

Ruprecht fell silent. His hips and back jostled with the bed of the wagon as it rolled over divots in the country road. He began to feel stupid again. He began to feel like he had been tricked into playing a child's game. He began to feel like Geoffrey, inside that infuriating hood, was laughing at him either for getting tricked into playing along, or because his answers had been weak. For the briefest of moments he had a vision of separating that hood from the rest of Geoffrey's cloaked body and placing it on a tall spike against a distantly familiar backdrop of fire-red for all to see. But the sun's warmth was also urgently tugging him back to the momentary enthusiasm he had felt a moment earlier, and it led him to conclude defensively, "So I guess that's what I meant when I said *the sun's pretty.*"

"Seven!" Geoffrey exclaimed triumphantly.

"What?" Ruprecht was confused.

"That's seven beautiful things, Ruprecht. You said the sun, that it's big and bright, that it's brightness is special, that it's warm, that it causes everything to glow, that those two birds seem energized by its light, and that little flower-petal faces follow it through the sky.

Those are lovely observations you've made about beauty around us at this very moment. Thank you, Ruprecht."

Geoffrey drew gently on the mule's reins and the wagon creaked to a stop. He half-turned to Ruprecht, who was now facing forward, and reached his right hand back to grasp Ruprecht's right forearm. Ruprecht blinked involuntarily. At Geoffrey's touch every inch of his skin felt like it was being lightly pinched by a chill air. The next thing he knew they were seated facing each other on top of a grassy hill, a short distance from the road.

"You have asked who I am," Geoffrey began, before Ruprecht could articulate his surprise, "and I think it's time I told you." He stood up and began pulling his jet-black robe off over his head.

The first thing Ruprecht noticed as the folds lifted was Geoffrey's mangled right foot. It was missing the three toes in the middle, and the smooth part that normally leads to the ankle was a caved-in discolored valley of scar tissue that continued up to where his shin would have begun and then disappeared up under the hem of his pants.

Dropping his robe in a pile next to them, Geoffrey sat back down cross-legged. He fixed Ruprecht with an intense gaze, but Ruprecht found it hard to look back at him. Geoffrey's head and face were completely hairless. Ruprecht had never seen someone with no eyebrows or eyelashes before. Moreover, the skin on all the prominent points of Geoffrey's face—his nose, his lips, his cheeks—seemed to be melted and runny.

"You'll have to pardon my face." Seeing Ruprecht's aghast expression, Geoffrey attempted a crooked smile the effect of which was more unsettling than reassuring. "I had a nasty disagreement with a very unpleasant earth crawler recently, and she left her mark upon me, I'm afraid."

Chapter Twelve

Ruprecht had no words.

"But it's not the scars on my face I wish to talk about today, Ruprecht," Geoffrey continued in his kind way. "The scars we must discuss plunge far deeper than those, and I believe they are borne by us both."

"Dad would let me carry things, or mess around with tools nearby, or pile small armfuls of wheat next to the wagon. It felt important to me at the time."

Chapter Thirteen
GEOFFREY

———————

"When I think of my boyhood, Ruprecht, I see sunshine. I remember the warmth on my skin, and especially the smell; the smell of warm green thickets filled with buzzing insects," Geoffrey began reverently.

"My father tended wheat fields for the lord of the Southern Plains. I went with him when he did his rounds. He had a rickety cart and a mule, not unlike the one I've got over there actually," Geoffrey chuckled pointing down the hill, "and we trundled far and wide through the huge flat fields that surrounded our little farmhouse."

Unable to look at Geoffrey's distorted features for long, Ruprecht stared down at the grassy earth beneath his own crossed legs.

Chapter Thirteen

"Sometimes he filled buckets with water and took them to dry patches, sometimes he would scatter seeds. The hardest days were tilling or threshing. I still marvel that he was able to will his old body to lift those heavy tools over and over again, for hours at a time, day after day."

Ruprecht was getting bored. He found himself listening only partway, hoping the story would end soon, hoping he would be left alone.

"Of course, at some point I was old enough to help, but as a boy I didn't really do very much. Dad would let me carry things, or mess around with tools nearby, or pile small armfuls of wheat next to the wagon. It felt important to me at the time."

Geoffrey concluded this last bit in a wistful tone, and the pause that followed was so long that Ruprecht began thinking this was the entire story—began thinking that now he was supposed to say something smart or sensitive.

"The lord of the plains died when I was fifteen." Geoffrey broke the silence, saving Ruprecht the need to say anything. "Dad's health was failing by that point, and I had really taken on most of the farming duties. I had a friend who also worked the land named Friederich. After dad stopped going out to work, Friederich and I would meet each day and work along side one another. We'd take breaks and lie down on the grass and stare up at the sky and talk. Sometimes we would talk long into the night even. I was feeling down about my dad's poor health, my mom was talking less and less by then, and Friederich..." Geoffrey trailed off.

"And Friederich?" Ruprecht's sudden interest surprised even himself.

"Ah yes, Friederich," Geoffrey returned. "One night he invited me back to his place. Friederich's parents hosted a gathering most nights in secret. At first I didn't know why it was secret, but it was exciting in a way to be part of something special that not everyone was supposed to know about, you know? I started attending their meetings whenever I could. They spoke in whispers about things I'd never heard openly discussed at home, things like love, and forgiveness, and generosity. And they invited the people there to share their own stories. I think earlier in my life, I wouldn't have had patience to listen to stuff like that, but with dad fading—and mom too, I suppose—some part of me was really hungry for the compassion of those evenings huddled together."

After another pause, Geoffrey went on, "Finally one night it was my turn. There we were, crowded into this little farmhouse. Friederich himself had lit the big red candle that you had to sit in front of if you wanted to say anything. There was barely enough light to see each other. And I..." Geoffrey faltered, his voice was becoming thick with emotion. "I felt The Great One for the first time Ruprecht. Just getting ready to talk about dad and mom—just forming the thoughts I had to form to share the confusion and fear I was feeling— brought me before the light you and I both know so well."

Geoffrey began to cry. Tears slid quickly down the unnaturally smooth melted grooves in his cheeks and pooled above scarred lumps of skin, before spilling over and falling into the warm air.

"What did you say?" Ruprecht asked gently, he found himself staring now at the wrecked face of the man before him.

"I didn't say anything," Geoffrey said softly. He took a deep breath and continued. "Remember I told you the lord had died? Well his sons had taken over and I soon learned about why the meetings were secret. It was because the new rulers of the plains didn't want any of us to be lifted up, didn't want any of us to organize, to find power within ourselves, to believe in anything but their supremacy. I never got the chance to say anything, Ruprecht, because their men ambushed us that night in the farmhouse."

"You're talking about Carlton and Bertrand Ingroff, aren't you, Geoffrey?" the light had dawned for Ruprecht.

"Yes." Geoffrey replied, looking his companion squarely in the eyes.

"And you know that Friederich was my uncle, don't you?"

"He still is," Geoffrey's darkened face cracked into a lopsided grin.

"You've seen him recently?" Ruprecht's heart was pounding now. His mind was racing with a mix of hope and fear.

"I have, Ruprecht, and I have seen your mom too." Geoffrey reached out and touched Ruprecht's mangled left hand, "They are well. Getting older, you know, but peaceful, and safe. Grisella is quite concerned about you."

Friederich's parents, Ruprecht's grandparents, were killed that night as was most of their congregation. This was a story Ruprecht had heard many times. Ruprecht's uncle Friederich had escaped along with Geoffrey and several others, however, and with time they established a secret school deep in the Bryker Woods in which to deepen their faith, hone their teachings, and organize their resistance to the brutal rule of the Ingroff brothers. They came to refer to themselves as The Brykerlings.

Geoffrey actually recalled Ruprecht's arrival with his mother, Grisella, on the back of Friederick's brown mare the day they fled from home. It was the day after Ruprecht's own first communion with the

GEOFFREY

Brykerling deity—that day when the fuel of his desperation had obliterated the marauders invading their home and delivered his youthful plea to his uncle Friederich through the ether.

But the demise of the Ingroffs came not long after that, and as stability returned to the Southern Plains, Geoffrey felt his faith calling him to the north, to solitude, and ultimately to build a lone cottage in the woods about a half-day's walk from the village of Westover.

"...And that brings us back to the discussion of the deep scars we both bear, Ruprecht." It was the middle of their second day talking on the hillside—up from the road where Geoffrey's mule waited patiently near the simple flat wooden cart that had borne them here.

A new heaviness tugged at Geoffrey's voice, and Ruprecht—who until this moment had settled into a comfortable reverie listening to the stories of a man he had once met, a man who knew his mom and his uncle—felt a sudden twinge of defensive anxiety, a powerful urge to protect himself.

"Oh, those," Ruprecht forced a casual ease into his words. "I feel a lot better now about all that. It was bad for a while, I realize, but I think this whole journey with you has really helped. I think I'm recovered."

Geoffrey eyed Ruprecht appraisingly. The ruination of his features made his expression hard to read, but to Ruprecht it appeared like skepticism mixed with disappointment.

"Several things, Ruprecht," Geoffrey began patiently. "First, I agree. This journey has helped. You have come a long way since a few short days ago. The Great One cleansed you, and our conversations have helped to bring light into some dark places. But I'm afraid you are far from recovered, my friend. In fact, neither of us will ever be the way we were before the orbs."

It was too much. At the word "orbs" Ruprecht jumped into the air and began to run. He had no more words for this ugly old-timer, this man he barely knew, who claimed to know everything about him. *For all I know he's trying to get them for himself!* Ruprecht thought wildly as he dashed down the hillside.

He made it a little distance down the road, too, before the now-familiar pressure of the atmosphere seizing him, closed around his upper arms and lifted him from the ground. Sailing backward through the air to Geoffrey, Ruprecht absurdly pumped his legs back and forth as if he thought he was still running away.

"My point exactly," Geoffrey sighed heavily, as the struggling Ruprecht was deposited back on the ground in front of him.

"Shall we continue?"

He needed something strong, something resilient.
He did not yet know why.

Chapter Fourteen
THE BOOK

A few months ago...

The goblins and the dwarves and the eyes and the hermit were a distant memory for Leopold when he finally came upon the shapeshifter. He needed something strong, something resilient. He did not yet know why.

He was deep in some forest when the massive brown bear lumbered into view. She was sniffing at the ground for berries and grubs, blowing small bits of leaves and dirt with each warm heavy exhalation.

Leopold hated her instantly.

The first thing he hated was her interest in eating berries and grubs. Such force she had. Such teeth! And to waste all that weaponry

Chapter Fourteen

was galling to the extreme.

The second thing Leopold hated was her apparent awareness of him.

Usually when creatures encountered him they crumbled, they weakened, they cowered, or they gave in to their darkest desires. They had no idea why. But not this one. She sensed him immediately, almost as quickly as he had become aware of her. And she ran.

At first she ran swiftly—deftly cutting through terrain she clearly knew. Her massive paws sank into the earth, claws the size of hunting knives cutting into the dirt as she swerved this way and that in an attempt to shake the unseen presence pursuing her. Leopold flew behind, taunting her with his penetrating dark thoughts.

The bear began to tire. It was little things at first, little stumbles, late turns around underbrush, low leaps that barely cleared obstacles in her path. Slobber formed around her muzzle and began foaming and streaming in two sticky strands as she panted, desperate to evade the terrifying foreign presence behind her.

Ghostly rags fluttering, Leopold flew atop the fleeing bear and set down on her forward haunches like a rider on a horse. Her deep anguished groan was delightful.

His bony hands sizzled the skin on the back of her neck right through her thick brown fur as he leaned forward and began to hammer on her mind.

The she-bear made it home. Stumbling, delirious, she swayed and dragged her hulking form between two moss-covered natural stone walls. She collapsed with a heavy defeated gasp onto a tidy, wood-slat floor, beneath a meticulously-constructed wood and thatch roof. The room was situated within walls of clean-scrubbed natural stone. Iron tools, a fireplace, and handmade furniture of wood and fur were arrayed neatly throughout.

As soon as she hit the floor she began to morph. Her form shrunk, her hair receded, her paws thinned and elongated. At last a tall, brown-haired woman lay, face-down, on the floor of her woodland home. Two large frost-blistered patches of skin showed brightly on either side of the back of her neck. She was unconscious, and Leopold would have to wait for her to recover.

It did not take long.

When she stirred a short while later, the blistered patches on her neck had already vanished thanks to the power of the shapeshifter blood coursing through her veins.

Perfect, thought Leopold viciously.

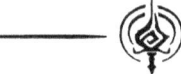

The book was constructed of several things. A mushy pulp of wood and saliva was spread, dried, pressed, and cut into pages. The black covering was two squares of hide flayed from the bear herself, twice, from the same wide flat place on her abdomen—each time those wounds took several maddening days to heal.

But the main ingredient was servitude. She had to make it, against her will. This Leopold somehow knew.

In bear form, over the course of several weeks she clawed into living trees, extracted hunks of wood core from the exposed trunks, and then sullenly chewed them into slush.

Hers was a powerful mind. Controlling it was not easy. She bucked against him like a wild horse, and frequently would break free and run, or lunge savagely toward the emanations of cold she had come to associate with his horrid presence.

But a week of brutal domination, of chewing splinters and

spitting out bloody pulp, of spreading and pounding and pressing, left her exhausted mentally and physically. When the time came to make the leather binding, she had barely any strength left to resist.

Leopold did not normally feel pain. At least not his own.

But he had a keen sense of others'. He could sense it from miles away, and gorged on its essence like a human might ravenously inhale the smell of a favorite meal roasting over a roaring fire.

But writing the book was excruciating.

He had left the were-bear gasping on her once-clean floor amidst piles of bloody muck. The creature was so weakened she had gotten stuck somewhere between human and bear forms.

With the finished book grasped in his skeletal fingers he drifted absentmindedly through the forest. At last he held the book before his empty eye-sockets and turned to page one.

Searing fire bored a hole through the base of his spine. It raced through his insides cooking his mind. The power was uncontrollable.

Fire-red ethereal ink spewed out of both eye sockets onto the pages, which fluttered with a life of their own and drank up every last bit of the terrible otherworldly wisdom.

The young man in Rockmoor was perfect.

Smart, proud, ambitious, curious, and alone, he used his intelligence to gain resources, and his resources to buy secrets.

Leopold came upon him walking by the docks to a meeting in a dark corner of a seaside bar. He witnessed the young man offering a fat trader nearly everything in his possession to buy a square of fabric he understood would make him invisible.

Placing the book in the trader's crate beneath the cloak had been easy enough indeed.

It did not register to Leopold that this was a young man he had once known in life.

X'andria pulled the remainder of the mysterious cloak from her bag, set the bag aside, and smoothed the coolness out on her lap.

Chapter Fifteen
X'ANDRIA

Much of X'andria's personal time was spent so intensely focused on whatever she was studying that she became oblivious to the world outside of her head. Ironically, it took a quiet and uninterrupted period to get her to that place, but once there, all the ambient sounds—the crickets outside, the distant waves, the swish of her own feet rubbing methodically together beneath her blankets—were shut out completely by the thoughts whirring between her ears, by the blood pulsing on the inside of her skull.

Night was her time. At night the rest of the world slept. Night was when her small candle was the only light, when rhythmic snores were the only sounds made by her slumbering companions—all but Gnome, who slipped out most evenings only to return just before

Chapter Fifteen

daybreak.

It took a week of persistent nagging to convince Ohlen to allow her examination of the book and two parchment rolls Boudreaux had cleared from Elias' hellish sewer-study. Now here she was, grasping the precious items with her thin, sensitive fingers, palms moist in anticipation.

She selected the longer of the two rolls. This one had a familiar look to it, and she wanted to confirm her suspicion. Laying on her stomach, propped on her elbows, she coaxed open the thick leathery parchment to the point she could see the first angular etchings.

Sure enough, with a tinge of disappointment, she confirmed it was just what she had thought. It was the exhaustively detailed guide to conjuring fire that Elias had used to teach her what seemed ages ago.

But disappointment was not the only emotion she felt as she allowed the parchment to go slack between her fingers and retreat back toward its natural curvature. X'andria also felt sad. Until this moment she had not mourned Elias. She had been furious at him, horrified at what he turned out to be. She had contributed to his demise, and would willingly do so again if placed in the same situation.

But there was another side to him that the others had not seen. X'andria didn't know if it was his former self she had met, or just another aspect of his personality. He was smart and ambitious, perhaps sometimes a little impatient when he was teaching her, but he had been friendly and respectful and interested. In her.

She hoisted herself up into a sitting position with the intention of rerolling and stowing the fire scroll. But instead her hand drifted to her backpack, to the place she stowed the item of his she had retrieved when no one else was looking. Glancing carefully around to make sure everyone was really still asleep, she drew her bag to her and cradled it in her lap.

The fabric inside felt cool, almost like it was made of liquid silver. Nerves tingling she pulled it partially out of her bag and studied the scintillating material for the first time in the candlelight. Even though she held it, it seemed to race around her hand, reorganizing and reforming itself in response to her soft exhalations, to her tiny movements, to the heartbeat within her fingers.

What are you? she wondered, transfixed.

X'andria pulled the remainder of the mysterious cloak from her bag, set the bag aside, and smoothed the coolness out on her lap. And then she froze, unable to believe what she was seeing. Or not seeing. Her legs had disappeared. The cloak had taken on the appearance of the bedding around and beneath her, making it look like the lower half of her body had vanished completely.

At this discovery X'andria's heart began pounding and she hastily wadded up the cloak and stuffed it back inside her pack. As soon as it was securely hidden she looked around once more, to be certain no one had stirred. No one had seen. This little treasure was her secret, and she planned to keep it that way.

And this feeling of protectiveness brought to mind another item taken from below ground, another acquisition she had not divulged to her companions. When the blood-sack had burst and sprayed hot muck all over them, one of its ruby eyes had sailed through the air and landed before her. She had stowed it in one of her many pockets before departing. She extracted the glinting red gem now, studied it briefly and then slid it, also, into her backpack for safekeeping nestled deep within the cool folds of Elias' chameleon cloak.

X'andria's scalp and the back of her neck were uncomfortably hot and itchy as she reached for the second roll of parchment. This one opened with surprising ease, and she realized it was not made of parchment at all, but rather a very thin, well-worn leather or hide of some kind.

She did not understand everything she was seeing, but what she was able to make out was chilling, yet electrifying at the same time. This was a meditation on pain and injury. The runes themselves were messily scrawled as if the writer was in a huge hurry. The ideas were incomplete, more like shorthand sketches than the exhaustive detail of the fire scroll.

The first elaborate rune was new to her. She would need to know what it was. This, no doubt, was the power word. Beneath it she deciphered the following: *feel pain cause pain PRECISE speak mimic*. In smaller print, near the bottom, there was this list: *teardrops blood tool UNWILLING*.

It took her just a few seconds to lock the legible contents of the scroll into her memory. Only the ornate unfamiliar rune gave her a brief challenge as she etched the details of its line-widths, curves and dots into her mind's eye.

This left only the book.

She had saved it for last, the way one reserves a bite of the tastiest part of a meal to have something to look forward to while consuming the less flavorful parts. There was something about this book, even though it was not large, that made her think it was particularly significant—perhaps it was the long pause Ohlen had taken, hand lingering upon it, before he handed it over to her earlier that evening.

Cradling the book in her hands like a fragile baby animal, she gently lifted the thin worn cover from the pages it protected inside.

It was as if the blood-red ink of the first page jumped crystalline into the atmosphere, tore through the air, and assaulted her eyeballs.

Forced wide open and hopelessly glued to the now-fluttering pages, X'andria's eyes became unwilling conduits for an overwhelming glut of incomprehensible proportions.

There was information. Formulas, recipes, stories, images, but it was way too much, way too fast. Somewhere inside her, amidst the sickening overload she realized in horror, *I'm not reading this, it's reading me.*

You, you, you, it chanted. Objects were swirling around her, fire was bleeding from her body. *You, you, you*, the pulse was mesmerizing in her ears. The fat man was choking, clutching his neck, eyes bulging red, as olives and figs rushed unbidden into his powerless mouth. *You, you, you*, came the enthralling refrain. Boudreaux and the others were kneeling before her.

And suddenly it was over. X'andria's head was throbbing, she had a massive headache. The book was still on her lap but it was closed, Ohlen's hand lay firmly on top of the cover.

X'andria stared down at Ohlen's long resolute fingers feeling phenomenally weary with a mix of thrill, shame and resentment.

"I heard," the voice strained, like it was being forced through reeds to make a sound it was not originally designed to make, "that it ate them."

Chapter Sixteen
THIEVES AND SORCERERS

A silent but swift river of goods and information flows through the dark crevices and back alleys of every city. Its banks swell with a constant supply of valuables taken without consent, of secrets flung too casually by gossipers that land in the eager ears of eavesdroppers, of desperate people willing to pay for deeds too dark to be openly traded in shops and stalls. The problem with spying upon this world of bottom feeders is that it often places you in unpleasant situations.

Waif had stabilized three days after regaining consciousness, during which time Gnome spent every waking hour by his side. As the sun fell on that third day however, the urgent mystery of Rove's whereabouts and likely machinations pulled Gnome out into the muggy city night.

And, after three more days, pursuit of that mystery had deposited him here—clinging to a steep embankment beneath the slatted wood floor of a fishy kitchen stall, stuck alongside countless insects to layers of discarded oily sludge so thick not even rats from the drainage ditch below bothered to excavate whatever morsels

Chapter Sixteen

might be encased within.

"What more 'ave you heard 'bout that little guy an' his crew?" the one-eyed man growled through sunken oil-slick lips. When he spoke his mouth barely moved from the deflated grimace carved there by years of scowl and disappointment. *Come on, guys*, thought Gnome, *it's been three days, give me something*. He unstuck a hand from the gunk, and edged closer to peer up between the grease-dripped floorboards.

Gnome had not properly seen the one-eyed man's companion, who was always shrouded by a deeply drooping hood. But three nights earlier, jumping from walls to rooftops and listening in on conversations of all manner of unsavory characters—listening for some mention of Rove—he heard a strangely wheezing voice rasp out something about a gnome from underneath that hood. He had been following them each night since.

"I heard," the voice strained, like it was being forced through reeds to make a sound it was not originally designed to make, "that it ate them."

The two were seated on a makeshift bench, and a sleek hairy arm shot out from within the folds of the companion's robes to grab a piece of whatever they were eating, probably fish. *No, not grab*, Gnome realized, *skewer*! This thing's fingers ended in thick, straight nails filed into long dagger points, one of which it used like a hunting knife to deftly select its next bite.

"Ate 'em? Sounds more like somethin' *you'd* do, Sunoor." One-Eye chuckled nervously and stole a furtive glance at the darkened hood.

The thing within the hood responded with a hiss and a low rumble before continuing in its tortured wheeze, "It has friends. Two arms and two head cooks. They slayed some elf-kind and a dockhand

and a few others, ate them mostly, and there's good coin for their heads."

Gnome's mind was racing. *What the hell are they talking about? Two arms, two head cooks and a little guy? That could easily be Arden, Boudreaux, X'andria, Ohlen and me. But we didn't hurt anybody, we...*

And suddenly the hooded companion was sitting erect. In response, the man next to him transformed from an old grouch eating dinner into a taut ruthless hunter, his eye searching his companion for any indication of a threat. One dagger-finger emerged ever so slowly and pointed straight down at the slatted floor, straight at Gnome.

In an instant the man fell on his knees, blade in hand, eye hovering over the cracks to locate whatever his companion had sensed. At the same time the robed figure exploded into the air and flipped backward out of Gnome's limited field of vision.

Ignoring the startled shrieks of the nearby vendor and gruff barks to halt from One-Eye, Gnome began slipping hastily down the slick and sticky oil-covered embankment toward the drainage ditch. Tumbling backward, he snagged his right elbow and heel on an ancient wooden pier, and this sent him spiraling out of control down the remaining descent to the damp ditch below.

The thing was coming—its pursuit silent apart from breaths tinged by audible aerated growling. It had displayed startling strength and agility, not to mention animal instinct and weaponry, but it was the hungry, vacant look transforming the old man's face— the mercilessness—that played in Gnome's mind in the seconds he lay inhaling the rank ditch-fumes after his fall. Gnome sprang onto his feet and whirled around just in time to see the compact animal form land catlike in the ditch not twenty feet away, amidst a flutter of trailing robes.

Chapter Sixteen

Gnome began backing away warily, his dagger had appeared somehow between his teeth. The one-eyed man's words echoed in his ears—*ate 'em? Sounds more like somethin' you'd do, Sunoor.* This thing was a predator, a killer.

It must have sensed his fear, because it sprang forward on a mix of powerful limbs. Gnome was sprinting down the ditch, heart in his mouth. He was fast, but this thing was faster. They sped through the twisty ditch, dodging support beams and refuse deposited haphazardly by a city that had long-ago forgotten its existence. The thought of those savage claws tearing through him pushed Gnome's legs to their fullest exertion. The ditch was rising, the embankments on either side became less steep, and they approached the subterranean firmament of a large building laid by the city founders in centuries past.

It hit him from behind at shoulder height. The impact was oddly soft, perfectly placed to knock him off balance, but not in a clumsy or desperate kind of way. Graceful at any speed Gnome tucked into a roll and hit the ground as lightly as could be expected given the circumstance. So too must have his attacker, because he did not even hear any other impact whatsoever, not so much as a grunt—only that rumbling wheezy breathing.

Regaining his feet Gnome found it was now in front of him, between him and the stone foundation, and he was able to see her for the first time. Hood back, she looked down at him curiously, emotionless. Her face, distantly human, looked like a lioness' head had tried to force its way out through her skin from the inside. Only the ears, whiskers and eyes made it to surface, the feline nose and saber-lined maw were barely contained within tightly stretched skin. She was purring.

She came in low, matching her joint pivot points to the level of her target. Her hands—paws—were a deadly slicing blur. Gnome rolled and dodged, merging with the darkness around him, cutting behind obstacles, weaving up and down over the uneven terrain, but she was tireless. Her ferocious attacks sprung relentlessly, silently, efficiently, beneath the methodical hungry hum of her rhythmic breath.

When the claws finally raked across his body they began low, around his mid-section, and arced up across his chest. He knew it was going to happen. Engaged as he was in their deadly dance, he could feel himself falling a step behind, he anticipated the upward swat, saw it unfolding as if time had slowed. It was not deep, but there were four thin slashes that split his sleek leather tunic, split the skin beneath, and released the blood pumping furiously inside.

Gnome hit the ground on his backside. This was not fatal, not yet anyway. She stood up tall and surveyed him, a mix of satisfaction and hunger in her golden feline eyes. It was time to play.

Verda'eiftu. Multiply. Gnome breathed the word after extracting a crushed and gloppy cricket from his shredded tunic. His brain seemed to separate and pull away. The middle part stayed in him, but the two sides drifted confusingly outward to occupy perfect mirror images of himself—also seated bloody and defeated on the ground—in both directions.

Sunoor seemed to comprehend what was happening because a low warning growl emitted from deep within her chest. Gnome, winded and injured but by no means fully exhausted, willed himself and his projections to move swiftly in and out of the pylons that thrust upward from the ditch in support of the street-level structures above.

She attacked. She attacked wildly now, furiously, claws raking through thin air at his visions darting around in the dim light. With tremendous effort Gnome piloted his likenesses behind him in jaunty evasive dances, but seized the opportunity to race his real self to the towering stone firmament on the other side of his foe.

Climbing the wall would require too much concentration to maintain his focus on bundling and directing the light and ether behind him, and so he abandoned those projections and strained to recover his full consciousness.

Eyes ablaze, Sunoor whipped around just in time to see him scuttle desperately up into the Rockmoor dawn and away from the death dripping hungrily from her claws. As he ascended, Gnome heard the empty streets beneath him fill with the deafening ring of a bone-chilling lioness' roar.

The book was closed. It lay still. With a grim look on his face Ohlen sat next to X'andria, placed a hand on her arm, and asked if she felt well enough to lead him to The Sorcerer of Rockmoor.

A short while later they were walking along the worn boards of Westwood in silence.

Ohlen had taken the hideous book back from her, and stowed it within a slim brown leather satchel with molded silver buckles that had been a gift from Arden two nights before.

"What just happened to me, Ohlen?" X'andria finally blurted out as they crossed The Torrent into Hillcrest. She was still weary and confused from the onslaught of the book's enchanted pages.

"I was going to ask *you* that very same question, X'andria," Ohlen replied, his tone somewhere between concern and disapproval.

"Hey, I was just trying to examine it," she fired back defensively. "It's not like I *wanted* any of that to happen."

Ohlen seemed to consider this carefully for several long moments before replying, "Of course you did not, X'andria. I know that. Do you feel up to telling me what it was that you experienced, as best you can recall?"

"It's like the secrets of the whole world are in there, Ohlen. But it's not a book you can read. It forced the ideas into me so fast I couldn't understand any of it. And," and here X'andria searched momentarily for the right words, "I honestly think it was reading me more than I was reading it."

They threaded their way east into Watertown, toward the docks, toward The Emporium.

"Why do you want to see The Sorcerer, Ohlen? I've never even met him myself," X'andria finally asked, shrugging her small backpack higher onto her shoulder. The knowledge that it contained two of Elias' scrolls, on top of a chameleon cloak, wrapped around a ruby plucked from the demon muck below ground, made X'andria's pack seem heavier than usual.

"My hope, X'andria, is that The Sorcerer will become an ally. We need all the friends we can get, especially powerful ones. And I believe this object," Ohlen patted the book inside his bag, "contains important mysteries that will require great power to discern."

The streets became narrower and more twisting as they entered the seaside district of Watertown, the oldest part of Rockmoor and home to The Emporium and The Sorcerer. The cobblestones beneath their feet were worn smooth by centuries of foot traffic, push carts, and rainwater.

At this pre-dawn hour, almost no one stirred. Which is why Ohlen so keenly sensed the first cool consciousness appear out of nowhere down the dark street before them. Cloaked in midnight blue, one of the Sorcerer's sensates stepped out of the air itself on a puff of silver mist that quickly dissipated.

"We are no longer alone," whispered Ohlen surreptitiously.

"I know," replied X'andria under her breath. "They sometimes appear near The Emporium," she explained, "but only when I'm returning something I borrowed from the library. I think they can sense the presence of magical things."

"I feel no malice," observed Ohlen, "but neither is there warmth."

They walked stiffly past the tall motionless sentry and rounded a corner. At the end of the next alley, preceded by a faint glint of silver mist, a similar stoic figure stepped forward out of thin air and silently surveyed their progress.

"Here we are," breathed X'andria a few minutes later. She pushed through a decrepit weather-beaten door into the shabby shop that was the entryway to The Emporium.

"This is where we will find The Sorcerer?" queried Ohlen skeptically, still using a low voice even though the shop was deserted.

"Not everything here is as it seems to be, Ohlen," X'andria replied as she led him past a counter behind which shelves held vials of luminescent multi-colored liquids.

X'andria continued to the far wall, Ohlen trailing distractedly behind as trinkets and toy animals came alive in his peripheral vision pulling on his attention and tempting his curiosity.

"This way, Ohlen," X'andria urged, as she stepped directly through an empty table and the wall behind it. Ohlen hesitated, dumbfounded. X'andria was gone, and the whirring and clicking of animated mechanical objects grew louder and more insistent behind him. He was about to turn around and look once more at The

Emporium's bizarre offerings when X'andria's hand reached back out through the wall, grabbed his arm with surprising strength, and yanked him forward into the space beyond.

"Stay behind me, but stay close," X'andria eyed Ohlen with a rare gravity. They were in a library with book-lined walls, an ornate red carpet, and an array of plush chairs and cushions. Ohlen was startled to realize that the comfortable warm lighting of the space seemed to emanate from the ceiling itself, like it was made of a piece of a pleasant late-afternoon sky. A young man with dark hawkish features glanced up at them momentarily from an enormous volume resting in his lap. A blotchy woman nearby—the only other person in the room—intensely scoured a parchment roll open before her, and seemed unaware of their presence. Her head was wrapped hastily in a gray scarf, her eyebrows appeared to be singed off, and parts of her face and hands had burn marks.

X'andria led Ohlen through several odd-shaped, book-filled chambers. They were passing out of the library and into a darkened hallway when Ohlen felt the cold presence of one of the Sorcerer's sensates and caught sight of a column of silver mist materializing before a nearby shelf.

"Where are we going?" Ohlen asked sounding uncharacteristically mesmerized.

"That was the library," X'andria replied matter-of-factly, "and now we're heading into Practicum. Practicum's a series of rooms where you can try things out. After that it's The Bazaar where they buy and sell all kinds of rare ingredients and tools of the trade. I've never been past The Bazaar, it's enormous, but I figure the further we go, the closer we'll get to The Sorcerer."

At the word "Sorcerer," however, everything changed.

They suddenly found themselves standing on a stone landing at the top of a wide curving staircase that wound down and out of sight. Dim but sufficient light was cast by white candles that floated along the ancient gray walls absent fixtures of any kind. If Ohlen were to guess, he would say they were in the turret of some great castle.

Set into the wall before them was a solitary wooden door with iron bands, and a knocker mounted in the middle in the shape of a serpent. Collecting himself, Ohlen stepped forward to try the knocker.

X'andria yelled, "STOP Ohlen!"

Ohlen froze.

"Things here aren't as they seem, remember? You NEED to let me go first," X'andria pleaded.

"I am sorry, X'andria, of course you are right. This part just seems rather straightforward." Ohlen had stopped and turned, wearing a curious expression on his face that might have been impatience.

"Look again," X'andria said flatly, indicating the door with her chin.

Where before there had been a stone wall, now there were the thick iron bars of a jail cell. On the other side of the bars, at the precise point where the illusion of the banded wooden door had been, a naked and hairless hermaphroditic monster stood lurking on two stubby, severely supinated legs. Above its pot belly, two long, stringy arms extended from a sunken chest covered by folds of mottled skin. Both of its abnormally large clawed hands were poised just outside the bars. It bore three lipless, fanged mouths: the first was where a human's forehead would be, but it was aligned vertically, not horizontally. The other two, parallel to the first, were where you might normally find ears. There were no eyes that X'andria or Ohlen could see, but it had two long slits on what might otherwise be its face that flapped open and closed as it inhaled and exhaled in a ceaseless search for the scent of prey. Mounds of cracked and gnawed bones were piled and strewn throughout the large cell behind it, and the floor was stained by the lifeblood of its many unfortunate victims.

"How do you like Gruder?" a wheezy voice penetrated icily through their revulsion and shook both Ohlen and X'andria out of their stupor.

They whirled around to face the speaker. In a stiff floor-length fire-red coat fastened in front by oblong ivory buttons, The Sorcerer stepped onto the landing from the stone staircase. His head lolled oddly toward his left shoulder, almost like it was too heavy to hold straight up. His left eye was closed tightly, but his right was a vibrant electric blue that fixed the two visitors with a piercing stare.

"Wh-what is it?" X'andria stammered, struggling to process the horror imprisoned behind them.

"Thadeus Gruder," The Sorcerer chuckled self-importantly, enunciating each syllable overmuch. "It was an experiment he tried some years ago—right here in Practicum—that left him in this state. I have never seen anything quite like it before or since, and I could not bear to let him go."

At these words, the three lipless mouths of the monster called Gruder began clicking vigorously, and it bounced up and down on its bowlegs, tightly gripping the bars of its cell like an impatient child demanding a treat. Ohlen was suddenly flooded by a deep sense of suffocating sadness mixed with insatiable all-consuming hunger.

Looking smugly satisfied through his one good eye at the two dumbstruck visitors, The Sorcerer spun on his heel and started heading down the stairs calling lazily back over his shoulder, "follow me."

Scrunching up his face so that even his brilliant blue eye became a small slit, The Sorcerer gingerly opened the rat's cage and deftly grasped the cowering animal in one of his spotted hands.

Chapter Seventeen
THE SORCERER OF ROCKMOOR

———————

Ohlen's disturbance deepened as he descended the staircase behind X'andria and The Sorcerer. Preoccupied by the overwhelming sadness of the tragic and terrible Gruder, he could not work out any justification for The Sorcerer's choice to imprison the unfortunate soul and use him as a grotesque and deadly gatekeeper devouring would-be visitors who lacked the vision to avoid the snare of his spidery claws.

As the stiff red conical form of The Sorcerer bobbed jauntily down the eerily-lit windowless circular staircase, Ohlen found himself wondering if anything surrounding them was, in fact, real.

Gruder's spiritual presence had somehow been masked from him, until the monster had revealed itself with its ravenous tantrum. The Sorcerer was similarly absent from Ohlen's probing awareness, a hole in ethereal space. It was unsettling, indeed, to be in a place where Ohlen's own senses could not be trusted.

X'andria, however, projected a wide-open ebullience as she hastened along behind The Sorcerer. Her inquisitive nature—a tendency to find interest in almost anything and anyone—normally inspired Ohlen and challenged his penchant for cautious appraisal. But in this strange environment her curious nature only deepened Ohlen's apprehension.

An opening melted into the solid wall before The Sorcerer, stone disappeared organically the way parchment recedes and evaporates into flame as it burns. The three passed into a domed chamber lined with narrow alcoves, and Ohlen felt the return of the cold sentinel presences—many of them—as the wall reformed itself behind.

X'andria's red hair turning this way and that as she absorbed their surroundings, and her voracious spirit presence, were like brilliant beacons in a sea of bleak gray. Stealing a glance into an alcove as they passed, Ohlen was mildly interested to see a grim-faced sentinel in midnight blue stepping back out of an interior wall that looked like a glassy image of an early-morning seaside market. Each successive alcove contained a similar portal-wall through which different parts of Rockmoor could be seen shifting into or out of focus. Sentinels came and went, faint silver mist enveloping their forms and then dissipating upon arrival. Some lingered, absorbed in studying the scenes within their portals. Near a far wall two had emerged from their alcoves to whisper about a velvet-draped object hovering suspended between them.

The Sorcerer perched behind an expansive table that had massive wooden legs carved with curving muscular designs. Elbows on the surface, fingers intertwined lightly together, his crooked head seemed nothing more than a frame for the one brilliant blue eye studying his half-elf guest—he seemed to take no notice of Ohlen.

Objects and books overflowed the table, the shelves, and the floor of the vast round study. The space was far from neat, but in many cases several objects of a similar type were lined up next to one another, or precariously stacked.

"You have something that belongs to me." The Sorcerer said coolly to X'andria.

Ohlen's stomach clenched as his thoughts turned to the book in his satchel. He was not at all sure he was comfortable revealing it to the odd little man before them.

"I do," replied X'andria brightly, returning their host's stare. Ohlen did not know what they were referring to, and her enthusiasm took him completely off-guard.

"Here you go," X'andria stated matter-of-factly as she stood, retrieved a roll of parchment from her backpack and made to deposit it on the table before The Sorcerer. The fire scroll never touched the table, however, because without so much as a twitch of his eye, The Sorcerer sent it flying swiftly across the dim chamber to join its brethren in an innocuous wicker basket by an armoire hung with crooked doors.

"Did you…make use of it?" The Sorcerer pried, betraying genuine interest for the first time.

"Oh yes," X'andria replied disarmingly. "It's really, very helpful."

Did she just wink at him? Ohlen was mystified by this entire exchange. As uncomfortable as he found himself, X'andria seemed to be completely at home.

"...and the individual who gave it to you?" A seriousness settled around them.

X'andria's demeanor changed to match the tone of The Sorcerer's words. "Ah yes," she sighed, "Elias." The two looked at each other in silence, the name seemed to hang in the air between them like an accusation.

"Yes, Elias," The Sorcerer finally continued. "He has involved himself in some interesting things. A promising young man."

"Like Thadeus Gruder," Ohlen interjected sourly, he couldn't help himself. Both X'andria and The Sorcerer looked over at him only briefly before returning attention to one another.

"This place is amazing," X'andria enthused, changing the subject.

"It is the finest collection of sentient artifacts ever assembled," The Sorcerer replied authoritatively. "I feel as though I have a responsibility—a man in my position...you can imagine, I suppose—to preserve these items, and to protect people from themselves."

Like you protected Gruder and Elias, Ohlen thought privately. He found The Sorcerer's self-righteous tone offensive.

"You know Elias, then?" X'andria prodded, after a respectful pause during which she dutifully looked around the packed room.

"Oh, I know everyone, dear." The Sorcerer returned smugly. "But let's talk about why you wished to see me. My time is precious, and I do not think you sought me out just to return that little guide to making sparks."

"So then you know he's dead?"

The words hit the room like a bird flying into a window. The Sorcerer's features froze.

"Well...I can't say that I'm surprised." He was clearly rattled by the news, but recovered his poise quickly.

The Sorcerer unfolded his hands and sat back now, placing them flat on the table before him. His eye darted momentarily to Ohlen, and then back to X'andria who was smiling politely.

"It's a bit complicated," X'andria continued, "but we recovered something unusual and we need someone of your wisdom and stature to help us understand it."

Here we go, thought Ohlen. He was not fond of The Sorcerer, and was not sure he wanted to place the book in his hands.

"First, I'd like to draw something for you," X'andria stood and approached the table.

"I am not here to play games with undereducated girls," The Sorcerer retorted haughtily.

X'andria froze, Ohlen felt a flash of the anger she was capable of dance briefly through the ether. "Of course you're not," she managed, "I've just heard so many tales of your unparalleled wisdom, and no one I've met can tell me what this is. I was just hoping..."

"Fine, fine. Draw it here, quickly." The Sorcerer interrupted, feigning annoyance. Ohlen realized that by allowing The Sorcerer to recover the upper hand in the conversation, X'andria was bending him to her will.

With a quill and blank parchment that materialized on the table before her, X'andria drew a rapid series of slashes and points before turning the page around for The Sorcerer's appraisal.

"*shra'muhrjnik*," breathed The Sorcerer in disbelief. He studied the symbol for some time before returning his gaze slowly to X'andria. "Where did you encounter this darkness?"

Ohlen was wondering the same thing. But in that moment— hearing The Sorcerer's aghast tone—he concluded that while the arrogant man clearly enjoyed his position and possessions, he was not the type to use an evil object like Elias' book for nefarious means.

"I have the book here," Ohlen declared, standing. He extracted Elias' small black book from his satchel and placed it on the table between X'andria and The Sorcerer. X'andria pushed it toward him while deftly recovering, folding and stowing the parchment upon which she'd recreated the rune from Elias' other scroll, the one hastily scrawled on some kind of hide.

Sweat beaded on The Sorcerer's forehead. He had alternated standing and viewing the book from afar with crawling partially on top of the table to bring his face so close to the worn cover it seemed he might stick his tongue out and taste it.

A brass monocle with multi-colored interchangeable lenses sailed through the air to his aid, as did a variety of powders and fluids which he pinched and poured and painted onto the surface of the table while muttering and heaving heavy, audible breaths. He did not appear to be making satisfactory progress in his evaluation.

The Sorcerer rapped his knuckles twice on the table top and within seconds one of his cloaked sensates stepped out of thin air beside him holding a small wire cage in which a large white rat dozed. As the sensate disappeared, The Sorcerer placed the cage carefully on the table. Waking suddenly, the rat raced twice around its cage before stopping and shuddering in the spot furthest from the book.

Scrunching up his face so that even his brilliant blue eye became a small slit, The Sorcerer gingerly opened the rat's cage and deftly grasped the cowering animal in one of his spotted hands. Ohlen sensed screaming in its mind as it was brought closer and closer to the book. The rat fought madly against the fingers holding it, and bit The Sorcerer just inches from the book. One drop of blood fell to the table, as did the rat. The rat scurried away and dropped off the far edge of the table and out of sight. The blood splatted on the dark wood, but immediately pulled together into a perfectly round drop. The drop was sucked oozing into the nearest edge of the little book.

The book flew open.

Blood red ink swirled into a powdery dervish above fluttering pages before plunging into The Sorcerer's blue eye just a few feet away.

He started shaking. Breath and spittle and snot emitted from his nose and mouth in spastic bursts. At first he just murmured, "uh, uh, uh," between various guttural utterances. He sagged almost as though the strength had left his body but the energy pouring from the book held his frame suspended by his eyeball.

"Elias." he blurted suddenly. Words then came tumbling out, among them was "Dwarves! GEOFFREY!" the pitch was rising. "ALZBEDA!" they heard distinctly before the pleading began: "TOO MUCH!" he wailed, "HIDE!" he cried, his lopsided face contorted with pain.

"Under here, Ohlen!" X'andria hissed, and she threw her invisibility cloak over them both. Not understanding what she had done, but sensing that The Sorcerer could not take much more, Ohlen reached out and closed the cover of the book much like he had when it assaulted X'andria earlier in the night.

The Sorcerer plunged to the ground convulsing. Immediately

sensates began appearing all around them. As Ohlen stowed the hellish book back in his satchel, X'andria tugged him down to hide beneath The Sorcerer's table, just feet away from his body which twitched glistening within the stiff, conical red coat. Ohlen stared in wonderment at X'andria, who simply placed her finger in front of her lips, the silver fabric shimmering over them both.

All around them was shouting, running, searching. At some point the Sorcerer's limp body was lifted magically into the air and transported away.

*"First," Gnome scowled at the pain he was clearly experiencing,
"I need you to get me one of those." He pointed a greasy,
bloody finger up at Boudreaux's cup of ale.*

Chapter Eighteen
THE IRON AXE

———————————

"How did you get out?" Arden asked, enthralled.

Boudreaux's jaw had gone slack early on in X'andria's description of the wild adventure at The Emporium, and he moved from his stupor only slightly to take sips of ale from the square, wooden cup before him.

They were whispering in what had become their usual booth in the darkest corner of The Iron Axe—a tavern near their lodgings that Boudreaux first discovered shortly after their arrival in Rockmoor. Waif, Zarina, and the girls had stayed home.

"We escaped through a portal in one of those alcoves," X'andria's eyes were bright with excitement. Ohlen, mindful that she had left out certain details of the story—like the dark rune she had drawn for The Sorcerer, her mysterious cloak that made them invisible, and the two empty green stoppered vials she swiped during their tip-toe escape from the study—eyed X'andria with a new consideration.

"It was amazing," X'andria continued. "How would you describe it, Ohlen?" She caught his eye momentarily, stuttered for an instant, and then prattled on, "like being rolled and squished between two cold, wet blankets that weigh a ton but are actually dry—but feel wet. Yeah, something like that. Does that make any sense? Anyhow, we came out near The Torrent and raced all the way back here."

Boudreaux managed another sip of ale.

"Do you really think they'll blame you for what happened to The Sorcerer?" Arden asked earnestly.

"There is no question about it," Ohlen spoke up for the first time. "We find ourselves now in a predicament, being alienated from the very people whose help we need. We can only hope that when— if—The Sorcerer regains lucidity he will recall that we meant him no harm."

These days Gnome had a practice of coming and going unnoticed. Gravitating toward shadow and cover of any kind, he also seemed to enter and exit spaces as frequently from above or below as at ground level. The first oddity about Gnome's arrival this night at the Iron Axe, then, was its obviousness. He walked toward them straight through the middle of the room weaving between tables filled with all manner of guests from woodsmen, to ruffians, to bent hoods whispering or listening in anonymity.

Something was wrong. Gnome was limping, and he was clutching his mid-section. Voices hushed and heads turned as he ambled by. Gnome was dirty. And when he finally slid with a wince onto the bench beside X'andria they all discovered he was smelly too.

Boudreaux had recovered from his stupefaction at X'andria's tale. "What the hell happened to you?" he asked Gnome in a tone that could possibly have been interpreted as concern.

"First," Gnome scowled at the pain he was clearly experiencing, "I need you to get me one of those." He pointed a greasy, bloody finger up at Boudreaux's cup of ale.

"I'll be *fine*, Arden," Gnome squeezed through gritted teeth as Arden fussed with a stinging balm over the parallel claw marks Sunoor had left on his abdomen. "They're not that deep!"

"They don't have to be deep to cause deep trouble," Arden retorted firmly, ignoring Gnome's attempts to squirm sideways.

Gnome's ale arrived just as Arden became satisfied that the wounds were acceptably sanitary.

"So I've been following this pair of thugs for a few nights now," Gnome growled softly, pulling the square cup of ale down from the tabletop. "There's an old creep with one eye and a companion I didn't get a good look at... until tonight."

"Looks like he got a good look at you, too," Boudreaux interjected.

"It's a she," Gnome countered, "and she's some kind of cat. Like a cat and a woman got smushed together or something."

They all sat motionless at attention.

"And she's fast and deadly." Gnome allowed himself a big gulp of ale, which spilled over the edges of his cup and down his cheeks.

"But none of that is what's important," Gnome continued intently. "What's important is that the word on the street is we did all that stuff in the sewer. Word is that we," Gnome made a vague circular motion indicating the booth, "killed and ate those poor people down there. That we're the ones responsible for all the terrible stuff that happened. There's coin for our hides."

Arden, Boudreaux, X'andria, and Ohlen all began speaking at the same time. Boudreaux was upset, "What?" he blurted incredulously, "Like I nearly drowned in that muck just for fun?" Arden was interested in the catwoman. "She's part cat, Gnome?" he asked, "like human and cat together?" Appalled, X'andria just repeated, "But that's not fair! We were trying to *help*!"

"Hush everyone, please," was Ohlen's refrain, which he emphasized by methodically touching and squeezing every arm he could reach. Ohlen had a way of transmitting his thoughts and feelings through touch. It was not long before a steady, calming warmth was flowing through each of his companions and the booth settled into silence.

"Ale!" Boudreaux shouted, shattering the stillness. He raised a massive arm and signaled one of the bustling servers. The others fixed him with a collective glare.

"What?" Boudreaux replied, clueless.

"Friends," Ohlen began very softly, cutting off the admonishment Gnome had been about to deliver, "come close."

With their heads bent together, Gnome standing on the bench to join them, Ohlen continued. "We are in precarious circumstances. Eyes and ears surround us even here in The Iron Axe. Gnome has uncovered false rumors spreading about us in the underworld. It is just a matter of time before the Sorcerer's sensates discover us. This, then, is one of the insidious ways in which our enemy engages us. Its darkness will turn people against people. It has, I believe, already tried to turn us against one another."

"You've lost me, Ohlen," Boudreaux murmured earnestly. "Just because you and X'andria had some bad luck with the magician, and that twerp Rove is whispering lies in the shadows... what's the connection? I don't see why we don't just find and silence the jerk thief and go have a talk to clear things up with the head cooks?"

"I appreciate your perspective, Boudreaux. There is something more, however. We were followed from The Den by an evil force. I was not conscious during our travel, but when I awoke at our lodgings it was among us. Can you each cast back in your memory to the morass of malcontent that surrounded us at the moment I awoke?"

Boudreaux's eyes had glazed over. Gnome looked intently from face to face. X'andria was nodding.

"I do." Arden affirmed. "Just thinking about it makes me sad. We were arguing about Waif's arm, it got out of control."

Boudreaux recalled, "Oh yeah, you all ganged up on me. I remember now. But I still don't see the connection." He sat back noisily and took a swig of ale.

"So what do we do, Ohlen?" It was Gnome. The others were all still huddled together.

"We must attract as little attention as possible while we figure this out," Ohlen said carefully. "Misunderstandings are best settled person to person, but the stakes are high and if I am correct, if the enemy is among us, then chaos will continue to be injected into our midst."

The meaning of Ohlen's assessment settled in, as the friends sat quietly back in their booth and puzzled through the predicament in their minds. Arden stole furtive glances about the room to see if he could detect any likely spies. There were a lot of good candidates. Boudreaux looked around sourly, bored. Gnome's fatigue and discomfort from his exertion, his wound, and his greasy filth seemed to catch up with him—the one swig of ale he'd had was not helping—and he slumped forward exhausted on the bench. X'andria stared into space while her small hand found its way into her backpack and absentmindedly rolled the red ruby nestled within the silken cloak between her fingers.

And it was this newly-settled silence, this apparent need for anonymity, that made the olive-skinned visitor's arrival so particularly unwelcome.

"I've found you!" the squat, portly young man announced cheerily looking between Boudreaux and Arden. He stood with a wide staunch stance, directly in front of the party's booth. He had a round ruddy face touched ever so slightly with age, a mop of reddish-brown hair, and he wore a green silken shirt flowing out beneath a black vest with small, colorful sequins.

It seemed all conversation in The Iron Axe ceased and that every ear was straining to hear what this young visitor had to say next.

Spinning like a dervish, Gruder fell onto the searingly cold floor and flailed about like a child throwing a tantrum.

Chapter Nineteen
FREEDOM

Pangs of hunger beat like drums inside Gruder's addled brain with each pulse of his powerful heart. The long, deep-rooted fangs lining each of his three mouths ached with a never-ending need to feed. He clicked his jaws together constantly to mollify the nerve-endings in his teeth that clambered for stimulation.

His days were spent waiting. Waiting and anticipating. Sniffing in short huffs, the membranes covering his long nostrils fluttered with each desperately hopeful sampling of the dank air. From time to time Gruder would leave his position—the place he had learned would, once in a very long while, bring a warm and juicy victim into his clutches. At these times his hunger was so overwhelming, his patience frayed beyond reason, that he would seek the hollow comfort of gnawing on the clean-picked splintered bones littered about his cell. Pitching himself forward, he'd worm about, rolling this way and that, so each mouth could fill itself with the dry tasteless shards. But these episodes were deeply unsatisfying, and soon the fear of missing a rare visitor would overcome Gruder, and he would return to the tortured stillness of his post.

Gruder had not eaten in a long time. He was intolerably ravenous. Sometime in the not-too-distant past two delicious-smelling morsels had wandered near, but then The Sorcerer had taken them away from him. Gruder had smelled the foul little man's arrival shortly before the delicious odor of the new visitors had dissipated. The Sorcerer had taken everything away from Gruder—including his freedom.

Gruder began to feel cold. Gruder never felt cold. But he felt cold now. The cold was not a good feeling, but it was an odd distracting relief from his sole obsession with eating. His fatless muscle-corded arms extended through the metal bars of his cell, and his spiderlike hands were upturned and ready to ensnare prey the instant it neared. But the bars grew colder and colder. Colder than ice. Frigidity began to seep into Gruder's arms, and radiate out toward his naked body. He knew if he stayed in place much longer, his arms would freeze solid.

Was this some new torment of The Sorcerer's design? Gruder backed away from the bars and grew angry. Stomping and clicking, the anger welled inside him. Spinning like a dervish, Gruder fell onto the searingly cold floor and flailed about like a child throwing a tantrum. He hurled bones at the wall, and pounded his fists. Gruder was angrier than he was hungry, and he did not even know why.

But he knew at whom.

Gruder had lost his eyes and ears in the accident in Practicum. But he saw The Sorcerer now clearly in his mind. He imagined ripping into The Sorcerer's flesh, tearing him apart. And suddenly he was on his feet. He madly rushed the bars of his cell. His bare skin screamed and split on contact with the impossibly cold bars, but the bars themselves shattered too, as if made of ice.

Gruder was free.

Patrick's team was arguing in the portal vault. Mayhem had followed The Sorcerer's incapacitation, and his team organized quickly. They searched The Emporium in vain for the two interlopers, and thoroughly scoured Watertown in a rapid and methodical outward-radiating pattern. The white-robed man and she-elf were nowhere to be found.

The Sorcerer himself was nonresponsive. Still alive, though, his sweat-dampened body was motionless apart from the occasional involuntary twitch. Shortly following the attack, Patrick had transported The Sorcerer to his inner chamber and now Eleanor, The Sorcerer's protégé, was trying her best to revive him.

"Calm down everyone!" Patrick noticed a rare agitation creeping into his own voice as he tried to make himself heard over the din. Hoods back, the normally-stoic sensates, hurled accusations and insults at one another. No one had breached The Emporium's defenses in recent memory, much less injured The Sorcerer himself. *They must be frightened*, Patrick thought with increasing frustration, *but they're acting like imbeciles!*

Keidu'aqadu. Hold. Patrick's hand trailed slowly left right at eye-level before him releasing a pungent brownish powder the main ingredient of which was mold spores carefully harvested from the gills of giant, slow-growing mushrooms in the swampy forests near the Southern Plains. The powder bloomed into a thin, nearly transparent membrane and spread over the six bickering sensates.

It was an extreme measure to silence his team. As a rule, sensates did not use magical countermeasures against one another. *But they're the ones who lost control!* Patrick argued defensively in his mind, bristling at the imagined inquisition that was surely to come. Jaw set defiantly, Patrick surveyed the men and women before him, each suspended awkwardly in mid-gesture.

Patrick had been interested in magic from an early age. The youngest by far of three siblings, his older brother and sister thought it would be fun one day to have their little brother drink one of the more adventurous liquids they'd heard were available at The Emporium in Watertown. Born to a wealthy merchant couple in Hillcrest, the older kids had become involved in the family shipping business, and thus passed through Watertown regularly on the way to the docks.

The bright green syrupy liquid tasted vile. The effects were at first unpleasant and bewildering and then grew to become utterly terrifying as young Patrick lost control of his senses. He would never sample The Emporium's commercial mind-altering potions again. What hooked him on magic that day had been the dragon.

Giggling nervously, his brother and sister had led him into the shabby Emporium shop where Patrick spotted the metallic green toy dragon on a shelf. It looked at him! It had woken up, steam rising from its nostrils, and turned its head right toward him. Patrick imagined it hissing, "Welcome young squire. If I were larger, or you a wee bit smaller, I would eat you here and now. But I guess we'll have to be friends, instead."

Long after the headache cleared, and his siblings' teasing abated, Patrick absorbed himself in a fantasyland where he was no longer just a boy, and the green dragon was not a small toy.

Adolescent Patrick was not encouraged toward the family business. His parents were often away or distracted, and his older siblings became too singularly concerned with their own advancement within the company to welcome another familial competitor.

With plenty of resources, however, Patrick had access to excellent tutoring, and he was frequently left to his own devices. During a rare lengthy stay at home, Patrick pestered his mom and dad daily to allow him to seek an understudy position at The Emporium. The position would require he move out of their Hillcrest villa and live within the walls of the mysterious Watertown Emporium complex for an indefinite period of time. His parents eventually relented, directing a family servant to make the arrangements, and then returned to studying their maps and charts.

Patrick met Eleanor at The Emporium two weeks later. They were both fourteen years of age. Smart, educated and hardworking, Patrick threw himself into his studies. Patrick was good, but Eleanor was better. He was so blissfully happy learning the laws of ether, ancient runic symbology, and dimensional theory, that Eleanor's scholastic superiority never bothered Patrick, even when she ultimately garnered the special favor of The Sorcerer himself. Patrick and Eleanor became good friends, study partners, and finally, colleagues in The Sorcerer's inner circle.

Patrick had always been mild-mannered, content with his circumstances, willing to gaze inwardly when change was needed before casting outside himself to find fault in others.

Nothing in Patrick's character or history would suggest the

behavior he was now exhibiting, as he surveyed his brethren, ready to defend his aggressive actions against some imaginary interrogator.

Leonora's inert torso exploded in a spray of blood that showered over the two sensates nearest her. Shaken from his uncharacteristic ill-tempered reverie, Patrick lost his control over the five others he had been holding in suspension.

Gruder's giant gore-glistening jaws had already gotten hold of Philippus' arm by the time Patrick realized what was happening—realized that The Sorcerer's hideous monster had escaped and was now devouring his team. Philippus was screaming and trying unsuccessfully to pull away from Gruder's relentless jaws, each of which worked in seamless concert with one another to ensnare, reel in, and obliterate his prey bite by devastating bite.

Patrick's disoriented team was getting slaughtered before his eyes. Gruder's ambush came full force out of nowhere, and the waking sensates—coming out of their held state—had no chance to summon the impressive magical arsenal they possessed between them.

Keidu'aqadu! Hold! Patrick spewed the word desperately once more, focusing now on the monster churning toward him through the bodies of his precious team. A dusting of the mushroom powder was still clinging to his shaking fingers from before, and he flicked them wildly into the air to release it into the ether.

Patrick felt the familiar constriction of the spell, felt his mind engage with the subjects—it was impossible to affect only Gruder and not his groggy friends in the vicinity—but it was not enough.

Either he was too distracted, or he needed more of the powder element, or perhaps Gruder's polluted mind was somehow impervious to Patrick's influence.

The last of his sensates was being chewed up before him, and Patrick stumbled and fell backward in horror. His entire team had been destroyed in what seemed like mere seconds, and he was next. Dribbling the team's blood from his mouths all down his sunken chest and pot belly, Gruder halted momentarily to assess his surroundings with loud, bubbly sniffs.

Dru'iidfae! Push. The force of the word exploded from behind Patrick. It was Eleanor. Splayed awkwardly on the stone floor, a powerful fist of air blew over Patrick's head and caught the monster squarely in front. The impact dented and smoothed Gruder's grey wrinkly flesh and pushed his head backward, as if a large and heavy clear ball had plowed into him at great speed.

The monster was blown backward off his feet. He sailed sputtering through the air, blood trailing from his clawed, bony feet. Gruder flew into one of the alcoves, through a portal, and out into the crisp evening air on a dark street somewhere in Watertown.

And Leopold's work here was done.

He had followed the two in possession of his book at a distance. The tall man had shone with a particularly unpleasant brightness. He had witnessed his book rip satisfyingly into the bent little magician. He had lingered long enough to unleash the singular and somewhat amusing monster.

It was time now for Leopold to recover his stolen property.

It felt like the air closed around his torso—like an extension of her fingers—and carried him backward into the wall.

Chapter Twenty
PETRIC

———————————

Petric's confidence was flagging. The ebullient smile he had forced onto his face began to slacken.

There was no question in his mind that he had found the two fighters the grizzled older man at the training fields had described. Eyeing Petric closely as though sharing privileged information the man had hoarsely whispered, "One's got a big brown beard. He's deadly with a sword, but a right terror with two. An' the other. Some kinda elf freak. Powerful like I've never seen, pointy ears, rugged lookin'. You'll know 'em when you see 'em. An' them two could help ya with whatever yer dealin' with. I'd start at The Iron Axe if I was you."

Petric did not necessarily expect a warm reception, in light of the fact that the two fighters didn't know who he was, and were not expecting him. But he had a knack for setting people at ease with his enthusiasm, and so he went for it. After all, what choice did he really have?

At Petric's tableside arrival in The Iron Axe the bearded swordsman looked shocked and at a loss for words. The big man in the far corner seemed cagey and annoyed, but in a lazy sort of way—like he might grab Petric by the collar and interrogate him harshly, if only he didn't have to put down his square cup of ale and reach all the way across the table to do so. Perched between the two fighters was a slight she-elf with medium length red hair and huge green eyes both of which bored intensely into Petric's own as though trying to see right through him.

Across from these three was a tall, thin, dark-complexioned man with very short white hair matching his clean robes. This mysterious man had bowed his head slightly as though he was more inclined toward listening than seeing. And finally there was a small person, dirty and bloody in torn black pants and tunic, who had jumped to his feet on top of the bench at Petric's pronouncement, with his eyes narrowed in a particularly unpleasant scowl.

No one said anything for a moment. In fact it seemed that every guest in the entire establishment had stopped talking.

Toting a worn leather backpack, the she-elf slid lithely out of the booth over and past the dazed-looking bearded fighter. Without a word, she grabbed Petric's left upper arm with surprising strength, spun him around, and half-guided, half-dragged him back toward the exit of the crowded pub. Several times he stumbled and looked back over his shoulder at the others, but the she-elf just squeezed tighter and tugged him along with greater insistence. Passing the last table of staring strangers Petric began murmuring an ill-conceived protest, but her threatening sideways glare was enough to keep him quiet until they were out the door.

"Pardon me, but do we know each other?" Petric stammered the most polite protest he could think of, as she hurried him up the dark stone steps to street level.

"Not here," she hissed curtly.

Petric stopped resisting and worked to keep up with his captor's quick, purposeful strides. The she-elf kept a firm hold on his arm, but the pressure released slightly. Two blocks away from The Iron Axe she guided him into a narrow alleyway, darkened between two long wooden tenements.

Ten paces in she released him, but something happened that he could not explain. It felt like the air closed around his torso—like an extension of her fingers—and carried him backward into the wall, forcing his shoulder blades firmly against the damp rough boards of the building behind him.

"Now tell me," she purred dangerously. "Who the hell are you?"

"I am called Petric," Petric replied hastily, rattled by the entire affair. "I need help, and a nice old gentleman at The Fields told to me a tale of two strongmen I might find at The Iron Axe."

Heavy footsteps pounded up the wet street toward them. The big fighter's hulking form filled the entrance to the alleyway.

"Does this one need to go away, X'andria?" The question was lobbed so casually, it took Petric a moment to realize what the fighter was suggesting.

The she-elf, X'andria, was somehow pinning Petric to the wall with an unseen power. She lifted her left arm, and to his own amazement Petric started sliding up the side of the building out of reach of the advancing fighter. Petric's back rubbed uncomfortably along the rough boards. He could feel his fine sequined vest snagging and tearing as the invisible hands of the atmosphere dragged him upward. This was not going especially well, and Petric did not have time to lose.

"Not yet, Boudreaux." The she-elf named X'andria replied coolly, "Not sure what we're dealing with. I think he heard about you and Arden at The Training Fields, wants help with something."

Petric was trembling. Suspended helplessly against the alley wall, his undergarments clung to his skin, saturated with sweat.

"You've come at a bad time," this was a new voice, emanating just inches from his right ear. With some effort, Petric managed to turn his head to the right, and came face to face with the small person, somehow clinging like a spider to the wall beside him.

"We must go now," another new voice, this one deep, reverberated up from the alley below. "We are discovered, and must seek shelter immediately. I feel them closing in."

It was all too much for Petric. As the force holding him aloft dissipated and he slid toward the earth, his frayed nerves gave out to unconsciousness.

At Ohlen's solemn pronouncement in the alley, the party hastened back to their cottage. Boudreaux carried the stranger's doughy limp body. Waif and Zarina were up waiting for them with the girls, but it was clear from the silent and somber arrival that it was not the time for light conversation.

The door closed behind them, the stranger was lain on Arden's fur bedding like a sleeping child, and all the candles save one were snuffed out.

"What is it Ohlen?" Arden's whisper broke the tense silence.

"The air is alive with danger, my friends," Ohlen began. "Our guest's arrival aroused much interest at The Iron Axe. I felt the eager anticipation of more than one mercenary spy racing through the night as soon as we left. But that's not all. The Sorcerer's sensates have entered into Westwood, and there is deep concern in their auras. Something has gone very wrong at The Emporium. I fear perhaps that The Sorcerer did not survive our visit."

X'andria seemed about to interject something, but Ohlen raised a finger ever so slightly and continued ominously, "and the cold, creeping darkness that's been haunting us. I'm afraid it, too, is nearby and infecting the space all around and between us."

Arden sat down heavily, and let out a low whistle through his teeth.

It was Zarina who stepped forward to break the eerie silence that followed Ohlen's assessment. Placing a hand on Arden's shoulder, her voice was reassuringly steady and carried with it palpable warmth, "You five are the most heroic souls I've ever had the privilege to meet. You not only saved my life, and my daughters' lives, you rescued our spirits. They destroyed my sweet husband, Mordimer, and I thought I would not be able to face another sunrise. But through all the confusion and danger you have shown us nothing but kindness. I, for one, am confident you will meet this new challenge, and many more to come."

The friends all stared at the floor, allowing the gratitude in Zarina's voice to wash over them. It was a moment of unexpected calm.

"And now has come the time that we must leave you," Zarina continued. Arden twisted his face up toward her with a quizzical grimace. "Waif and I have been talking, and we have decided that not only do you have bigger concerns than looking after us, but we have our own concerns too. We have seen enough to know that the darkness that took my poor Mordimer is spreading of its own accord. Am I not correct?"

Ohlen's eyes clicked suddenly open. He looked directly at Zarina, and nodded.

"My friends, I want to fight it. I want to lead legions against it. But my weapons are not swords or spells. My weapons are words and understanding. Waif and I and the girls will return to my home in Watertown for the present. And there we will stage our own sort of resistance. We'll flood darkness with light, we'll meet hate with love. And while you face the terrors that surely await you, we will work quietly to weave the good citizens of Rockmoor together in solidarity for the day you call upon us to make a stand."

Waif was on his feet now. He held a packed bag in his remaining hand. Zordim and Mara were standing too, alert and looking older than their years.

The goodbyes were hurried but hearty, before the young thief, the widow, and the two small sisters slipped away into the night.

"Maybe we should just take him back to The Iron Axe, and leave him in that alley." Petric heard a measured but hurried voice floating through to his waking brain.

"Well it seems to *me*," Petric roused himself and decided to push his luck, "that we should listen to what the stranger has to say. You know, perhaps have a *conversation* with him."

The five strangers stopped talking and turned to look at him, mouths open. Propped up on an elbow, Petric continued with a dose of defiant sarcasm complimenting a winning smile. "He certainly seems nice enough. Who knows? Maybe there's a reason he found us at the pub, *might* be worth an ask."

"He's up," the owner of the measured voice—the brown-bearded fighter—said aloud as if all of them were not already staring.

The small, bloody, black-clad person, standing, was not much taller than Petric propped on his elbow. Even so, he had a big presence, and spoke up, "Listen, you've arrived at a really bad time. We... wait, what's your name?"

"Petric," said both Petric and the she-elf named X'andria at the same time.

"Alright Petric, X'andria said you need help with something. What is it you've come for? We're not usually quite this rude, but things are a bit...*complicated*. So be quick about it." For the first time, Petric became aware of the strain behind the little person's mask of ill manner. Unease was, in fact, in all the faces peering down at him.

"As you wish," Petric sighed, righting himself into a cross-legged seated position on the bedding. "I am from Meriden, in the mountains. It is forty hours' hard ride from Rockmoor. Few have been to our remote village, but many have heard tell of the grains we grow for ale and bread, or of the red Abgoa leaves we cultivate for smoke."

"You grow *Abgoa*?" The brown-bearded fighter burst in, suddenly exuberant.

"We do." Petric paused with a purposeful stare.

"*Arden*," hissed the small person impatiently at the fighter. Looking back at Petric he urged, "and you're here because...?"

"I am in your midst because something unspeakable happened to Alzbeda, our village elder. She is gone and there was much blood. I do not know who to trust or who to turn to, but things are spinning out of control in Meriden. And if things spin out of control in Meriden it could be very unfortunate for many people. It is complicated, I am afraid. I have horses, a carriage, and I have gold. But I do not have much time."

"Alzbeda," X'andria repeated slowly. "Ohlen do you remember?"

The man called Ohlen had again bowed his head, eyes closed, as though experiencing the world around him by some means other than sight. "I do not X'andria, remind me." He replied, his voice richly reverberant.

"Alzbeda…" X'andria pronounced each syllable slowly, and scrunched up her face as if trying to recall an elusive detail, "I think it's one of the names The Sorcerer yelled when our book was attacking him at the Emporium!"

Petric's eyebrows knitted densely together as he tried to comprehend X'andria's words. He had not expected anyone to have heard of Alzbeda. But he did not get a chance to ask about it, because just then, there came a loud and insistent rapping at the door.

"It is here," Ohlen murmured through chattering teeth.

Chapter Twenty-One
VISITORS IN THE NIGHT

A wave of trepidation washed over Ruprecht as Geoffrey secured the mule to a hitching post at the edge of Westwood. Ruprecht's concern only intensified as the thumps of their footsteps amplified on the Rockmoor district's elevated boardwalk, and the worry mixed with guilt as they passed the spot he and Dortmund had last encountered Boudreaux.

They arrived at the cottage. As Geoffrey raised his staff to knock, Ruprecht recalled his first sorry arrival at this place what seemed ages ago.

Ohlen—the only person who had come close to empathizing with him after his corruption—had left them on the road to Rockmoor. Gnome had scouted the place. He and X'andria were so close to one another, and immediately they took to exploring every nook and cranny together. Ruprecht had not really gotten to know Boudreaux, but it seemed the big brutish half-elf waffled between being drunk and sneaking suspicious looks in Ruprecht's direction. Boudreaux and Arden had become friends, it seemed—training together and sharing laughs—and they, too, had entered the cottage where they jokingly laid claim to different spots for their bedding and belongings.

That had left Ruprecht hovering near the door alone—incessant need gnawing at his heart, aching pain throbbing in the half-healed mutilation of his hand and chest. He stood there, feeling removed from his body, watching four people he used to know bustling through the banal motions of occupying a new space. He wanted to run away that very instant, and he might have, but X'andria had looked up, caught his eye, and invited him gently to come inside. So he had.

Knock, knock, knock—it seemed like Geoffrey was trying to wake the entire neighborhood.

"Pssst!" It was Gnome. He motioned frantically for everyone to move toward Petric, who was still seated on Arden's fur bedding, looking bewildered.

Gnome quickly studied the details of the fur beneath Petric, the patterns in the wood behind him. He then hastily produced a small fistful of brownish dried leafy matter and dashed to the lone candle.

The rapping repeated on the door, even louder this time.

In seconds, Gnome's leaves were smoking. He willed his motions to slow, in spite of his hammering heart. Waving the smoking incense before his eyes in several long fluid motions, Gnome bent the light around his compatriots, channeling a vision of an empty bed and a blank wall out of his mind, through the smoke, and into the ether.

The latch lifted and the door swung inward just moments after Gnome's illusion was complete, and he had dashed across the room to hide in the shadows.

Two cloaked figures entered the dim space.

"It seems no one is home," the first one said. He lowered his hood and revealed a shockingly scarred face with no hair of any kind.

"That's odd," said the second, still hooded his voice sounded quite familiar. "They wouldn't leave a candle burning, and what's that smell?" He turned and closed the door carefully behind him, as if he was entering his own home.

"Ruprecht," a third booming voice entered the conversation. It was Ohlen. His tone was inscrutable.

There was a collective gasp. The party, moving now, materialized out of thin air, their motion eliminating the potency of Gnome's light-bending spell. Gnome bolted forth out of the shadow exclaiming accusatorily, "What? Ruprecht? Is that you?"

It seemed everyone had something to say. Boudreaux began muttering darkly about how much he'd been waiting for a reunion, both Arden and X'andria seemed ecstatic at their friend's unexpected return. Ruprecht found himself speechless.

But it was Ohlen's rich baritone that commanded their attention once more, "Please everyone," he projected. "If I am not mistaken, I believe we know Ruprecht's companion also—though his appearance is rather different than the last time we laid eyes upon him."

Excitement hung tenuously in the forced silence.

"Though I know not how, I believe it is none other than Geoffrey who stands before us in the flesh." Another collective gasp issued, X'andria's most audibly. "When last I sensed your presence my friend, you had fallen to your doom upon that accursed slithering worm beneath the great hall of the dwarves."

"Indeed I had, Ohlen. And she left her marks upon me as you all see. But in those desperate moments of struggle before I fell I reconnected with my deity. With *our* deity," he added the last bit looking back toward Ruprecht, "and it seems The Great One had other plans for me than being seared and swallowed in the bowels of the earth by that frightful depth crawler."

Geoffrey continued, "But come, let us sit and visit like civilized people. Time is short, but if we do not commune and share smiles and laughter, then we risk forgetting what it is we are fighting for."

With that, all eight of them bustled into motion. X'andria lit candles, Arden set out the last of his dried berries from Westwood Forest, Boudreaux poured several horns of ale, Gnome helped Petric to his feet, Arden clasped Ruprecht in a tight embrace before taking his and Geoffrey's cloaks, and they all squeezed tightly together onto the two long benches astride the cottage's sole dining table.

"We are in trouble, Geoffrey," Ohlen began. "The evil we both know from beneath the mountain was waiting for us here in Rockmoor in the form of an ambitious and troubled young man named Elias, along with his minions. We found them and fought them, but now it appears lies are spreading about us. Whisperers accuse us of the mayhem we in fact stopped. There are rewards for our heads."

"What else?" Geoffrey asked sagely.

"Elias had a book." X'andria jumped in. "It's a moody tome, has a mind of its own, and likes to grab hold of you when you open it. We took it to The Sorcerer of Rockmoor but it attacked him. He might have died, we're not sure. And now his people are out looking for us too."

"Interesting," Geoffrey was nodding, looking up and to the left like he was putting pieces together in his mind. "And do you have the eyes?"

Blank stares.

"The eyes. The black orbs that invaded Ruprecht and me? Do you have them?"

"I carry them," Ohlen announced, a tinge of wariness in his voice. "They are eyes?"

"Yes," replied Geoffrey. "Those horrid things were plucked right from the skull of a being I barely saw and can hardly remember. He hurled them at me in my cabin in the woods near Westover. One entered into me, as you will recall." Geoffrey shuddered at the memory.

"So that's what it is!" Ohlen exclaimed. "We are plagued by a cold, creeping anger that has been following us since our trials with Elias. Even now I feel it—it must be this spirit you are describing. It must be chasing its eyes."

Looking around the table, both Gnome and X'andria were, in fact, hugging their own shoulders. Ohlen felt cold as well, and thought he might even be seeing Petric's breath creating small foggy puffs at the other end of the table.

"I have a question," Boudreaux blurted out, holding horns of ale in both hands. "What the hell's HE doing here, and why are we talking when we oughtta be outside settling our differences?" He indicated Ruprecht with one hand, sloshing ale over his fingers and onto the table.

"Boudreaux, please don't," Arden protested. He had been worried about this confrontation from the moment he recognized Ruprecht's voice.

"I would like to offer a few words of explanation…" Geoffrey began, but he was interrupted.

"It's a fair question, Boudreaux," Ruprecht said softly but with conviction. "Honestly, it's a question you all should be asking. I was a monster. I was dangerous. I was starving and willing to do anything—to sacrifice anyone—to get what I needed. These things are true." As he spoke he looked intently at each of the taut faces huddled around the table. He lingered especially on Boudreaux's hard stare, willing himself to accept the accusation seeping from the big man's narrowed eyes.

"I don't ask for your pity. But while you have all been fighting the enemy around you, I have been fighting the enemy inside of me. And I have been losing. I cannot describe its enormity. Had I not experienced it myself, I would not be able to comprehend it. Geoffrey has, of course, shared this burden. Ohlen glimpsed it within me. I am sitting here today because of Geoffrey. Indeed I owe my very soul to him, and to the patience and insistence with which he has guided my recovery and my reunion with The Great One. While I am not the same as I once was, I believe I am no longer a danger to you."

It was truly freezing now. Every breath formed a visible mist. Poor Petric was shaking.

"Boudreaux, if you'll let me, I ask for the chance to prove myself to you. This foe robbed me of time, of friendship, of trust, and of dignity. I will not rest until I have done all in my power to set things aright." Ruprecht concluded.

"It is here," Ohlen murmured through chattering teeth.

"Fly now, all of you!" Geoffrey commanded hastily, "I will delay it. This is an adversary I know."

The wall opposite the door began to shake, a layer of frost was forming on the inside as though an invisible painter was methodically sloshing layers of translucent white crystalline upon the boards with an enormous brush.

"To my carriage!" cried Petric, fog erupting from his blue-cold lips.

The frozen wall cracked diagonally all the way across.

"Run!" Geoffrey urged frantically, standing to face whatever was coming, and bringing his palms together, so that his fingertips came to rest against his ruined lips.

And so they ran.

PART TWO

"Well the toad hated that. It backed up and shook its head, and made an angry, slobbery whistling sound I've never heard before or since."

Chapter Twenty-Two
THE ALCHEMIST

───────────

The carriage was unusual indeed.

It was like the same artisan who made Petric's fine—though now torn—sequined vest, had also appointed the interior of his surprisingly large enclosed wagon. Silken fabric was arrayed in opulent folds over luxurious cushions so thick and plush they almost completely muted the bumpy terrain over which the team of four massive black horses now sped.

The frantic flight from the cottage the evening before—on the heels of Gnome's encounter with the were-lion Sunoor, Ohlen and X'andria's dealings with The Sorcerer at the Emporium, Petric's unwelcome arrival, the revelation of Geoffrey and Ruprecht's return, and the chill of the darkness plaguing them—left the party thoroughly exhausted. They had followed Petric, who was not a terribly fast runner, to the training grounds where they came upon his great carriage and steeds looming large on the wide moonlit field. Not knowing if they were being pursued, they piled haphazardly through heavy folds of fabric that hung over the entrance. In a language unfamiliar to the rest of them, Petric gave their mute driver a quick, terse, directive and the horses took off like a shot.

The soft enveloping comfort, and the rhythmic swaying of the transport, allowed each of them to drift easily into their private, addled thoughts, and then eventually off to sleep.

"It's funny, Gnome, I don't think I've ever known much about what you and X'andria got up to before we all met?" Arden asked mid-morning the following day.

Petric's carriage had numerous compartments concealed beneath its plush beds and benches, and from them he had produced deliciously soft and sweet rolls and a cold, forest-green brew that was slightly bitter in a bracing sort of way.

"I remember you said something about nicking things for two creeps who lorded over a gang of street kids?"

"Mama and Papa," offered Gnome sourly.

"That's right, Mama and Papa!" Arden continued amiably. "How'd you get away from those two, anyway?"

"Whew," Gnome let out a long slow sigh and studied his hands. He waited a moment or two, almost like he was hoping a new topic of conversation would arise, but none came. Instead, when he looked up he was greeted by five eager faces all pleading silently with him for a story. X'andria, reclining against the far wall, was absorbed in one of her scrolls. A grin played at the corners of her mouth.

"Alright," Gnome finally consented. "But stop me when you get bored, and X'andria," he called, "Chime in if I get off track will you?"

Gnome took a leisurely swig of the coolly refreshing greenish brew out of an ornately filigreed bronze goblet that looked comically large in his small hand, and he began.

"You all know—except Petric—that X'an and I met near the coast up north in the city of Greenlee. X'an was on the run from the men who'd taken her from Atolia, and I was on the run, too. I'd had a huge fight with my father. It was bad, and I left the Gnome hills for good. Anyway, that's a different story.

"I lived with a bunch of kids who stole for their supper, under the leaky roof of two mean old losers we all called Mama and Papa. I wasn't a kid, but I was small. I didn't say much because I only knew Gnomish, and I was pretty good at stealing things—so I guess that's why they put up with my strange looks.

"One day X'an showed up. She was the first person I'd met since leaving the hills that looked different than all the other big people, and—correct me X'an—I'm pretty sure I was the first person she'd met who looked different too, since she'd run away. So we started roving together. X'an had a knack for spotting valuables, and I'd generally do the taking. Along the way she taught me how to speak your language. And she learned some Gnomish.

"One day we were out, and X'an saw an old guy sitting in the sun. Actually, she spotted a book he was reading and recognized it was in Elfish. I'm sure you all know this already, but X'an is amazing at reading and remembering anything. She hadn't seen Elfish since before they took her, and still she knew it at thirty paces.

"The old guy didn't seem much of a threat, so I raced over and plucked the book right out of his hand, and away we ran! But we didn't get far. It turned out that the old guy was quite a master of the magical arts. We weren't but ten steps away when he did something that caused the air to clamp down tight all around us, and hold us still in mid-step like we'd been frozen solid.

"He wasn't mad at all, believe it or not. He seemed more amused than anything. When he got near to us, I guess he was able to sense we had a little magic of our own, and after taking his book back, he invited us to come to his place and study magic with him. The truth is that we had been thinking about running away from Mama and Papa anyhow, and the man—he called himself The Alchemist—seemed nice enough. Plus, X'an and I were fascinated by his powers. Both of us had caused some magical things to happen on accident before, but we didn't know how.

"The Alchemist didn't live in Greenlee. He lived a few days' walk from there, down in a valley in an old mossy cottage near a stream. A special place, really.

"Our lessons started right away. He worked us from sunrise to sunset, and then we studied by candlelight. I remember he used to say that when he was younger he went for years sleeping only every other day, so that he could spend more time studying. I actually tried it myself at one point, but I barely made it a week before I was so tired I started seeing things that weren't there—and I don't mean my own illusions! We Gnomes need our sleep.

"The Alchemist was incredibly particular about everything. He taught me how to find and catch the bugs I use for my visions, how to select them, and store them. But he would get so mad if we so much as clipped the wrong part of a plant. He made us practice everything over and over again, and drilled us on our pronunciations. Oh how he'd yell when we got it wrong! It was bothersome, to be honest. I can get worked up myself, too. So we got into it from time to time.

"Mostly he combined our studies with chores he needed doing. He taught us how to mill rare and potent dried berries, but had us practice by grinding corn and wheat for days on end. At least that's what it seemed like. He taught us to find rare plants, but honed our technique trimming the trees and shrubs all around the cottage. You get the idea.

"Upstream a ways was a Fisher clan. A man came to The Alchemist's cottage wailing about something terrible that was scaring the children. So The Alchemist raced away with him and left X'an and me on our own. That was a good day. Things were so much more peaceful without the grumpy old man ordering us around.

"He came back late that night in a foul mood, sopping wet, with a wild tale about some enormous toad that had hopped out of the trees and pinned one of the villagers to the ground like it was going to eat him, before getting scared off. It was so exciting, X'an and I asked a whole lot of questions.

"I'll never forget the first time The Alchemist showed X'an what she could do with Rotweed. We found the giant leaves growing in a dark scummy pool under thick clouds of gnats. After I wrenched the first one free I made the mistake of swatting at the buzzing air in front of my face. The big, leathery leaf brushed just under my nose and boy oh boy did it smell bad.

"Anyhow—X'an can explain this better than I can—the trick to turning Rotweed into a lethal weapon is imagining the effect it'll have on your foe. So we stood outside and The Alchemist explained things to her carefully, made her repeat the ancient power word, explained the precise ethereal conversion and then demonstrated. He took a piece of the Rotweed, said the word, and then this grey puff came out of him. It looked like it plumed right out of the top of his bald head, then it floated forward like a loose jiggling jelly, and landed on the ground about twenty paces or so away. I'll tell you, whatever was in that thing, smelled way worse than the plant itself—almost made me gag.

"So then it was X'an's turn. She grabbed her piece of the weed, scrunched up her face like she always does, and the word came spitting out of her like she had been hit in the gut with a tree limb. All of a sudden this massive ball of angry gray, hissing, steam erupted out of her, flew across the field like lightning, and hit the ground so hard bits of earth blew up into the air all around.

"The Alchemist and I just stood there stunned. A few moments later, when the first hints of that cloud began wafting back to us, it was clear we might not survive if we stood our ground. And that's when he and I realized X'an was passed out cold. All the power she'd conjured was more than she could handle.

"X'an was out for a few hours, it was scary. And even after she came to, she had a splitting headache. But here's the odd thing. The Alchemist was all mad about it. Even though her spell was so good, so much better than his, he had nothing but mean things to say about it. Told her she'd lost control. Told her the only reason it had worked at all was because he'd shown her how to do it.

"So the toad continued to plague the Fisher People, and The Alchemist spent several months answering their calls for help. But at the same time he was showing X'an and me more and more ways to harness our magic. I had started out using different kinds of smoke to bend light. Not long after the whole noxious Rotweed cloud thing with X'an, The Alchemist explained to me that with certain bugs and proper focus I could make other people see things in my imagination, scary things if I wanted.

"The Alchemist had to go back to Greenlee for something. He

was going to be gone for a week or so. The day after he left, a Fisher Woman showed up at the cottage all hysterical because her baby had been swallowed whole by one of the monsters. She begged X'an and me to help. What could we do? She was crying and carrying on, it was just so terrible, and there was no way to say no.

"I grabbed a few heavy hunting knives and the three best bugs I'd collected, and X'an got her stuff together, and we took off downstream after this bent little woman who ran way faster than either of us would've thought.

"It seemed the whole village was out by the bank milling around, looking sad and nervous. They had expected The Alchemist, of course, and they got X'an and me instead. But the Gnome in me took over. I asked where the baby was, and they pointed, and away we ran. We Gnomes tend to get to the point of things.

"X'an and I were sneaking along pretty quietly, it was just the two of us. I guess the villagers were too scared to come along. As we made our way into the trees, X'an asked me for the knives I'd brought with us. I pulled them out of my bag and dropped two on the forest floor. You know how when you drop a knife by accident, you jump out of the way, because the point might land on your foot? Well I did that. The knives clanged, and I landed on some dry sticks that crunched. This huge brown beast jumped out of the gloom and rammed me from the side. I flew straight into the air, I don't know how far. So X'an was collecting those knives, and this giant knobby toad was lumbering toward me, and I grabbed one of my beetles and thought of the thing I'd be afraid of if I was a toad. I thought of the tears in the Fisher Woman's eyes. I heard her voice. And just as the toad was getting ready to squash me under one of its huge webby feet, my beetle burst into the most brilliant swirling flame, like the sun itself had appeared right there in the forest.

Chapter Twenty-Two

"Well the toad hated that. It backed up and shook its head, and made an angry, slobbery whistling sound I've never heard before or since. And the second my flames went away, X'an commanded two of those big heavy hunting knives to fly through the air and bury themselves in the toad's face, one in each eye. They hit their marks alright, because about three twitches later that big awful beast slumped forward and never moved again.

"The Fisher People weren't as far away as we thought. Maybe they had heard the commotion. But as soon as the toad collapsed, they appeared out of nowhere and gutted the big nasty thing like it was one of their river fish. They pulled that poor little baby out of its bloody gut, and the next minute seemed like hours with them crowded around it, with its mom sniffling and blubbering and cooing, and with all of us hoping against hope that by some miracle the child survived.

"Well it did survive. And about a month later we were back at The Alchemist's cottage when that Fisher Woman came walking up at midday carrying her little baby. The Alchemist asked her how things were going, and she told him she wanted to talk to us. He was confused—we hadn't told him about our adventure. She went on and on about how brave we had been, how the stories of the fiery vision and flying knives were told each night in the village, about how grateful she was, about how we'd saved her little baby's life. And she presented us with two gifts."

Gnome shifted on the plush cushion and slowly extracted the dagger he always kept strapped to his waist.

"She gave me this blade, set just for me by a craftsman in the Fisher village with a wooden grip that fits my hand perfectly. And then she pulled out of her pocket the emerald necklace I'm sure you've all seen X'an wearing. It had been in the woman's family for generations, and she thought it matched X'an's eyes. Which it does.

"I honestly thought The Alchemist would be proud. The Fisher Woman left, and X'an and I sat there holding our gifts, with the old man hovering in the doorway. We had saved that baby's life! We had used his teachings to make a real difference.

"But The Alchemist wasn't happy at all. *You went to the village without telling me*, he groused. I remember he was shaking a little bit and the words came out one at a time, like he had to let them out slowly to keep control. *My teachings*, he kept saying. *You used my teachings.*

"We only stayed with The Alchemist one more day. It was terrible. He alternated between periods of yelling and then sitting in silence staring out at the river. We tried to apologize for keeping the adventure a secret, but each time we opened our mouths it just seemed to make things worse. At one point I looked at X'an and our eyes locked—we knew it was time to go. So that next afternoon we left the beautiful river behind us, and set out on a long hike that eventually took us to Rockmoor.

"I've thought about that old man many times since then. In fact, I don't think many days pass when he's not on my mind at least a little. I've imagined countless conversations. We owe so much to him. But I think something shifted when X'an outshined him that day with the Rotweed. And I think that Fisher Woman pushing past him to thank us for saving her baby, to give us gifts—I think her leaving without so much as a look in his direction—it was just too much."

Oh no, no, no, no, no!

Chapter Twenty-Two

Geoffrey pitched forward on his staff. Some part of him was vaguely aware that the others were running way. This was good. But it was a distant and fading good, like a fuzzy memory of childhood laughter in the delirium of life's last moments.

The freezing, probing penetration of blackness would have struck fear into any living soul. But for Geoffrey it was worse. This was his hell. He'd been here before. This blackness had been around him, in him. It had *been* him.

He had been destroyed by its might. And the memory was devastating.

His scarred, hairless body sagged forward on his staff. He put all his energy into simply maintaining his grip on the knotted wood handle, into staying upright.

The wall exploded. It shattered like ice—bits of petrified wood flew in all directions—and terror itself oozed inexorably through the jagged gaping hole.

Damn that Ruprecht! Geoffrey screamed in his mind. *The stupid, weak wretch of an excuse for a man!* Geoffrey's left knee was almost grazing the top of the layer of frost growing on the floor beneath him. The balls of his feet were inching backward on the icy floor. His frozen fingers were slipping. He was furious now, angry at Ruprecht, at the cold, the ice, at his own feet and hands.

It was in the room with him now. A shadow outline of a soul, floating slowly nearer, reaching out toward him, hell in man's form.

The pain was excruciating. It felt like white-hot coals were packed into the sunken place in his chest where the orb had previously nested. Geoffrey began to cry. The tears froze instantly in hard little streaks leaking out of his browless eyes. His anger melted away in a sea of despair.

The cold outside him, the fire within him, all were magnified by his memory of what was to come, of all that had come before.

In some abandoned reserve deep in his mind Geoffrey knew he had forgotten something important. He tried to fight against the pain to recall it. Something powerful, something warm and comforting. Something opposite to cold and fear and anger and blame and despair.

His frozen fingers slipped jerkily on the staff and both knees crunched into the frost layer. Geoffrey could no longer feel his hands.

What is it? He begged madly of his overwrought emotions. *I can't go back, don't take me back.*

The staff toppled. Geoffrey's face smacked dully into ice. *Help me*, was his last meek thought, but he had not the awareness even to know who to ask. He was too late. Steel-vise fingers closed around his ankle and dragged him away leaving thin spotty smears of dark crimson trailing haphazardly through the crystalline white.

"Alzbeda," X'andria piped up peering over the top of her scroll.
Her voice was darker and more serious-sounding than usual.
"What about her, Petric?"

Chapter Twenty-Three
THE ROAD

Gnome had run out of words. No one else seemed to have any either, and so for a few moments the only sounds in the heavy atmosphere were the muffled noises of hooves and wheels speeding over earth somewhere outside their plush cocoon.

Until Boudreaux—sprawled backward with his mouth lolling open—emitted a loud, ragged snore that rudely shook all the passengers from their respective reveries.

Gnome's eyes darted up from where they had been resting, on his own folded hands, and he said irritably, "I guess I went on a little long."

Everyone else made noises of protest. "Not at all, Gnome," Arden, who had asked for the tale, was the most vociferous. "We honestly didn't know what to expect. I had no idea of any of this."

"It seems to me, Gnome," Ruprecht said softly, opening his eyes and looking upward at no one in particular, "that The Alchemist wasn't able to see clearly through to his own heart."

This pronouncement was met with quizzical looks all around. "I mean," Ruprecht continued, "It seems the old man was working from the outside in, you know?"

No one knew.

"We all have our reasons for doing the things we do, right?" Ruprecht ventured on gently. "Our reasons anchor us, help us persist through challenges, help us focus through confusion. Those reasons are beliefs held inside, and they guide our words and deeds on the outside. It seems to me that The Alchemist knew he wanted to teach Gnome and X'andria, knew he wanted to use his gifts to help others, but he was not in touch with his own deeper beliefs. He knew *what* he wanted, but he did not know *why* he wanted it."

X'andria had returned to her scroll, Boudreaux produced another lengthy snore, and the others stared at Ruprecht expectantly.

"It is good to have you back among us, Ruprecht." Ohlen replied simply.

"*Abgoa Leaf,*" Arden changed the subject, "I have to know everything you can tell me about it, Petric."

"Oh my goodness yes!" their host said amiably, though he looked somewhat tired. "Have you had the pleasure of sampling the wondrous aroma of Abgoa?"

"Only in my dreams, Petric."

"Well you, sir, appear to me to be a man who would really appreciate its subtlety." The little round man smacked his lips together. "The plants themselves actually grow high up in trees," he made a vertical gesture as if pointing at a bird flying in the sky. "The roots are fine filaments that hang down like hair, drinking moisture out of the air itself." He touched his own hair to demonstrate. "Our growers place many specimins, but not all actually survive. Abgoa is a mysterious and precious form of life."

"Young leaves are shiny and broad, and each produces a single white flower. They're quite captivating, really. As the plants mature, the lustre fades, and that is when the time is right to harvest. The leaves cure in a special solution before we dry them in the sun, package them up, and sell them to select lucky buyers near and far. Oh," and here Petric laughed lightly waving his finger back and forth in front of his face, "and you need to watch out for the white flowers. They're deadly in any form."

"Alzbeda," X'andria piped up peering over the top of her scroll. Her voice was darker and more serious-sounding than usual. "What about her, Petric?"

Petric took a shuddering breath. He cast his eyes downward and seemed suddenly to appear older and more frail.

"Alzbeda," he began slowly. "Alzbeda is ancient and mysterious. She is the heart of our people. We Meridens were once nomadic savages," Petric's face twisted into a pained grimace, "but Alzbeda brought us to safety and harmony. That was long ago. She held us together." Petric's voice trailed off in the reverie and he rubbed his hand carefully along the fine cushion beside him.

"Fabric," Ohlen suggested, he was leaning intently toward Petric as he spoke, almost like he wanted to smell Petric's breath while hearing his words. Ohlen's eyebrows knit together. "She held your people together like fabric?" He elaborated.

"Yes," Petric seemed to suddenly return to his senses. "But now she's missing. There was blood all over her altar. So much blood. Everyone is terrified, and fear what may come." Petric's voice had diminished to a whisper.

"So what do you want us for?" Gnome asked bluntly.

"I want you to find her!" Petric was suddenly animated. "Find Alzbeda and bring her safely home. Meriden cannot last long without her, and I shudder to think of the consequences should we fall."

The carriage stopped suddenly. There were voices outside. Shouts.

Moments later the heavy rear curtain sealing out the late afternoon—sealing inside the passengers—parted to reveal Petric's driver, a gaunt middle-aged man with jet black hair and dark, sunken eyes in a simple grey robe.

Petric released a rapid stream of quick and surprisingly terse-sounding commands in his own language, before a ragged band of sun-baked brigands—men and women armed with hatchets, scythes and reapers—ambled into view behind the driver. The pale driver cast his gaze despondently downward, and stepped aside.

Mara's soft little hand lagged with the gentlest resistance as Waif followed Zarina and Zordim through the dark streets of Watertown. Her warm sticky fingers molded shapelessly into a limp round paw that Waif had trouble holding onto with his one remaining hand.

"Almost there," Zarina breathed conspiratorily into the night. "Anyone?" she asked tensely, even more softly.

"No one," Waif replied, taking one more look over his shoulder. They had passed only a few people on their hasty nighttime trek from Westwood, and Waif was quite sure none had followed them.

"Good," Zarina returned, with the steely edge Waif had come to expect from his new companion.

Zarina darted left into a low archway pulling Zordim close after. Waif tightened his grip on Mara's slippery hand and altered course quickly to follow. He stumbled slightly, his feet scuffing little whispered swishes over the cobblestones. The recent loss of his left arm made it difficult to keep balanced, and the pain of the raw wound served as a constant reminder.

Their steps echoed in the narrow corridor, damp with cool evening condensation from the seaside air, but they soon emerged into a small moonlit courtyard. Mordimer and Zarina's place was through a low warped and swollen wood door that swung out creakily on salt-rusted hinges.

Mara raced forward and, together with Zordim, darted into the familiar stillness before Zarina, almost as though they hoped to find their father smiling inside with some new treasure off a trading vessel. Zarina, on the other hand, looked sullenly at the threshold, and waited for Waif to enter first.

"What are we gonna do?" Waif asked several long, quiet, deliberate minutes later.

"We're going to sleep, my little friend. We will sleep, and then we will return to that dreaded place, learn what we can, and make a plan to avenge my Mordimer."

She began feeling confined, confined like Elias' underground cell,
confined like the hull of the fat man's ship all those years ago.

Chapter Twenty-Four
THE STAIRS

Fear washed over Ohlen—but it was not his fear, it was theirs. The tension emanating from the scrappy band squinting up out of the hot dusty road into the darkness of Petric's carriage was so palpable it felt like moist tendrils swimming in the air around him, tugging at the very sweat hovering in the pores of Ohlen's skin.

These people are hurting.

One moment Boudreaux was sleeping, and the next he had catapulted himself out the rear of the carriage like a wildcat with his weapon drawn. "GOLD!" he yelled maniacally. "Gold's what you're after is it?"

Ohlen pushed down into Petric's deep cushions, trying to get upright.

"Here's how it works!" Aggression came in waves from Boudreaux, competing in Ohlen's psyche with the apprehension of the villagers.

"We FIGHT! Anyone alive with TWO arms at the end gets a silver. One-arms get a copper. And I don't pay any dead. Got it?"

Ohlen scrambled past Petric and landed awkwardly on one knee on the dry dirt road behind Boudreaux, whose bulging taut skin already glistened in the hot sunlight.

"...not after gold..." Ohlen heard the feeble protest come from the shifting sorry gaggle as he righted himself.

Boudreaux took a stutter-step forward, kicking up a small plume of dust, and shouted, "Who's FIRST?" The armed band flinched collectively at the fighter's advance.

"We's not after gold!" the same thin voice whined through the air again. "We's lookin' fer a boy."

The voice, Ohlen now saw, belonged to a sun-wrinkled skinny man clinging to a scythe. This was no fighter, this was no robber, this was a farmer. In the same instant, awareness came to Ohlen that his companion Boudreaux had no real intention of harming these ragged people—Boudreaux was putting on a show of cruel lunacy in an effort to intimidate and scare away the sorry grouping he had assumed were bandits.

"Lower your weapons," Ohlen gained Boudreaux's side and placed a steadying hand on his friend's rocklike sword arm. "There is no need to fight this day."

Ohlen's serenity was contagious. Indeed it could be overwhelming. Boudreaux's adrenaline-fueled mask of violence began to relax, and the jittery band of villagers loosened their grips and lowered their shoulders.

"Tell me about the boy," Ohlen continued, staring penetratingly at the man with the scythe.

"He's my boy!" wailed a grey-shrouded woman near the back of the group. "Some'n took 'im," she cried, "Some'n took my boy..." and she broke down.

The scythe-man piped up again, "It's been two days. We're lookin' for 'im. Stoppin' travlers, jus' checkin', ya know?"

"How do you know someone took him?" It was Gnome. He and Arden had arrived, and X'andria was climbing down from the carriage behind them. Petric's driver had disappeared around the side, and Petric himself remained hidden inside, as did Ruprecht.

There was an awkward pause. Clearly none of the villagers had ever seen a gnome or an elf.

"Oh we know. We know a'right." It was scythe-man again, recovering himself. "Some'n took 'im. Took 'im in th'night. We know 'cause he's not th'first be missin'. Th'first was my little girl. My Callie."

And if ever there had been real menace in scythe-man's presence, it was there no more.

The carriage was rolling along again.

"We trade with the fieldlings. They are a nice, simple people. They produce great quantities of wheat primarily. I venture much of your Rockmoor bread and fermented ale originates in this very valley." Petric did not seem overly concerned about the missing boy and girl after Arden finished explaining all that had transpired in the dusty road behind the carriage.

The villagers mostly wore stiff heavy garments in greys and

earth tones with dirt and plant-matter ground thoroughly into the cloth. Ohlen had ascertained that the missing young people were similarly clad—he had promised to keep an eye out for them.

These were farmers tending fields generation after generation. They were close-knit, peaceful sorts, and the loss of two children in as many weeks had left the community reeling.

"Meriden is close now," Petric seemed genuinely excited.

And sure enough, several minutes later, the carriage slowed to a halt.

They found themselves beneath tall, thin, white-barked trees with few reachable limbs but a high canopy with dappled sunlight filtering through. With little underbrush, the effect was almost like being in a high-ceilinged cathedral built upon a multitude of sinewy white columns. The carriage stood before a wide but shallow stream burbling cheerily with crystal clear water over smooth rounded river rocks of brown, red and tan.

As they took in the pleasant surroundings, Petric's driver— thick black eyebrows knit together in a study of seriousness— secured the heavy flap over the carriage entrance and returned to his perch.

"Thank you, sir!" X'andria called brightly to him as the reins snapped and the wheels turned. But if the driver even heard her, he gave no indication.

Petric led them genially, turning and smiling every few paces, to a bend in the stream where several large, flat stones stood above the rushing liquid, allowing for dry passage. They gained elevation quickly after that. Without Petric to guide them, they would have run into a variety of challenging obstacles along the way, but he knew just where to go to find the graded footpaths leading around the rocky shelves and vegetation—far thicker here on the ascent than on the open floor of the airy forest they had left below.

"How far is this place, Petric?" Boudreaux was panting more from habit than fatigue.

"Meriden is nestled in the mountain," Petric replied lightly, smiling and nodding. "We are not far now, Boudreaux."

As if on cue, they emerged from their obscure path and stood staring straight into a sheer rock face that extended high above them and out of sight.

"Whoa, good luck getting up there!" Arden exclaimed, squinting skyward with his hands on his hips. "Gnome, I think you might be the only one that'll make it to Meriden today."

Gnome snorted derisively, a snort that sounded to X'andria like *I think this whole trip was a stupid idea.*

"Follow me please," Petric beckoned them along the uneven, rubble-strewn base of the high cliff. Stepping over and around boulders, the forest they had passed through to get up here was now on their left, the sheer rock rose high on their right.

"Almost there," Petric—picking his way forward—kept calling over his shoulder, like he feared losing his companions if he did not encourage them along.

At last Petric halted before an enormous round boulder. The boulder loomed twice as tall as Petric himself and cast a shadow over the mysterious little man. At first it seemed he was just taking a breather in a cool spot. But then a remarkable thing happened. Petric placed his left hand against the cool stone and a moment later it moved. It appeared, in fact, like Petric had pushed the massive boulder forward with only a gentle nudge.

The stone behemoth descended steadily down and backward into the base of the cliff itself and revealed a gaping pitch-black entrance into what moments before had appeared to be impenetrable mountain.

"What the hell?" breathed Boudreaux, for once giving voice to the exact sentiments of all his companions.

"Follow me please!" Their host chimed once more, as if giant moving rocks revealing hidden entrances was a commonplace occurrence. He hastened into the chiseled maw over top of the boulder, which had settled precisely into the smooth, polished floor of the entryway.

Exchanging puzzled glances, the friends followed slowly behind the little man, taking in what they could see of the mechanical marvel they had just witnessed. At the rear of the party, X'andria stooped low to examine the fine fissure outlining the space into which the boulder had descended as if a piece of the floor itself.

"Amazing," she breathed. "How did you make this, Petric?"

"We did not actually make this," Petric chuckled. "It's easier if I show you." He was hovering in darkness a little ways down the polished narrow passage, beckoning them past and within.

The passage was chilly, clean, and smooth. Everything echoed— their steps, their breaths, the smacking of lips. Once they were all past him, Petric manipulated some kind of lever set into the wall, and with a faint clunk the floor of the entrance behind them rose like a giant sea creature breaching the surface of the ocean, and materialized once more into the boulder that had previously blocked the secret passage. X'andria glimpsed a deep empty trench beneath the rising mass before its bulk sealed out the sunlight entirely.

X'andria felt a sudden panic. The dark, the unknown, the mass of stone surrounding them. She began feeling confined, confined like Elias' underground cell, confined like the hull of the fat man's ship all those years ago. Swooning, she placed a hand on the wall nearby— the cold surface a contrast to her rising temperature. Sweat beaded on her scalp.

Somewhere far away their curious little guide was urging them onward, insistent.

Nearer by Ohlen's voice broke through, it felt almost like it was inside her skull.

"Light, Petric? Do you have light here?"

Is Ohlen reading my thoughts? X'andria wondered feeling a little grateful, a little perturbed.

Petric had no light. Petric wanted them to move forward.

"I will summon light, Ohlen." Ruprecht was saying. There was murmuring.

And a moment later, the space filled with daylight-bright brilliance. Petric uncharacteristically shrieked with surprise, and the odd high-pitched wail echoed and amplified in the heavy press of the claustrophobic tunnel. X'andria found herself on her knees, hand still braced on the wall beside her. Ohlen was looking directly at her with a furrowed brow. Ruprecht was the very picture of serenity, eyes closed, calm, his mangled left hand cradled lightly in his intact right hand just before his lips. Boudreaux's hand hovered over the hilt of his dwarf blade, and he stared searchingly at Ruprecht as if seeing him truly for the first time. Arden was facing the wall, like he had been about to walk directly into it.

"What's up X'an?" It was Gnome, concerned.

"I'm alright," she heard herself saying. Everyone was looking now. "It's just so close in here, you know?"

"How long 'til we're outta here Petric?" Boudreaux barked.

Petric seemed flustered.

"How long. Out?" Boudreaux said slow and loud, pointing unhelpfully up at the ceiling of the tunnel.

Now, in the light, her head clearing, X'andria noticed the filigree.

This cramped, dark tunnel was gorgeous. Tight, confined beneath the unfathomable weight of a mountain of stone, but intricately carved with geometric decorations of straight and swirling gloriousness.

"How is this light possible?" Petric stammered. "I do not understand." It seemed to X'andria that their guide was somewhere between amazed and deeply disturbed.

"OUT!" shouted Boudreaux, now pointing forward, "You get us outta here, or this'll be the last light you ever see!"

Ruprecht's light was tremendously reassuring. As they resumed their march, X'andria felt her trepidation fading and her sense of wonderment returning.

The tunnel was perfectly uniform, fastidiously ornate. They turned left one time, then right, then continued straight for several minutes before emerging into a singularly spectacular open space.

They were at the bottom of a thin chute carved out of the rock—the sky above a sliver of bright blue. Straight, filigreed walls rose dizzyingly high above them on three sides, with the fourth side being the tallest staircase any of them had ever seen.

"Welcome to the land of Meriden." Petric offered simply, placing a foot on the first step.

"I saw 'im, boss!" Fig insisted. "There I was, in the Axe like you told me, an' he come wobblin' in all bleedin' like."

"I wouldn'ta figured the freak for an ale drinker," Rove retorted lazily. This got a low rumbling chortle from Boris, an enormous, hairy shirtless oaf standing nearby.

"He had a ale, sir," Fig countered, as if it was a detail of the utmost importance. "But he wasn't alone neither. He had four others with 'im, jus' like we been tellin' folks. First the big ones was there, then the head cooks hurried in, then the gnome, an' they all started talkin' up a storm."

Rove had made his camp just south of Rockmoor, south of the Grotto and The Den from which he was a fugitive. Here the Westwood forest stretched down to the rocky coast, here bandits and smugglers went stealthily about their nefarious business—so long as they managed to avoid gruesome fates at the claws of the kinds of things that lurked in shadows outside the relative civilization of the port city.

A small fire struggled and popped around damp kindling, its flickers illuminating Rove's angular face. "So they're at the Axe, then?" he mused dangerously.

"No sir. Not no more. This fancy little guy came in. Dressed nice like. He said somethin', the she-elf jumped up, an' then they all cleared out'n a hurry." Fig gripped and rubbed the stumps of his missing fingers as he shared the last of his news, as if hoping they would begin to grow back.

"How much for the lot?" A gruff gravelly voice interrupted from the shadows nearby.

"Who's there?" Rove's voice took on a higher pitch than usual, and he glanced over his shoulder to make sure Boris was still standing behind him.

"We heard there's a price for the little flesh eater, the two arms, and the two head cooks. We wants to know what it is." It was the kind of voice that had steeped for decades in smoke and ale.

"Git in the light ya coward," Rove barked. The interloper sounded old enough. A voice belonging to someone he could likely best in a fight—at least with Boris and Fig backing him up.

Chapter Twenty-Four

But it wasn't just one person. It was two. A hooded figure rolled out into the light on liquid joints. Its feline movement reminded Rove of The Master, and ice passed over his stomach. Behind the hood came a grizzled old man with one-eye—the owner of the voice they'd heard.

But the next noise came from beneath the hood, "I tasted it." The words were bizarre and haunting, a voice forcing wheezy sound through a throat full of perforated reeds. "I tasted it, and I want more."

The others lingered for several long moments at the bottom of the stairs, taking in the bizarre grandeur towering above them, before starting their ascent.

Chapter Twenty-Five
UP

_____

Petric had regained a measure of composure after his shock at Ruprecht's otherworldly light in the tunnel, but his effervescent enthusiasm evaporated somewhere between the unexpected illumination and Boudreaux's angry outburst. The others lingered for several long moments at the bottom of the stairs, taking in the bizarre grandeur towering above them, before starting their ascent. X'andria noted that the ornate patterns decorating the tunnel seemed to explode out of that confined space into huge swirls and sweeps that covered the expanse of these gargantuan walls extending beyond her field of vision. The effect was both awe inspiring and unsettling.

"Alzbeda," Petric began—even though he led the march, and

faced forward away from the others, his words rang clearly around them off the steps and walls, "has the most remarkable way of knowing what people seek, sometimes even when they do not know it yet themselves. When she delivered our people from wandering long ago, she sought the safety of the mountains. But she and the other Meridens soon learned that the mountains had dangers of their own shrouded within.

"The Rock Eater was a frightful beast. Artless, with no intellect, it churned through rock and soil, uprooted trees, and obliterated all life it encountered, including our people. I never trusted the Rock Eater, but Alzbeda believed its abilities could be harnessed. She used her gifts to create some kind of mist that enabled her to speak to it— and it to her. According to Alzbeda it was the first time the Rock Eater communicated with another being in centuries. It is the Rock Eater that created this stair and the tunnel below to protect us from the outside."

"What do you mean you never trusted the Rock Eater, Petric?" X'andria called up from several steps below.

Petric stopped and turned around, eyeing X'andria intently. "It's a savage beast, X'andria. It's unpredictable. I think Alzbeda came to trust it overmuch."

X'andria joined the little Meriden on his step. They were almost the same height, and she leveled a stare back at him, equaling his intensity. "That's not what I meant, Petric," she replied. "You said all this happened long ago, and that you never trusted the Rock Eater— as if you were there at the time. I'm confused."

It seemed to take Petric a moment to understand what X'andria was asking. But then his face broke out in a wide grin, and he chuckled lightly. "Oh, perhaps you'll meet the Rock Eater, and you'll see why I feel the way I do. But you're right, Alzbeda and the Rock

Eater met long ago, long before this time." Petric resumed his methodical steps upward.

It was odd to be back among his friends. There was no proper reunion, arriving as he had with Geoffrey in the midst of turmoil and flight. And now they were on this puzzling journey following a strange little man named Petric, who called himself a Meriden, and who seemed to want them to rescue some ancient lady who made mist and could talk to mountain monsters.

Why were they here? Because they had to get out of Rockmoor, away from false accusations, and from *It*. Because Petric had a carriage, and a job, and gold. And because apparently Ohlen and X'andria had heard the name of Petric's missing elder spoken by the Sorcerer of Rockmoor.

I have missed so much, thought Ruprecht as he took the final step out of the colossal stone staircase onto level ground. Everything that had happened in Rockmoor, the temple, Dortmund, Boudreaux, it was all like some terrible fever-dream.

They were walking now. It was a rugged, rocky terrain. The air was clear and cold, and wind came in gusts whipping across the naked rock. But they were sloping gently downward on a manicured pathway that led toward a smattering of tall green-needled trees in the distance. Everything about Petric, his language, his vestments, his transport, the tunnel, stairs and paths, it was all so refined and opulent.

That was quite a look Boudreaux gave me in the tunnel, like he was seeing me for the first time, thought Ruprecht, with mixed emotions. *He must despise me for what happened with Dortmund in Rockmoor. I wonder if I'll ever gain his trust?*

Boudreaux was clomping stoically along just ahead.

They were passing between the tall, thin trees now, the tops of which bent with each gust of wind. There was sparse chatter amongst the group. X'andria quizzed Petric about the designs on the stair and learned that the Rock Eater always left decorative grooves in anything it made. Arden made frequent observations to whoever was nearest about the grasses and trees, and the small quick animals darting around on the earth and in the sky.

Ruprecht was grateful his deity had come to assist him in the tunnel. He meditated on his gratitude with each step through the trees. After losing his humanity to the all-encompassing darkness, and thrashing about in lust-borne chaos, his spiritual reunion— thanks to Geoffrey's patience and guidance—had been at once the most challenging and most rewarding experience of his life.

Ruprecht's steps continued, guided by instinct. His eyes rolled skyward in their sockets, his lids fluttered closed, and he shifted his gratitude-focus to Geoffrey. Geoffrey was wisdom. Geoffrey was generosity. Ruprecht reflected on their lessons, on Geoffrey's gentle but unwavering elucidation of Ruprecht's former self—the one before the invasion.

Where is he now? Ruprecht wondered, recalling the frost-covered fracturing wall in their Rockmoor lodgings and his own screaming nerves as dark dread approached them. Ruprecht pictured—as though looking through a window—the pained resolve in Geoffrey's wrecked visage when he yelled for them to flee and offered himself up to face the torment—buying time and space for the others, for Ruprecht, to get away.

In this state of concern, grief, and gratitude, Ruprecht reached out to his deity once more. He asked for a connection to his friend and mentor, to his uncle's partner in spiritual deliverance. He drifted away from his body, submitting himself completely to fathomless compassion.

But he was jerked downward. His expanding mind was boxed in by a stabbing pain in his mangled left hand. Ruprecht stumbled, and his eyes clicked open, and he found himself looking over the edge of a sturdy but wobbly rope and wood-slat bridge, down into a deep chasm.

The trees were behind them now. They had emerged, they had walked onto this chasm-spanning bridge, and the missing middle finger of his left hand was killing him all of a sudden.

Everything's gone. They took it. That big, stupid oaf. I want him dead so bad.

Dortmund was a mess. He'd convinced some skin and bone old sop on the grimy bank of the Torrent to give him a few swigs of a vile, retch-inducing fluid in an earthenware jug. Or had he waited for the old guy to pass out and simply stolen the jug? Whatever.

I want to hurt him. Dortmund's head lolled forward, the stuff in the jug was hitting him hard. *And Ruprecht...just wish I could see him rot in some hole. I'd spit on him. Better than he deserves.*

Dortmund's fantasy world gave him less and less of an escape these days. He tried to go there, to see Ruprecht, and Boudreaux, and all the clerics begging for his forgiveness, begging for his mercy. But these dreary, bone-chilling nights on the Torrent, not to mention his growing hunger, dragged him back quickly to reality. His food from the Temple had run out after just a few days.

Dortmund's chin drooped forward. Another swig would actually take a bit of effort—he would have to lift his head up to make it happen. He wasn't sure it was worth it.

Lost in drunken self-pity, Dortmund did not register the sounds that must have preceded the warm spray hitting his face and hands. In the cold of night, even though the wet drops and chunks cooled quickly, the surprising warmth was enough to shake him to alertness.

But sounds had definitely happened. Crunching, slobbering, lust-addled bubbly breath, and a brief, shocked cry came in quick, messy succession as Gruder's three fang-lined mouths churned like hot razors through the passed-out old wretch—the former owner of the jug of foul drink.

Dortmund dropped that jug in his lap. The cool contents mixed with his own hot urine leaking onto the riverbank between and around his thighs. Gruder's glistening jaws advanced forward twisting this way and that, dripping gore. The long nostrils flapped open and closed as the horror advanced, sniffing ravenously, toward its next victim.

And Dortmund disappeared to his other land. A land where a terrible dragon approached him. *His* dragon.

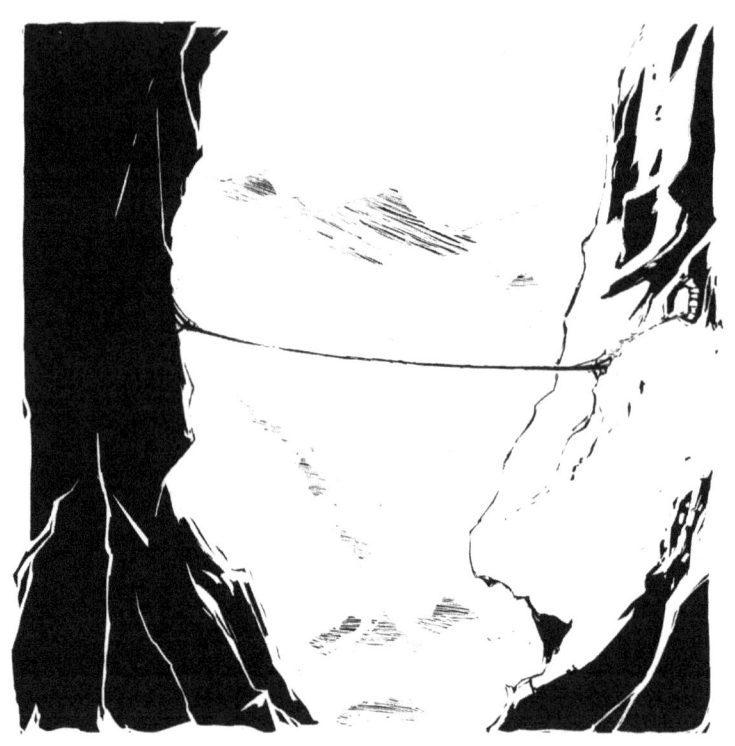

*Ohlen coaxed his imagination over the edge of the bridge
into the swirling air beneath. He began to feel chill.*

Chapter Twenty-Six
THE CHASM

───────────

Petric was a mystery to Ohlen. He seemed nice enough, open, articulate, and genuinely distressed by Alzbeda's apparent abduction. But something else was going on. Something hidden. And Ohlen wanted very much to tease it out into the open.

The little man was leading them across an enormous bridge spanning a deep chasm. *This is an odd country indeed*, thought Ohlen, reflecting on the mute driver of the opulent carriage, the spectacular hidden tunnel and stair, and now this suspended passage—itself an engineering marvel. It seemed what the Meridens may have lacked in physical prowess, they made up for with wealth and ingenuity.

"There's an interesting story about this bridge," Petric

announced to the wind swirling around them.

Ohlen was interested to hear more. "Tell us, Petric." He encouraged.

"Well a young Meriden some years ago, by the name of Bodomek, cast himself off of this bridge." The bridge swayed slightly from the weight of their alternating steps as they clomped across. "He had gotten into a disagreement with Alzbeda and became very sullen. So sullen, in fact, that he decided to come here and end it all."

"But that's crazy!" piped up Arden. "What were they arguing about?"

Ohlen coaxed his imagination over the edge of the bridge into the swirling air beneath. He began to feel chill.

"An excellent question, Arden," Petric replied. "We were all mystified, to be honest. It turns out that he had become quite enamored of Alzbeda. Obsessively so."

"En-what?" Boudreaux shouted from the rear.

This earth has a story to tell, Ohlen sensed. There was heaviness here.

"*En-am-ored*, Boudreaux," X'andria hissed. "Means he fell in love with her."

"That's right," Petric concurred, "Bodomek was deeply in love with Alzbeda."

"Eww!" Boudreaux whined. "That's gross, didn't you say she was super old?"

They were approaching the end of the bridge. Petric arrived on solid ground and turned to wait for the others to follow.

"Hush, Boudreaux," implored X'andria. "Let him finish."

Petric smirked, it made the wrinkles around his eyes crinkle up into little folds. "You are right Boudreaux. But Alzbeda had...has...a youthful air about her, and has certain charms that are hard to describe."

Ohlen stepped off the bridge and caught Ruprecht's eye. He was startled to see Ruprecht looking as pale and ill at ease as Ohlen himself was feeling.

"So he loved her, and she did not love him, and it drove him to end his life at the bridge?" X'andria seemed enthralled by the story. "But that's so sad!"

They had resumed walking.

"You are exactly right, X'andria. It was extremely sad for everyone, especially Bodomek's mother and father, and for Alzbeda herself, who regretted not being able to recognize Bodomek's passions for what they were."

Boudreaux seemed to be chewing on all this information with unusual interest. "So this Alzbeda," he began, "she's the one we're supposed to find?"

"She's the one," Petric grinned, knowing exactly where the big fighter was going.

"And it sounds like you'd say she's...pretty good looking?" Boudreaux ventured, over disapproving noises from X'andria.

"Something like that, Boudreaux," Petric was smiling now. "But be careful, you don't want to end up like poor Bodomek."

"Whoa," Boudreaux exclaimed loudly and he stopped in his tracks. "Looks like I may not have to find Alzbeda at all!"

They all followed Boudreaux's gaze down the path and immediately saw what he was looking at. She had come, it seemed, out of nowhere. She bore the same, dark features as Petric, but had none of his portliness. Straight jet-black hair hung down over her shoulders. Her lithe form was fitted snugly in a ruby red silken vestment that seemed to be one piece fashioned perfectly just for her. She stood frozen like a wild animal seeing something strange for the first time—trying to decide if it should flee or pounce.

"Petric..." she called when she recognized he was among them. But the words that followed made no sense to any of them. Except Boudreaux, who believed each successive syllable to be the most sensuous entreaty ever uttered. Her smile was devastating.

But all the levity was gone from Petric. The smile was a distant memory, obscured by a mask of complete disdain. They did not need to understand his words, to comprehend the tone of his livid reply.

Her smile only widened as Petric seemingly berated her in their language. This Meriden woman seemed supremely confident. X'andria found herself wondering if someday she herself might be able to track down the maker of the fabulous outfit. Arden wondered the same thing. The woman in red gave one last goading look at Petric, spun on her heel, and marched briskly away from them.

"What the hell was that?" Boudreaux whined, "I didn't even get her name, Petric."

"Nezka and I have a...disagreement," Petric replied coolly.

Eleanor was at a loss. Days had crawled by. She held The Sorcerer's warm moist hand. She stroked his hair, trying to ignore the disease-black lines snaking like webs from his ears out across his ash-grey cheeks.

Come back to me, she breathed pleadingly into the dense, humid air stagnating over The Sorcerer's inert body. He had been lying flat in his inner chambers ever since those two bastards attacked him with some kind of cursed book. A dark, blood-drinking, brain-addling book. At least that is what she had pieced together from the stories.

And from the rat.

It was dead now, of course. Feeble minds could not withstand thorough scraping. When she had arrived at the scene—The Sorcerer sweating and convulsing, collapsed in his signature red conical garb—there had been only one thing on his desk: an open cage.

They had searched frantically for the two interlopers. And then the bad dream turned nightmarish. That freakish human-monster Gruder was somehow unleashed on Patrick's team. No doubt more work of the nefarious duo.

After Eleanor expelled the hideous creature out into some unsuspecting Rockmoor neighborhood, she ordered the remaining sensates to search for it unceasingly, in pairs, with explicit destruction orders. It had yet to be found.

Frustrating was Patrick's helplessness. He had hardly spoken since his team had been devoured in front of him. So Eleanor found him a place in The Sorcerer's study where he spent most of his time staring despondently at the walls of artifacts.

It was the middle of the second day following the attack that Eleanor ventured from The Sorcerer's side and busied herself straightening things in his study. Anything to keep her mind occupied, to allay the dread. She closed the little door to the cage, preparing to return it to The Conservatory when it occurred to her. *Something must have been in this cage.*

"Patrick…" she called matter-of-factly, before stopping herself. Patrick would be no help this day. He hardly even moved when she called his name. From the hysteric gibberish that had poured from him following the slaughter of his team, it was clear he took full responsibility. Patrick even claimed to have charmed his sensates all to defenseless stillness before the assault—which was incomprehensible, of course, a violation of their most basic

Chapter Twenty-Six

precepts—it must have been his guilt talking.

I'll do it myself, Eleanor groused. Just a few ingredients. She relished the few opportunities she had had working in The Sorcerer's study when she first became his protégé—everything she needed was always right here.

Powder of any enchanted nocturnal predator's eye would do. Rifling through The Sorcerer's many-drawered armoire, the first she came upon was that of an ancient giant salamander—a huge lethal beast that could spend decades beneath the surface of the swamps it lived in, dining on any being foolish enough to place a paw, or hoof, or foot in or near it's murky waters.

She tapped two pinches of the heavy algae-green powder into one of The Sorcerer's shallow brass mixing bowls. Next was conveyance. Fresh spinal fluid was best. Eleanor summoned a sensate from the Conservatory and asked him to extract fluid from whatever unfortunate creature had been selected as today's living donor.

Dripping the solution into her eye would be the hard part. *Narasi'iku.* See. She whispered, as she arched her back over top of the ornate desk and slid the mixture down a narrow pour-trough into her rapidly blinking left eye.

The stinging was terrible. She doubled over, dropping the trough and brass bowl, and splattering what little remained of the salamander eye juice. For several minutes she could not get either eye to do anything but squeeze defiantly closed. At last, however, she managed to coax them gently open.

What an odd sensation it was. Her right eye saw normally. Her left saw only grey outlines on black. Cupping her right hand over her right eye she focused on the signals coming from her left. She turned toward Patrick and everything changed. His huddled form lit up her vision like a burning star.

Time to hunt.

Bumping into things here and there, still covering her right eye, Eleanor stumbled about the study. Slowly scanning in each direction, it was a matter of minutes before she detected the rat, radiating its little life force from behind one or another of The Sorcerer's many treasures—night-predator vision was good for seeing warmth, but not much else.

Keidu'aqadu. Hold. Eleanor flung brownish mold-spore powder casually out before her, and directed the paralytic power through space to overtake the small quivering rodent, which immediately ceased its quivering. Both eyes uncovered now, and ignoring the brain-twisting dual ocular signals, Eleanor stormed determinedly across the room, reached into the cobweb-dusty narrow gap behind The Sorcerer's tallest bookcase, and extracted the immobilized animal.

She had a sudden desire to chomp down directly onto its juicy, crunchy head. It was impossible—so far as Eleanor knew—to bring into oneself the powers of any creature, without also inviting a bit of the creature itself.

Huh, I'd forgotten about that, she mused, easily mastering the vague prehistoric instinct to feed.

With Eleanor's prize laid prone on her master's desk, she sat and prepared herself for what was about to happen.

Sorry little friend, she caught herself thinking as she pulled the fur directly above the rat's left eye back tightly, forcing open the lid, and revealing the shiny, twitchy black eye beneath. She held the little body up, placing the teeny, hairy, scratchy eye, against her own, normal, right eye. Eleanor fought the urge to blink with every ounce of her self-control.

Kushbaa'age. Reveal. She commanded.

Another otherworldly rumbling cry filled the night, preceding a second shattering percussive crack. The sound came just as the toe of Arden's boot nudged into a foreign object on the forest floor.

Chapter Twenty-Seven
MERIDEN

———————

This place is so enchanting! Arden trailed closely behind their intriguing, smartly attired guide. They ascended the third of three short sets of elegant stone steps in the forest path. *Must be a clearing up ahead,* Arden mused, observing a wide vista of deep blue, late afternoon sky emerging through a growing gap in the treetops.

Their brief encounter with Nezka—if that was her name—made Arden appreciate Petric's sequined vest anew. *These people know how to dress!* Petric's carriage, the artistic bridge construction down to the fitted cast iron couplings, and the spectacular stonework, the Meridens' attention to detail was mind-blowing. Arden definitely felt he had found his people.

And all of that was before he saw Meriden itself.

Chapter Twenty-Seven

In front of them stood a great colonnade. Tall perfect columns stood twenty or so across, and the same number deep atop a giant stone square. Advancing forward, mesmerized, Arden saw the columns were at once polished and sheer but also covered with the finest swirls of thin lines, as though each decorated by a spider. Petric was speaking, welcoming them to his home. But Arden's mind was too busy swimming in the wonder and elegance before him to really process the spoken words.

They were walking along the perimeter of the square now. Each new step gave an optical illusion of solidity or vacancy depending on the alignment of the columns relative to the vantage point of the viewer. Close in, though, Arden was fairly certain he detected an open space at the center of the compound with no columns at all.

"Petric," he chimed in, squinting, unaware if this had already been discussed. "Is there a gap in the middle?"

"Indeed there is Arden!" Petric replied enthusiastically. "Our colonnade runs eight pillars deep from any side, and we have an open courtyard in the middle surrounding Alzbeda's Altar To The Wind And Sky."

"Fascinating..." Arden mumbled in response, studying the large rectangular pieces of slate-grey stone making up the surface beneath their feet, and then allowing his eyes to drift outward to the tree line a short distance away.

"But where do you live, Petric? Is the village nearby?" Arden asked.

Petric laughed out loud. "Great question, Arden!" he managed. "Believe it or not, we are actually standing right in front of the door to my home."

Still chuckling, Petric walked several paces over to a column one place in from the exterior row. Glancing around, Arden observed that each uniform column differed in its decoration. At least no two in his field of vision were identically adorned.

Petric placed his left hand on the column before him at shoulder height and moments later a door-sized cut-out of the column itself began sliding straight down into the slate-grey floor. When this exterior section had descended about a third of the way, a second layer of identical dimensions behind it began to drop, and then a third. This whole remarkable progression was accompanied by a muffled grating sound similar to the one they had heard inside the mountain when the boulder had ascended to reseal the tunnel entrance.

The slabs nestled themselves progressively deeper into the stone floor, the top of each becoming a step leading down into subterranean space beneath the colonnade. The center of Petric's column had transformed mechanically into a doorway.

"We have finally arrived!" Petric clapped his hands together and turned to face his guests. "It has been a long journey, and you all must be very hungry and tired. Let us eat and rest, my home is your home. In the morning we shall set about the business before us."

And with that, the little Meriden disappeared down the dark column steps, leaving the befuddled party to stand awkwardly for a few moments, before following him within.

Earth and rock and wood blended seamlessly together forming rounded walls and ceilings over sloping floors. Gentle natural rises connected Petric's numerous alcove-rooms. Curved honey-comb nooks for lounging or resting—lined with plush cushions and soft-woven throws—could be found in each unique space. Smooth white walls were backdrops for rich colors in textile drapes and rugs, and soft-edged shelves sculpted out of the living rock were teeming with countless unique treasures.

"What's the blanket on the wall for?" Boudreaux slipped in between noisy guzzles of delicious ale from a gem-studded ceramic vessel. Petric bustled to and fro somehow producing new beverages and platters of nibbles on each trip. Boudreaux, sprawling back in cushiony comfort, continued, "Do you people sleep standing up or something?"

Petric stopped his scurrying and considered the wall-hanging for a moment. "I was traveling some years ago, Boudreaux, quite a distance from here near the Macken Coast. I met a man whose hands were stained different colors, one green and one red. It was seeing those hands, rough and scarred and stained, that stopped me and led me to try and communicate. I learned that the man's hands were stained because he mashed roots and certain berries to make tinted pastes. Then he used the pastes to color strands of fiber that he wove into colored mats like this one. It is meant to capture the vision of the sea, and the sky above it, off the Macken Coast. I thought it was quite beautiful, and brought it back here for my wall to remind me of my trip there."

"The Macken Coast is near my birth-place," Ohlen's rich voice filled the room. "I have not seen work like this in many years. It pleases my eyes to see this beauty once more."

"Is that so?" Petric mused. "Where are you from exactly, Ohlen? I enjoyed my visit there immensely."

"I am from Toyath, near The Watchhill." Ohlen replied.

"Ah, the big tower!" Petric enthused. "Watchhill had the big tower, right?"

"It still stands, yes." Ohlen confirmed. "I spent hundreds of hours in that dark place, Petric, and I am one of the few ever to leave alive."

The room quieted, and—beyond the crunching, slurping, and lip smacking—they fell to eating in silence. Petric's food was delicious. Gnome and Boudreaux fell asleep. Ruprecht and Ohlen closed their eyes and may have been sleeping as well, or meditating, it was hard to tell with those two. X'andria was up, closely studying Petric's many peculiar objects, picking each one up and turning it over in her hands.

Arden began to feel a yearning for the outdoors.

"Petric, I think I might like to take a short walk. Would that be alright?" Arden asked their host.

Petric, who was quietly clearing platters and empty drinking vessels, got a pained looked on his face. "I know you are very capable, Arden, and I probably should not worry, but whatever has befallen Meriden remains a mystery, and until we uncover its source, I fear for your safety out alone near dark."

"I will join you, Arden." Ohlen must not have been sleeping after all. "I, too, could use a short walk before turning in."

"Very well," sighed Petric, and he made for the entry chamber. Ohlen and Arden followed closely behind.

From within, the partial stair looked odd—like a joke a frivolous decorator might have placed in a room as a conversation-starter. The five ascending steps led straight up into solid rock. Before either guest could comment, however, their host placed his hand on what appeared to be bare wall beside the stair and the now-familiar earthy rumble activated once more somewhere within the floors or walls. Massive individual slabs of stone, that before appeared as one, began sliding individually downward into the floor, and open space appeared above the partial staircase as a sixth, seventh and eighth step settled into place and the dim light of dusk filtered in from the open doorway above.

Without a word, Petric led the way up to the surface and out into the still evening air. "Do be careful," he told them, a hint of disapproval in his tone. "The most important thing is that you remember which one is mine. They do all look similar. If it helps, mine is the fourth over from the southeast corner, one row in. Knock four times anywhere on the column and I will hear and let you in. Only I can activate this doorway, it was designed to be that way."

"We won't be long, Petric," Arden said reassuringly. "I just have a thing about quiet time in nature. Calms me, you know?"

"Oh, and don't go that way, toward the peaks," Petric added darkly, pointing north beyond the colonnade. "The Rock Eater lives that way, and I would very much like to be able to look upon both your faces once again."

And with that, Petric stalked back down the steps, the column resealing itself to polished seamlessness behind him.

"He doesn't seem to be happy with us," Arden said matter-of-factly, turning toward the trees.

"The Meriden is fearful, I can sense it." Ohlen replied sagely. "His fear has increased since our arrival here, and he tries to hide it."

"Wanna walk back down the path a bit?" Arden queried, ready to get moving.

"You lead, I follow," Ohlen said simply.

The temperature had dropped with the setting sun. Arden had not spent much time high in the mountains—just a few short trips he and his father had taken years ago—but he remembered the chilly nights. As intriguing as the perfect colonnade was, it felt really good to step off the precisely hewn stone onto natural earth.

They were halfway across the shrubby, weedy expanse between

the colonnade, and the point where the forest path entered the trees, when they heard what sounded like crackling thunder coming from the north. The echoing boom was followed by a long low rumbling moan that sounded as though the mountain itself was wailing in despair.

The two friends froze in their tracks and waited, but the evening returned to stillness. "Our Rock Eater?" Arden whispered. Ohlen gave a barely perceptible nod. On they walked, toward the path into the trees, away from the origin of the troubling sounds.

"Who's Alzbeda, Ohlen? What do think is going on?" They were ambling amongst tall thin shadows along the path now, with probably an hour left before pitch dark.

"X'andria and I went to see The Sorcerer of Rockmoor, Arden. She and I brought him the small black book Boudreaux extracted from that dreaded dark sewer where the demon spawn was growing," Ohlen conveyed in a near monotone. "The book is powerful and evil, I believe it may have the same origin as the Eyes of Darkness I now carry. It nearly consumed X'andria when she attempted to study it. It was frightening."

Arden paused a moment and turned to study Ohlen's stony features. *Frightening*, seemed an unusual word for Ohlen to use.

"So we delivered the book to The Sorcerer, seeking his advice, and I fear it may have destroyed him." Ohlen continued.

"That's what X'an was telling us at The Axe. So that's why all The Emporium's sentries were out after you two." Arden recalled the crazy tale X'andria had hastily regaled them with at the Iron Axe before Petric's arrival.

"Correct," Ohlen said coolly, clearly preoccupied, "and before he lost consiousness, The Sorcerer uttered several names. One of them was Alzbeda. That is why we are here."

Chapter Twenty-Seven

"What's bothering you Ohlen?" Arden asked sincerely, before adding more lightly, "I mean, beyond the obvious!"

"I am concerned that she..." Ohlen began, but he stopped abruptly when Arden halted mid-step, raised his right hand in a closed fist, and placed his left on the hilt of his forefathers' sword.

Ohlen immediately left his conversational logic-space and probed outward with his senses into the earth and air—eyes closed. Arden was moving, Ohlen followed, sensing.

Someone had departed the path. Faint tracks, bent blades of grass, groundcover struggling to recuperate. Divots nearby indicated something had been dragged, something light, with no hard gouging edges. Half a day ago, give or take.

Nostrils flaring, Arden searched smell and sound for the presence of life or activity. Nothing revealed itself beyond his friend Ohlen trodding and breathing lightly behind.

In the cover of trees, the waning light was insufficient. Arden's pupils were huge, trying to drink up as much detail as possible in the absence of any non-visual clues. With no other indication, Arden continued along the vector established by the entry point into the brush. It seemed, though, that they had best turn back and possibly return in the morning.

Another otherworldly rumbling cry filled the night, preceding a second shattering percussive crack. The sound came just as the toe of Arden's boot nudged into a foreign object on the forest floor.

"It is time for us to return, my friend," Ohlen breathed into the darkness behind Arden's head. "*Tomorrow is another day*, as my mother used to say."

"I've got something, Ohlen." Arden replied, kneeling. He felt with his hands for the object. It was dry, like leaves or parchment. *No, wait!* It had different surfaces. *Is that fur?* Arden had encountered countless dead and dying animals at all stages of demise. In those cases there had been blood, smell, and there was always substance. *This is pretty light, but not featherlight.*

"I need to see it, Ohlen, I'm lighting a torch." Arden decided.

"I would not advise it," Ohlen warned, "Sudden bright light in a place like this will bring unwanted attention."

But the sparks were already flying, the flame was already sputtering, and light began to struggle forth in Arden's hands. "Just for a moment," he was saying.

But he said no more. Neither of them did.

It was like a small person. But like a big doll. Or a terrible nightmare of a baby scarecrow. The skin was brown and wrinkled and dry like parchment left out in the sun and rain for years. The hair was stark white, stringy. *Are those teeny holes all over?* They were so small it was hard to tell. But they were everywhere, in the face, the arms, even through the clothes.

The clothes.

It was dressed in a stiff, heavy brown shirt, with greyish pants stained thoroughly at the knees with ground-in dirt.

Grey-green goo oozed from the rat's eye by the time Eleanor—hands trembling—laid its stiff little body back down on The Sorcerer's table. She felt sick. Sick from exertion, sick from the bilateral vision—part prehistoric predator, part rat—and sick from the all-encompassing terror the rat transferred to her as she probed its visual memory and discovered the book, the bite, and the drop of blood.

Pressing the rat's eye tightly against her own, she had

demanded its memory return to the two characters sitting in the dim light beyond the book and table. The rat had been singularly focused on the horrid book, so the images were quite obscure. Over and over again—her own eyeball scratched and bleeding—Eleanor forced it to replay the peripheral edges of its memory until the little mind gave out completely. But she had gotten enough. She pieced together a tall, thin, dark-complexioned man with white hair and white robes sitting next to a confident-looking, red-haired, she-elf.

Eleanor had identified her marks.

The Sorcerer looked dreadful. Black weblike lines crawled across his sunken, pale face.

I don't know what to do for you!

How could it be that in this most desperate moment of her life, Eleanor was without her beloved teacher, the man who always knew everything. Even Patrick, her best friend, had abandoned her—catatonic and nonresponsive.

Hours passed. The bizarre effects of the night-predator vision spell wore off her left eye. Her right eye, however, was swollen shut and quite painful from the prolonged contact with furry rat face.

Wait!

Eleanor had a rash inspiration.

It worked once tonight, maybe I could try it again.

She stood up and walked over to The Sorcerer, whose breaths were coming in erratic and deep shudders.

He would want me to do everything possible to find them.

Ever so slowly Eleanor leaned close over her mentor. She

placed her finger lightly on the eyelid of his large dominant eye, and pushed upward.

The lid was crusted closed and resisted opening. She had to stretch the skin uncomfortably tight before the seal gave way and the skin slid over the thick viscosity beneath. Eleanor felt nauseous all over again.

The Sorcerer's brilliant blue eye had lost all its brightness, all its life. The eyeball itself was bloodshot, but the hairlike lines were black and not red.

Keep it together. Eleanor steeled herself for the grim task before her.

She leaned in closer still, left eye fluttering in anticipation of contact.

But just then The Sorcerer gave a light, shuddering sputter.

Eleanor sprang backward. "Sorcerer!" she cried.

The Sorcerer's breathing became quick and shallow.

Eleanor fell to her knees beside him and put one hand on his heaving chest, the other on his upper arm. "I'm here, my Sorcerer, I'm here." She fussed.

"Eleanor," he coughed out, his voice raw and unfamiliar. "I need..."

"Yes, tell me," she said hurriedly, "anything."

"Hillcrest Temple," his eye was open now, staring straight up.

"Hillcrest Temple?" Eleanor was confused.

"The Brotherhood!" The Sorcerer wheezed—it would have been a shout had he been able.

Eleanor's mind raced. The Sorcerer hardly ever even mentioned the Hillcrest Temple Brotherhood, and when he did, it was only to make fun of their silly monastic customs and faith and rules.

Eleanor had just made up her mind to send sensates

immediately to Hillcrest Temple to request an audience when The Sorcerer said one more word. This word was one she was positive she had never heard before.

"Dormarion!" The Sorcerer gasped. His tormented eye swiveled toward her imploringly.

"Every sundown, for as long as I can remember, Alzbeda has gone to work atop her Altar To The Wind And Sky."

Chapter Twenty-Eight
INVESTIGATION

What a fascinating collection of objects. X'andria was in awe of Petric's many treasures. Ohlen and Arden had gone out, the others were sleeping, and she found herself drawn from one carefully arrayed tableau to the next—room by enthralling room. She wanted to understand each item, to know its origin, its use, its spirit.

Petric continued to bustle about, tidying up after the arrival of the six guests and their ensuing meal. Catching glimpses of him out of the corner of her eye, X'andria noticed his face seemed strained—somehow older than when they first met at the Iron Axe in Rockmoor. But any time he caught her watching, he quickly smiled and the worry and fatigue seemed to vanish into his good-natured grin.

"This looks Elfish," X'andria remarked, turning a wooden cube over in her fingers. The tall slender runic script was unmistakable.

"It is indeed," Petric approached. "Are you…" He paused awkwardly, clearly at a sudden loss for words, "from Atolia?"

"Yes," X'andria replied coolly. She was unsure exactly why Petric's hesitation annoyed her, but there was something in his tone that made her feel like she needed to explain her personal history— and she was not about to do that.

"I mean, of course you are," Petric rushed, a deep crease scrunched between his dark eyebrows. "It's just that when I have met elf-kind away from Atolia, they have often been…gone a long while." Petric was clearly uncomfortable.

"You mean they were slaves," X'andria said bluntly.

Petric opened his mouth, but nothing came out. X'andria eyed him closely.

"I have to confess, X'andria, that I have not been to Atolia myself. And yes, the elves I have met on my travels have all been indentured."

"Enslaved," X'andria corrected, a touch of hostility making its way into her tone.

Petric licked his lips. "Enslaved," he acquiesced.

Just then four reverberant knocks echoed out of the entry hall. With an apologetic look, Petric excused himself sideways out of the room, and soon X'andria heard the mechanical grating that signaled the opening of his bizarre columnar door.

Moments later Arden and Ohlen entered.

"Oh, hi X'an," Arden blurted, but he was clearly distracted. Ohlen said nothing but instead looked dolefully into X'andria's eyes, then at the elfish wooden cube in her hand, and then back up into her eyes. Ohlen had been acting strangely toward her ever since they visited The Sorcerer together. She was getting quite tired of it. In her mind Ohlen's look was patronizing and seemed to be saying: *X'andria, I'm exhausted, please don't do anything stupid with that, and don't steal it, either.*

Mercifully, both Arden and Ohlen walked straight through into another room, leaving her alone again with Petric, who shifted nervously nearby.

X'andria's eyes narrowed as she spied something new across the room. "Tell me, Petric." She was looking over his left shoulder at a black and red tray displayed behind several wooden figurines on the far wall. "Where did you get that?"

"Ah, that is a classic specimen from Stark Island." Petric slipped easily into the familiar role of host and guide. "I picked it up from a trader in Greenlee some years ago. They say no two are alike. I just love the savage strokes, and the sharp contrast of pure black against the deep red, don't you?"

"I should go to sleep," X'andria mumbled. The last time she had seen a tray like that, it was falling from her tiny hands, olives tumbling over the edge, her fat captor leering while a man was being burned alive nearby.

She walked from the room leaving her perplexed host standing alone, still holding his precious tray.

Gnome was the first to rise. He had eaten well, and slept comfortably, but he awoke anxious to get to work and then get the hell away from this whole bizarre situation. *Petric better have that gold he promised us back in Rockmoor*, Gnome groused in his mind as he poked his head out above the veritable mountain of cloudlike white-fluff blankets within which he had spent the night.

Gnome roused everyone from their slumber—even Boudreaux and X'andria—and after breakfast they found themselves above ground following Petric briskly toward the center of Meriden's colonnade.

"Every sundown, for as long as I can remember, Alzbeda has gone to work atop her Altar To The Wind And Sky. But ten days ago she just vanished. When we went to look for her the following afternoon, we found only blood around the altar, and nothing more."

Shapes darted in and out of the columnar shadows. At first he was not sure if he was seeing anything more than odd light-effects from the many uniform columns in daylight, but soon Gnome's eyes narrowed as he tracked the rapid motions around them.

"It's breathtaking, Petric." X'andria was the first to react to the sight of Alzbeda's Altar To The Wind And Sky.

Gnome tore his attention away from a hunched old Meriden man in flowing garments stealing out of one column and into another four spots away. Gnome was quite certain that the bent little man paused ever so briefly and scowled at him, before disappearing once more below ground.

The altar was spectacular indeed. Everything they had seen in Meriden thus far looked cut or chiseled. Alzbeda's altar, however, appeared to have splashed out of the stone like sea-spray exploding on a coastal rock. It twisted and grew organically out of the square plaza, reaching toward the sky with its central apex. Scalloped and undulating levels—Gnome could not really call them steps— ascended unevenly on all sides toward the middle. The material itself was mysterious also—grayish-blue, Gnome was nearly able to see right through it. When he drew near enough and looked upward, he realized the top of the altar blended perfectly into the sky above it—

like it was a piece of the sky itself, fallen down to earth and frozen in place.

What an odd group we are, Gnome thought as he looked around. Arden had bounded up to the top of the altar and was on his knees, sniffing around like a dog. Boudreaux had followed him to the top and stood looking out over the columns, hands on his hips. Ohlen was seated, crosslegged, on the lowest level of the near side of the altar—eyes closed. Ruprecht had dropped to his knees right in the middle of the plaza, fingertips pressed to his lips. And X'andria was chattering brightly with Petric asking for every minute detail about Alzbeda's rituals, materials, and powers.

"Petric," Gnome butted in, "Is there anyone here that disliked Alzbeda? And tell me a bit more about the Rock Eater you keep talking about."

"Certainly Gnome," Petric seemed eager for the subject to veer away from X'andria's probing technical questions. "I cannot think of anyone in Meriden who would wish her harm. Alzbeda has been our guiding star."

But he moved closer to Gnome, leaned in close, and whispered, "In her absence, though, cracks developed quickly here—that's why I flew to Rockmoor to seek help from the outside. Now that I am returned, and you are all with me, I will see what I can learn."

"The woman we met on the path," Gnome's voice was scarcely more than a breath, "Is she...one of the cracks?"

Petric nodded slowly, backed a step away, and stood up straight. "The Rock Eater, however," he was speaking normally again, "I have never trusted that fearful beast."

Chapter Twenty-Eight

It was Ohlen. Ruprecht recognized him immediately.

Ruprecht had knelt in the plaza before Alzbeda's altar to ask his deity for direction. But instead Ohlen greeted him, rushing into his mind, up out of the stone itself, up through his legs, a gentle but insistent presence.

Yes, Ohlen. Ruprecht accepted the request, offered his attention.

Follow me. Ohlen wanted to share something.

They were walking—Ruprecht's vision became splintered around the edges, like peering through a jagged hole cut out of thick, dark fabric. A path stretched before him, the path to Meriden! But they were going, not coming. It was dark. Arden was leading. Suddenly X'andria appeared, stone-faced, intent, eyes faintly glowing. Then Arden was walking away again, leaving the path, fading from view. Then X'andria reappeared, her eyes were fire now. She was crying fire, flame was bleeding from her face, trickling out of her nose and mouth. Branches whipped him in the face, Arden was ahead, it was too dark, confusing. The fire was snaking from her, probing forward like animated ropes, menacing the air with the promise of white-hot immolation. Arden had stopped. They nearly collided. Arden stepped aside, ashen-faced. There on the ground lay a shriveled human doll. Dry, sunken. He drew closer, his hand extended to touch the parchment-skin, covered in tiny holes. There was no life within. No soul! But once there had been. Fire licked at the edges of his vision. Flames engulfed everything.

And Ruprecht found himself in his own thoughts once more. Kneeling in the plaza, fingertips pressed to his lips. Ohlen was seated cross-legged on Alzbeda's altar some ten paces away.

INVESTIGATION

X'andria was grateful for Gnome's intervention into her conversation with Petric. Perhaps he was ignorant of Alzbeda's methods of conjuration, or just unwilling to share what he knew, but either way X'andria had learned all she thought she could from Petric about the workings of the stunning altar. He just kept on about how Alzbeda had received her abilities from some kind of spirit, and how she had a special gift for knowing precisely what each individual needed most desperately. *A lousy liar*, X'andria appraised inwardly.

For the moment, X'andria became more interested in the shadows flitting around between Meriden's mysterious columns. She drifted away from the group to investigate.

One row in and X'andria could no longer hear her friends in the plaza. The wind in the columns had an odd muffling effect making only the sounds in her immediate vicinity discernible. *One could easily get turned around in here*, she thought. At two rows in, X'andria actually did turn around once and was startled to note that Alzbeda's altar was no longer visible at all, but was instead replaced by a forest of identical columns both near and far.

Three rows in. Or was it four? X'andria found herself face to face with a positively ancient man. Stringy white hair, deflated cheeks, the spotted, knuckly fingers of his right hand rested atop an alabaster white cane inlaid with thin lines of turquoise. He wore a gold ring on his middle finger inset with an enormous iridescent multicolor opal that lolled to one side in the absence of flesh firm enough to support its weight.

The man hissed. It was not a pleasant sound. Had he not been decrepit, X'andria might have been frightened. His eyes bore into hers, as his flappy, wrinkled lips settled back together into a severe grimace. And then he shuffled away and disappeared into the maze of columns.

Alright! X'andria thought, *I guess not all Meridens have Petric's charm.*

She continued outward to the edge of the colonnade. *Goodness it's beautiful here*, the mountain peak loomed before her. Mist hugged the snowy summit, but the sky was otherwise cloudless. X'andria drew her midnight blue cloak tighter over her arms in response to the crisp cool air, and she leaned her shoulder up against the nearest column.

Someone was coming around the edge of the colonnade. X'andria heard feet scuffing the stone. She retreated a few steps into the shadow of her column. *I can play the hiding game too,* she thought. It was three people. One was clearly a Meriden woman, also quite old, her compact and slightly hunched frame was clad in loose-fitting sky-blue trousers and an ivory blouse of quilted silk over which she had draped a spectacularly bright multi-colored shawl.

The two trudging behind her, however, seemed at once out of place and yet oddly familiar. It was a man and a woman, tall, wearing simple grey robes, dark features, expressionless eyes. No one spoke.

The threesome proceeded somberly past X'andria's hiding spot, about halfway down the outer row of the north-facing columns. The Meriden woman must have worked the hidden door, because moments later they disappeared within.

X'andria was intrigued. *Why are those two so familiar?* She wracked her brain.

It was six columns away. X'andria had not taken her eyes off the spot where they had vanished. Staying one row in from the exterior, and darting quickly from shadow to shadow, she made her way closer.

This was it. *How do these things work?* X'andria wondered,

slowly circling the broad stone cylinder. She trailed her fingers along the cold surface and could just barely feel the faint etchings of the ornamental swirls.

On alert, X'andria's sharp ears picked up the faint rumble of a mechanical stone door operating nearby. *If only I'd brought Elias' invisibility cloak with me*, she wished, positioning herself on what she thought was the far side away from the noise. The guttural hissing of the odd Meriden language wafted through the whistling wind between the columns. It sounded like two people. X'andria peered around the corner. A Meriden man and woman were walking away, talking animatedly. They were young and fit. X'andria was pretty sure the female was the one from the path, Nezka, but she had changed into a flattering new skintight fitted ensemble beneath a white cape that fluttered behind her as she moved.

But at that moment the door to her own column—the one where the odd threesome had vanished—began faintly grinding into action. Heart pounding, X'andria dashed away toward the center of the maze. She backed her shoulders up against an interior column and tried to steady her breathing.

Two grey robes emerged. And it came to her, why they looked so familiar. *Petric's carriage driver had jet black hair, and wore these same style robes. That's where I've seen this before!* But these were not the same two people that had gone in minutes earlier. Long, straight black hair hung down their backs as they ambled quickly, nervously away. Two adolescent girls.

As soon as he placed a foot on Alzbeda's clear-blue altar, Arden felt a rush of energy. The cool mountain air and the bright morning light seemed to fill him with a levity that almost felt like he might be able to fly if he just tried to jump high enough. Arden bounded up the wavy, twisty edifice like a child on a grassy hill, but stopped cold upon reaching the summit.

A narrow and flat alcove was surrounded on three sides by the curious glassine material. Arden imagined Alzbeda stepping into that space, and calling forth whatever mysterious powers she must have possessed. The altar material was translucent, but the blood sprayed liberally all over the interior walls of the alcove was not. Arden's heart sank. It was a lot of blood. He fell to his knees and tried to read the dark crimson blotches, streaks, and smudges.

Boudreaux was close behind Arden. Scaling the odd structure felt great, Boudreaux filled his lungs with crisp mountain air, and bounded effortlessly from one curvy ledge to the next. Arden was on his knees examining the scene of the attack. Boudreaux took the opportunity to survey the area.

Meriden was a perfectly square colonnade at the center of which was a plaza, at the middle of which was this lady's altar, at the very heart of which Boudreaux now stood. Dense forest extended in all directions but north, where a final steep ascent began toward the mountain peak. A handful of trees were broken and downed to the east near a particularly dramatic rocky rise. To the south Boudreaux could just see where the path to the gorge entered the wood.

Ohlen and Ruprecht were clearly busy thinking their deep thoughts, Gnome was chatting up their Meriden host. *Where's X'andria?* Boudreaux wondered. He turned around and scanned in all directions, but could not spot her anywhere.

*Nezka spun around once, noting with pleasure her slender shape
beneath her black flowing hair and twirling fire-red scarf.*

Chapter Twenty-Nine
THAT AFTERNOON

———————

The blood told a complicated tale. Droplets had been flung quite far, actually, farther than would result from puncture wounds to the torso—even deep ones. This would indicate a flailing extremity, or a truly wild melee. There was a concentrated pool at the altar's apex where, Arden assumed, the attack had taken place. Some kind of tussle must have ensued, however, because there was much smearing, including manic hair-brushed streaks up onto the lower parts of the sky-clear walls surrounding the altar's apex on three sides.

So Alzbeda was attacked, blood was spilled, and there was quite a struggle. But that was not all Arden deduced. It was clear to him that she had been dragged a short distance, and then carried away. Arden slithered, head first like a snake, down the north side of the altar—face close to the undulating surface, eyes straining for each dried droplet. They grew fainter and further apart as he descended to the level of the stone plaza, but the trail was clear enough.

"Petric," Ohlen's deep voice broke through the steady hiss of the mountain winds, "How large is Alzbeda?"

"How large?" Petric squinted up at Ohlen and the bright sun that had climbed high in the sky behind him. "Normal sized, I suppose, Ohlen," he continued. "We Meridens are not all that big, but I would say she is just about my size, but thinner, you know, and just a little bit shorter." He held up his right hand to eyebrow level. "Why do you ask?"

Ohlen exchanged a dark glance with Ruprecht and replied, "When we find something, Petric, I would like to be certain it is her."

"Well guys, she went that way," Arden proclaimed pointing toward the mountain peak. He and Boudreaux were walking around the side of the altar to join Ohlen, Petric, and Ruprecht in the plaza.

"How do you know, Arden?" Petric asked.

"Pretty simple, Petric. The blood goes that way. It looks like whatever attacked her, picked her up, and carried her away afterward, and dribbled bits of evidence in the process." Arden had been speaking conversationally, but his tone grew more serious as he continued, "Alzbeda was gravely injured, Petric. She lost a lot of blood. You may be best served not hoping for too much."

"Hope," Petric matched Arden's gravity, "is the only thing keeping Meriden together at all, my friends."

"Well let's get on with it," Gnome announced conclusively. "If she went that way, then let us all go that way, find her in whatever form she's in, and be on our way."

"Hey, where's X'andria?" Boudreaux cut in.

Ohlen, Ruprecht, and Gnome followed Arden back around Alzbeda's Altar To The Wind And Sky, where he began threading his way north through the thick crush of perfectly arrayed Meriden columns. Now and again he would rush forward to some dark speck on the stone to verify if it belonged to the waning trail of blood he hoped would point them toward the missing Alzbeda. Boudreaux had elected to stay back with Petric to hunt for X'andria.

"Arden and I came upon a dead child in the woods last night, Gnome," Ohlen stated somberly as soon as they were far enough away from the columns to not be overheard by unseen ears.

"A child?" Gnome was aghast.

"Ohlen has shared the vision with me, Gnome," Ruprecht joined in, "The body was definitely that of a child, but it looked ancient and shriveled, dried up like driftwood, and I did not detect even the shadow of a soul within."

"I hate this place," Gnome replied, whistling through his teeth and looking around at the sparse grasses between them and the rise of the mountain peak. "I don't like rich people, I don't like secrets, I don't like dead children, and I don't like rock monsters."

"You've never met a rock monster," Arden called from his knees, several paces away. He appeared to be examining a blade of grass.

"Could it have been Alzbeda?" Gnome ignored Arden's interjection.

"The thought had occurred to me," Ohlen replied evenly. Arden was moving again, and so they were walking once more. "That is why I asked our host about the size of Alzbeda."

"But you said it was all shriveled up," Gnome countered. "Maybe it used to be her size before whatever killed it, killed it."

"The truth is, Gnome," Ohlen spoke patiently, "that it wore the field clothes of the villagers we met on the way here. I am convinced that the body we discovered was that of the missing boy about whom we were questioned by that poor farmer on the road."

"Well I'm out of blood," Arden stood up and wiped the dirt off his hands. "But there's no question in my mind that we're heading over there." He pointed northeast, where the foot of the mountain peak met the forest, and where—they could now clearly see—a number of trees had been uprooted or broken.

"That's where the rock monster lives!" Gnome exclaimed. "I knew it. Petric said he never trusted it."

"Why's everyone here so old and mean?" Boudreaux blurted out loudly as he and Petric threaded their way through Meriden's western quadrant in search of X'andria. They had run into several wizened grouches whose eyes grew wide at the sight of Boudreaux, but then quickly narrowed to illustrate the hissed derision they directed at Petric before ambling hurriedly away.

"It is rare for us to have visitors in Meriden, Boudreaux, and many of my brethren do not approve of your presence here. I am sorry if you feel unwelcome."

"Oh I don't care, Petric," Boudreaux quickly replied. He meant it. "Just keep that ale flowing again tonight, and I'll feel all the welcome I need." After a pause, he continued, "I would sure like to see that lady we met on the way here again, though, she was fine."

"Boudreaux," Petric wheeled around and came to a sudden stop.

"Stay away from Nezka, alright? She's dangerous."

At this Boudreaux threw his head back and laughed out loud. When he regained his composure, he said in his best menacing tone, "Oh Petric, Petric, Petric... *I'm* the one here who's dangerous."

X'andria was pressed flat against the dark side of a column when they came upon her. She seemed startled to see them, but recovered quickly.

"I was hoping to find you, Petric," she exclaimed. "I was just thinking a nap back at your place would do me some good." Then she added brightly, "Hi Boudreaux, where is everyone?"

"Arden thinks he knows where they took Alzbeda after the attack, and they all went to investigate," Boudreaux explained. "And I came with Petric to find you."

"Oh, great," X'andria said vaguely.

"What have you been doing, X'andria?" Petric asked pointedly.

"I'm a curious sort, Petric," X'andria's attention seemed to return to the present conversation. "I enjoy investigating this and that, you know, learning about stuff, comings and goings, that sort of thing. I like to find out," and here X'andria's bright tone became flatter and she leveled a weighty stare into Petric's eyes, "*exactly* what is going on and why."

Petric looked like he had been slapped and was about to reply when Boudreaux, oblivious, chimed in, "You want some company for that nap, X'andria?"

"Sure!" X'andria's brightness returned. "Oh wait, no!" She added. "Gross, Boudreaux. No."

Chapter Twenty-Nine

Nezka spun around once, noting with pleasure her slender shape beneath her black flowing hair and twirling fire-red scarf. Brunka had brought her many things over the years, but her favorite by far was the floor-to-ceiling sheet of thin Atolian silver polished so thoroughly she could watch herself dressing and then spend time admiring the results from many angles.

What a year.

Losing their child seventeen years earlier had been the second greatest tragedy of their lives, right behind losing their very way of life long before that.

Of course the two things were connected. To Alzbeda.

Nezka and Brunka hardly even spoke to one another after Bodomek's death. Brunka had long ago stopped bringing her new garments, stopped noticing how they stretched and draped upon her. But each year they had walked sullenly to the place it happened. Seventeen trips they had taken when the unthinkable occurred.

The child returned.

Slice she did, though. Myrtle screamed.

Chapter Thirty
THAT NIGHT

———————

X'andria was glad to be left alone. An hour or so after they had returned, Boudreaux and Petric had ventured out again to try and catch up with the others. This gave her time to think.

She gently pulled Elias' invisibility cloak out of her backpack and let its fluid coolness rush around her fingers. Hidden beneath the precious garment were, among other things, her remaining scroll and the two green, stoppered vials she had nicked during their hasty escape from The Emporium. The red ruby, however, she had kept on her person in one of the many pockets of her night-blue robes.

"I think I'll take all of you with me, this time," X'andria breathed softly into the curvy subterranean space. Donning her backpack, she stood up and looked around, absently letting the cloak's scintillating fabric slide from one hand into the other and back again.

Chapter Thirty

Petric seemed to have had several lifetimes of travel. *Perhaps he's older than he looks*, X'andria mused, recalling the wrinkles and spots of gray hair she had detected for the first time on their walk back to his home earlier that afternoon. There was no doubt in X'andria's mind that the red and black tray from Stark Island was procured on the seas and brought to Greenlee by the fat man. She had been imprisoned in his compound near Greenlee after all—it was in that sprawling opulent hell that she remembered using a similar serving tray. And Petric had admitted purchasing his specimen in Greenlee. For all X'andria knew, Petric may have bought it from the fat man himself. X'andria might have even witnessed the transaction. The thought made her shudder.

But the colorful tapestry was from the Macken Coast, from Ohlen's homeland. Petric seemed to have a clear memory of the area, like he had visited more than once. And the tapestry and the tray were just two items in an enormous collection of widely varying treasures. *Perhaps if I trusted him, and if we weren't in the middle of this macabre mystery, I would actually enjoy getting to know Petric the Meriden*, X'andria thought.

For the moment she was stuck in Petric's abode, since he was the only one who could operate the ingenious transforming columnar door. Wandering from space to space, eventually X'andria found herself at the foot of the bizarre unfinished staircase.

"How does he do it?" She wondered aloud in the hard echoey entry chamber.

Each time Petric operated a door he placed his left hand on a shoulder-height spot on the wall or column nearby. *It is always the same spot*, X'andria's superior visual memory insisted. A moment later her nose hovered inches away from the wall as she scanned for any clues about the door's operation.

What in the world? She wondered. Running her fingers over the spot, she felt nothing at all, but as she moved her head ever so slightly back and forth her eyes detected the tiniest texture in the stone—were they miniscule divots? Holes?

The door mechanism was suddenly operating. Stone plates were shifting, sliding down into place. Heart racing, X'andria jumped backward and hastily threw Elias' invisibility cloak over her head, taking care that it covered her protruding backpack and obscured both feet.

X'andria melted back toward the stone wall opposite the stair.

Arden's voice carried down through the open doorway. "It's knocked down tons of trees all around its lair," he said excitedly. "It must be absolutely enormous."

X'andria worked to quiet her startled breathing. *Gnome will hear*, she thought.

"I don't see why we didn't go in there and get her," it was Gnome, clearly annoyed. "If she's alive at all, she won't be much longer."

X'andria's fingers found their way to her small prized ruby.

"If the beast is all that it seems to be, Gnome," Ohlen's deep voice always seemed disapproving to X'andria these days, "then it would be prudent to have Boudreaux and X'andria with us for the encounter."

And then they were all down the stairs. Petric was the last to descend. X'andria, unseen and unheard, raced by him as he lifted his hand toward the imperceptibly dimpled spot on the wall. A split second later her small foot leapt deftly from the last step as the stone shaft rose smoothly back into place.

X'andria was out in the waning daylight, in the cool air, free, invisible.

Chapter Thirty

Gnome would love this, X'andria thought fondly, as the sun sank to the horizon and filled the mountain sky above the column city with vibrant oranges and yellows. It was spectacular.

Rapidly, however, the light diminished, the temperature dropped, and night fell over Meriden. As the last rays of graying sunlight faded, a long low wailing moan sailed out across Meriden blanketing the nightscape in despair.

Though it sounded as if the mournful wail was issuing from the mountain peak itself, X'andria still whirled around to see if her elf eyes could detect the source.

She was uncomfortable. The cry sounded huge, dreadful, and the air was cold—she looked nervously down at her toes to make sure she was still completely hidden by the cloak. She saw only moonlit stone.

You didn't come out here to enjoy the sunset, X'andria, she scolded herself, and began walking to the west side of Meriden, to the place she'd seen the grey-clad couple arriving, and the grey-clad girls departing, each escorted by the old Meriden woman in the many-colored shawl.

Another tortured behemoth moan echoed across the sky punctuated by a startling crack that sounded as if a piece of the mountain itself had been split in two. Beneath the weightless chameleon fabric of Elias' invisibility cloak, X'andria tugged her night-blue robes tighter around her goose-pimpled arms.

The Rock Eater must be the one crying out tonight, X'andria decided. She was hovering near the column where she had seen the odd coming and going earlier in the day. Perhaps the Meriden people were inactive during the night, or maybe Alzbeda's disappearance—or the Rock Eater's apparent unrest—were enough to keep them below ground once the sun was down, but X'andria's sharp eyes and ears picked up no foot traffic for several long, chilly hours.

After some time waiting, shivering, and cringing from the occasional night-rending wail, X'andria heard the sound of several pairs of feet scuffing along the stone once more.

The Meriden man leading the couple was youthful, handsome even. He wore a fitted vest over a flowing tunic, and seeing him immediately reminded X'andria of the first moment they had met Petric, wearing his sequined vest and that pasted-on smile, in the Iron Axe back in Rockmoor. The couple behind him were tall, an older man and an adolescent boy who could easily have been the man's son. No one spoke, but as they drew nearer X'andria noticed a confident smirk on the youthful Meriden's face.

Rapping a quick staccato series of beats on the column, the vested Meriden stood back for just a few moments before the familiar stone grinding began whirring beneath them. With the columnar door open before them, the Meriden, his two stoic guests, and X'andria in her invisibility cloak, marched wordlessly down the stone steps.

The Meriden woman with the many-colored shawl was standing at the foot of the stairs, except she was no longer wearing the many-colored shawl. Upon seeing the vested leader, she launched into a protracted series of what sounded to X'andria like furious exclamations. The youthful Meriden breezed past her—ignoring her outburst—and passed through into the next room with her riding close on his heels.

The father and son—X'andria had decided they were related—

looked genuinely afraid and exchanged several alarmed glances, but still said nothing. X'andria, careful not to get too close, followed them into the next, much larger, room.

Many things about this room struck X'andria at once, and caused her mind to race. First was the old man behind a massive carved desk. It had intricate insets in the shapes of fantastical beasts, and what appeared to be a taut leather writing surface laid seamlessly into the top. He was wearing gold. For all X'andria knew these people had figured out how to spin metal into fabric—it certainly looked that way as the torchlight reflected off the many folds draping his sunken shoulders.

The shawl-woman—X'andria now noticed the shawl itself was thrown across a plush chair nearby—was still in a state of great agitation. The old man, who seemed immersed in a stack of parchment in front of him, looked up slowly, raised his hand as if to say "enough," and let out a long, slow sigh.

"You are late," the old man said simply. But he was not addressing the arrogantly smirking Meriden youth, he was speaking to the pair in grey.

The whole exchange, amidst such spectacular opulence, was odd indeed. But the most shocking thing was the jail cell, to the old man's left, in which stood the grey-clad couple X'andria had watched arrive earlier in the day. The prisoners' eyes were fixed on those of the father and son. The father and son were, in turn, staring alertly at the old Meriden seated behind the enormous, ornamented desk.

"Eighty-three," the father said simply, stepping forward and producing a black velveteen bag—cinched tight at the top—that emitted metallic clinks when he placed it in the middle of the desk, beside the stack of parchment.

"Eight-y three," the gold-clad Meriden repeated slowly, penning symbols onto the parchment before him with a long black-tipped quill. "That is most certainly disappointing, Renfro," the old man continued. "What is your explanation?"

The father's fingers twisted together, and he shifted weight from his left side to his right. "Road passage is slowed, sir, our riders are being stopped. It seems there is fear in the valley."

The shawl-woman sputtered briefly from her perch before the old man put his hand up to silence her once more. The Meriden youth, still smirking, stared vacantly into the middle distance. The old man said callously, "It is unacceptable, Renfro. Fix it or there will be consequences."

And with that, he beckoned the Meriden youth forward toward the desk and lifted a large round iron ring from which hung a single key. The young Meriden took the key, walked to the cell, and unlocked and opened the heavy iron-grate door. The couple within stepped slowly out, and the father and son stepped slowly in. The two pairs stole brief furtive glances at one another as the exchange was made.

"Two bales, tonight," the old man piped up reedily from behind the desk. At this, the young Meriden stooped low and foisted two similarly sized bundles into the hands of the just-released grey-clad visitors. Without goodbye or hesitation they turned and began walking for the exit. Moments later the steps descended into place, and the couple walked up and out into the cold night, followed closely by a perplexed and profusely sweating invisible she-elf.

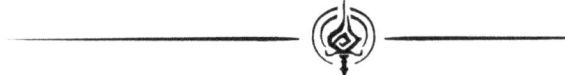

The couple walked quickly. *Do these people ever say anything to one*

another? X'andria wondered as she stepped lightly behind, careful to stay as quiet as possible.

What had she just witnessed? These humans from down the mountain were somehow being forced into serving the Meriden clan. The Meridens kept them imprisoned in pairs—presumably to keep them in line—and appeared to have some kind of trade relationship as well.

The longer they walked, the more outraged X'andria became. *The Meridens are slavers!* She fumed. *That's how they've managed to get so filthy rich, so well-traveled, so cultured.* Her fingers found their way to her small red ruby and began compulsively rolling it back and forth.

They were hustling down the forest path toward the bridge. The night was cold, but something even colder, darker clawed at the base of X'andria's spine. *I want some answers*, she decided.

"Excuse me," X'andria called, she couldn't think of anything better to say.

"Wh-who's there?" came the man's trembling response a startled step or two later. Both he and his companion had turned around, but continued walking slowly backward. He had transferred the package to under his left arm, and held his right out protectively in front of the woman.

"I'm not going to hurt you," X'andria replied.

"Show yourself," the man cried out, looking frantically back and forth at the empty moonlit path before them.

"I don't think I will, sir. I just have a few questions I need answered." X'andria was already tiring of the cat and mouse game.

"Run Myrtle, now!" The man shouted. And the two of them bolted toward the vast bridge.

Ruby rolling methodically between her left forefinger and

thumb, X'andria extracted her gold loop from an interior pocket, breathed deeply, and seized the atmosphere around the woman's ankles with her mind.

Myrtle face-planted on the grassy path with a squeal, the package she carried hit the ground and bounced awkwardly away.

"Myrtle!" the man yelled, five paces ahead, "Get up darling, get up!" he was frantic.

"I can't move!" Myrtle shrieked, "I can't move my feet!"

X'andria approached slowly, some part of her felt bad for this couple, regretted their fear, and confusion, and sadness. *Just tell me what I want to know*, even X'andria's thoughts were tinged with frustration.

"Seriously, I just have a few questions, and you two can go."

The woman sat whimpering, the man was speechless, aghast, still staring wildly around looking for the source of the voice.

"Like what's in this package?" X'andria pressed, gripping her gold loop and causing the spilt package to drift slowly through the night air and land softly by the seated, sniffling woman.

"Abgoa," came her muffled reply.

"And they keep you there, in the cell, and trade you out each day, to make sure you keep doing what they want?"

"Who IS this?" the man piped up again with new fervor. "You know we're sworn to secrecy about this. Who ARE you? Is this Nezka? Are you trying to trick us? Haven't we done ENOUGH?" And with that the man lunged in X'andria's direction.

It was a good lunge. It was not exactly at her, of course, since he couldn't see her, but it was close, and he was big, and it unleashed anger in X'andria's gut.

He was in mid-step, when she seized his entire body with her mind, lifted him up into the air, and turned him upside down so that

Chapter Thirty

his hair and grey robes inverted and dangled toward the ground.

At this Myrtle began repeatedly yelling "No!" But X'andria was not to be deterred. "Just a few QUESTIONS," was her retort, and she began nudging the dangling man toward the bridge, and chasm beneath it.

"Oh my GODS, put him down!" Myrtle yelled. "I'll do anything!" She pleaded. "Yes, they lock us in there, and trade us out, alright? That's what they do. We sell their stuff, they get the money. What else do you want?" Myrtle was hysterical, and now it was the man's turn to begin whimpering as he floated nearer to the edge of the chasm.

Myrtle was crying. Myrtle had asked *What else do you want?* and this gave X'andria an idea.

"I'll put him down," she said in a low voice, approaching the distraught Myrtle. "You just have to stay really still for a moment. Then I'll let you both on your way."

X'andria lowered the terrified man safely back to the ground. Beneath her cloak she shrugged off her backpack and rifled blindly inside until she located the two green-stoppered vials.

"Stay still," X'andria murmured, and reached quickly out to Myrtle's cheek and collected a tiny smear of the glistening wetness shining beneath her left eye.

"Almost done," X'andria did her best to sound reassuring as she dislodged one of her barbed darts—with the heavy polished tear-drop shaped handles—from it's holster on her thigh.

It was an awkward thing to do. To try and slice Myrtle's arm with the tip of the dart, and collect some of her blood in the other vial. X'andria saw the succession of motions clearly in her mind, but neglected to account for the time it takes for blood to well up.

Slice she did, though. Myrtle screamed. Her husband screamed too and started running toward them. X'andria grabbed Myrtle's wrist, dropping her dart in the process, and frantically, desperately pressed the lip of the vial against the struggling woman's maimed flesh.

Myrtle swung with her other arm. She didn't hit X'andria squarely, but her arm caught the draped invisibility cloak, which slid sideways from X'andria's head.

And there they were. Face to face. X'andria and Myrtle. X'andria was no longer anonymous. Myrtle was no longer prey. Their eyes locked for a split second in the moonlight, before X'andria started to run. Clutching her backpack, and her two vials—one with blood, one with tears—X'andria tore back down the path toward Meriden, her cloak streaming out behind her like oblivion itself flapping in her wake.

One brain-constricted moment later, the cricket morphed into a faint orange glow blooming from Gnome's left palm—exactly as he had imagined it.

Chapter Thirty-One
SUNLIGHT

X'andria streaked back into the clearing around the Meriden colonnade. She had raced down the path, away from the couple, away from her anger and frustration, from her need. The empty space left behind filled with something heavy indeed.

They were not pursuing her. *Of course they aren't*, she thought bitterly, *they've been terrorized by an invisible monster.* Another distraught howl filled the air. The voice was immense, filled with anguish, but it was coming from nearby this time—from in or around the colonnade. X'andria shuddered.

Taking a last look behind her, X'andria hastily placed the jumble of items she was clasping on the ground at her feet. She realized she was still gripping the red ruby between her left thumb and forefinger. She had been squeezing it tightly, and so when she slipped it back into a small pocket on the inside of her night-blue robes, deep grooves were left on her skin.

On one knee, staring out into the darkness for signs of the Rock Eater—whatever those might be—X'andria felt around for her stoppered bottles, and placed them gingerly into her backpack. Still looking in all directions, still listening for noises of motion, she shrugged the pack onto her shoulders. Standing, she pulled the cloak back over herself and disappeared from sight.

It was early morning when Petric heard four even knocks echo from his entryway. Only his guests from Rockmoor knew to knock four times. *But they're already inside*, he thought. Puzzled, he made his way to the stairs and operated the door mechanism. Cool morning air rushed in just before a haggard-looking X'andria.

"You lied to us," she hissed, her face pressed close to his. "I know everything, and this," she made a circular motion indicating the two of them and the entryway, "This never happened."

It had been a long, cold, and scary night. X'andria had not seen the Rock Eater, but she heard its cries, and she heard its movement throughout the column-city. It sounded almost like slithering more than stepping, snorting more than breathing, and when it howled into the night, it was so loud X'andria had to cover her ears.

But even through the cold, sleeplessness, terror, and the mounting shame for what she had done to that poor couple, X'andria was sure Petric looked worse than she felt. He looked underfed and had bags under his eyes. *How is it possible his hair has turned grey overnight?* she wondered. X'andria bustled out of the entry way, leaving Petric behind to stew in her brash accusation.

"Where were you last night?" Gnome arose a short while later and found X'andria—who had composed herself somewhat— drinking a hot cup of the Meridens' green morning brew by herself.

"Oh, I was here, Gnome, over in one of those other rooms—that way." She limply gestured in the direction opposite from the way Gnome had entered.

"No way," he shot back bemused. "I thought I looked *everywhere*. You could have at least answered when I called."

"I'm sorry Gnome," and she really was. "You know me. Sometimes I just need some space."

In a few minutes the whole party was up, helping themselves to another one of Petric's delicious breakfast spreads, and trading quizzical glances at one another each time he left to refill a platter. Everyone noticed the changes in Petric's appearance.

"So let's go get her," Gnome pressed. "We're all here. Let's get her, get our gold, and leave Petric here in peace, alright?"

"I need a few hours, Gnome, I'm sorry," X'andria replied. Everyone looked at her. All the eyes—Ohlen's eyes—they all seemed to know. "I got up and did some studying last night, is all," she stammered. "I just need a few hours more to sleep, and I'll be ready to go."

"What's going on with X'an?" Gnome groused to Ohlen a short while later.

At Ruprecht's request, they had all gone above ground with Petric.

"I have been mulling the same thing, Gnome," Ohlen's reply was slow in coming.

Ruprecht was seated on the grass not far away, facing south. Arden and Boudreaux were joking and pushing one another around like children. Petric had wandered off.

"She was not being truthful just now," Ohlen continued. "Generally when someone is not truthful it is because there is something to hide."

"X'an's always liked to work things out on her own," Gnome rushed to his friend's defense. "She goes off by herself to get that big brain working—I think other people's ideas just get in her way."

"X'andria possesses a great gift, indeed," Ohlen conceded. "But I fear—and I venture you do as well—that something may be clouding her judgment of late."

"It's there, Ohlen," Ruprecht announced, pointing south into the woods.

"What's there?" Boudreaux called, hands on his hips, panting lightly from his horseplay with Arden.

Ohlen glided over to Ruprecht, then past him and out into Meriden's southern field.

Everyone followed.

"We're going the wrong way folks," Gnome pouted. "Remember, Alzbeda is the other way."

"This place is faithless," Ruprecht explained halfway to the tree line. "In my prayers I've never felt such a keen absence of faith in any place with people living in it."

Ohlen was still drifting slowly toward the trees, but the others had stopped to listen.

"It's like the whole place is devoid of belief, except there." And he pointed in Ohlen's direction.

"Alright fine, but we should still be going the other way," Gnome nagged through gritted teeth.

"The thing is Gnome," Ruprecht spoke patiently, "the belief in these woods is cruel and desperate and...I think I recognize it."

"Wait a minute," Arden piped up, and immediately began running after Ohlen. "I see something."

"Fine!" Gnome cried, exasperated. "I'm heading back to the mountain. When you people are ready to get serious, you'll know where to find me."

Gnome wheeled around and stalked back toward the colonnade. A striking Meriden woman stood at the southeast corner, gazing after them. Nezka. But she stepped away from view as Gnome approached.

And below ground, X'andria eagerly extracted Elias' second scroll from her backpack. She silently formed the rune's ancient syllables on her lips as The Sorcerer had stated them, *shra'muhrjnik*. Methodically X'andria pulled another barbed dart from her holster. She opened her first green-stoppered vial—Myrtle's blood was smeared on the top and down the sides. She ran the tip of her dart around the rim, making sure to transfer some of the crimson onto the weapon. This process she repeated with the second vial, containing Myrtle's tears. It was harder to know if the transfer succeeded, but X'andria made a thorough effort of it. With blood and tears, gathered from an unwilling donor and placed upon the dart—the "tool" as the scroll's hastily scrawled list indicated—X'andria wrapped up the dart inside the runic parchment.

She pulled back her robe, to expose the skin of her left forearm.

She gripped the dart through the parchment roll.

She saw the effect clearly in her mind and said the word. *Shra'muhrjnik.* Wound.

X'andria screamed.

Chapter Thirty-One

So irritating! Gnome fumed as he stomped past the Meriden colonnade and made his way back toward the peak. He did not particularly want to face the Rock Eater by himself, but it irked him to see his companions get distracted by nonessential elements. So Gnome elected solo reconnaissance of the real target over watching Arden sniff around the forest in response to one of Ruprecht's silly *feelings*.

More trees were downed as Gnome neared what they had thought was the Rock Eater's lair. *This thing has been busy*, Gnome thought, passing one particularly large and splintery stump, the trunk of which lay broken some fifty paces away. Gnome wandered over to the maimed and downed poplar and with a little effort scrambled on top for an elevated vantage point.

There was quite a lot of destruction, actually. In addition to the downed trees, the many boulders strewn about did not appear to have arrived naturally in their present state or location. Each had at least one side cleanly cut or broken. It was also muddy—the earth ruptured and grooved in seemingly random places.

Here and there Gnome even saw what looked like discarded bits of stone that might have been meant for the Meriden colonnade but were abandoned for one reason or another. Gnome jumped from his perch on the tree trunk to investigate and, sure enough, one partially buried piece of finished stone turned out to be the top of a Meriden column with its faint ornamental swirls barely noticeable beneath the dirt and discoloration of time.

Now wait just a minute, Gnome froze, squinting at a point high up on a craggy rock face. *Is that where this thing comes from?* He walked to the base of the steep rock wall and looked up again.

The wall was covered in divots. Beneath his feet, Gnome realized, were countless shards of broken and flaked stone. *You've made it way too easy for me*, Gnome thought wryly as he gauged hand and toe holds to begin his ascent. *I'll just take a quick look*, he told himself, zipping upward from the ground like an insect.

The climb was easy enough. The mottled surface, though mostly vertical, was simple to navigate. Gnome was surprised to find, however, that the entrance to the Rock Eater's habitat was perfectly smooth. Sailing quickly up the heavily textured wall, the sudden change to smooth caught him a bit off guard, and his right hand slipped awkwardly from the curvy, polished lip.

Slow down, Gnome reminded himself of The Master's words. *Mold your fingers to the surface, become one with its contours.*

It was beautiful. The gray stone, polished to mirrorlike perfection, had depth and complex patterning. High above the ground, the clear mountain daylight at his back, Gnome was peering down into a circular, undulating tunnel winding its way toward the heart of the mountain. Bottom to top the perfect tunnel was easily six times Gnome's own height, far larger than it had appeared from below.

Gnome advanced quietly forward. He heard no sound from within. The tube-like tunnel twisted this way and that, but mainly went down. To avoid slipping, Gnome had to bring his full attention to his toes and the soles of his feet, probing through the deep-sea eel-skin slippers that had been a gift of The Master.

Every few steps he stopped to listen. His nerves were on high alert, ready to sprint back up and out at the slightest indication the host might be stirring. Gnome's eyes adjusted to the kind of darkness he was so accustomed to from his childhood within the narrow

Chapter Thirty-One

earthen passageways of the Gnome Hills.

A little further down, the tunnel opened abruptly into a vast space. It was so cavernous Gnome could not see to the other side. As far as he could tell the entire mountain might have been hollowed out. Directly in front of him, at the edge of the slippery polished tube, was a black void. *It would be so easy to slip off that edge,* Gnome thought warily.

To the right there was a landing of sorts. All was still eerily quiet, and so Gnome crept up to the edge, and peered around the corner. There was room to move, but there was absolutely no light. Gnome's lamplike eyes made the most of the faint traces of light reflected down the polished tunnel walls, but here, around the edge, was black as pitch.

Small, he prepared his thought, *so small, just the glow of an ember in the palm of my hand.* He fished around in a miniscule pocket of his tunic, and extracted a near-lifeless cricket. *Mjargi'lig* Gnome breathed as quietly as possible. Light.

One brain-constricted moment later, the cricket morphed into a faint orange glow blooming from Gnome's left palm—exactly as he had imagined it. It lit the small landing before him, bouncing off the gem-like walls.

There she was. Propped up against the sloping far side of the small landing, arms crossed, peaceful, beautiful, and covered in an ice-like transparent film. It had to be Alzbeda.

Horrifyingly, both of her hands were missing. Her wrists were mangled, gory stumps.

Terrifyingly, a huge roar emanated from somewhere far below. A complex cacophony of loud clicks and scrapes signaled the coming of the Rock Eater.

Gnome ran.

*He wanted nothing more than to rip into the host
and menace the cowardly voyeur behind the mask—
the voyeur in possession of Leopold's treasures.*

Chapter Thirty-Two
BLACKLIGHT

X'andria's blood was all over Petric's floor.

The flesh of her forearm had torn in a jagged line right before her eyes. She actually watched the cut open—exactly as she had envisioned it—a barbed dart inserted and dragged at medium depth from one side to the other. Except no dart had been used. Part of her had not expected it to work—certainly not on her first try. And she had not planned for the messy and painful results.

Slapping her right hand over the seeping wound, X'andria raced to her sleeping nook, and clumsily clasped the thinnest of her blankets using her elbows like a poorly designed set of pincers. Walking backward, still applying pressure to her arm, she tugged the blanket toward her workspace.

The light grey blanket was already bloody. A thick crimson drop had oozed from between her fingers when she tried to pick it up with her elbows. The drop widened as it sank deep into the fine woven fabric, like a stubborn witness to her duplicity.

Using a small knife, X'andria hacked off a long strip from the edge of the blanket. This action caused the wound to open afresh and cast droplets further onto the floor, on the blanket, and on X'andria herself.

Methodically she lay the center of the strip along her wound—the line of the cut instantly bled through the fabric—and began to wrap its entire length around and around her forearm. The bandage was uncomfortably tight, and Arden would not have approved of the tie-off, but at least no more blood was flowing from her body onto Petric's floor and belongings.

Now it was time to clean up, and dispose of the evidence.

Ohlen sensed Arden passing him on the way to investigate the forest south of Meriden, Boudreaux was close behind.

Ever since his first encounter with the orb in Geoffrey's wrecked cabin outside Westover, Ohlen had been honing his sense for the piercing, constricted energy it emitted. He had felt it in the demon statue beneath the mountain, he had felt it emitting from the oily black cretin in the sewer beneath Rockmoor, and he was feeling it now.

Knowing Arden would examine the physical evidence, Ohlen sat down cross-legged on the ground to meditate.

This ether is filled with a tumult of fear, regret, secrecy, and greed. Meriden is mysterious indeed, or is it what lies in this forest, or

Petric, or dear X'andria? Deceit is so thick here. Confusing.

Ohlen pushed deeper, into the earth.

Quieter, slower, so ancient, so patient. Fathomless rock hides not far below this thin layer of soil and grass and shrubs and trees. The earth here is hardened, packed by time and traffic, by the absence of worms and bugs and mice. It is not dead earth, but it is sorely wounded. Here in this place, is something that does not belong.

Ruprecht stood not far from Ohlen.

He bent his head and pressed his fingertips to his lips. He asked for guidance, for clarity in their current predicament, but to his surprise, his consciousness was instead yanked far away from the Meriden mountain into another's mind.

I can't feel my ankle! I think it's frozen off. It's the BEAST. The devil. The one that started it all. I know it.

The huddled man whose thoughts Ruprecht suddenly secretly shared was breathless, frantic.

Everything froze, the wall, the floor. OH MY GREAT ONE. I forgot. I forgot YOU.

This new place was muggy and damp. Ugh, the smell! Horrendous. Too dark to see. Water dripping somewhere.

It grabbed my ankle. Hauled me here. I can hardly remember. I need help, GOD!

The huddled man's addled brain strained through the pain and confusion for focus. Communion. Openness.

And light crept into their vision—first like a candle in an open room at the end of a very long hallway. It grew slowly, edging out the blackness, beckoning the visitors inside.

It's coming back, I FEEL it! Concentrate Geoffrey!

The vision shuddered. The light seized. But there shone, dimly, a symbol. It had three vertical slashes, the left-most angled out near the bottom. The tops of the middle and right slashes were connected by an elongated crescent that curved up and away. A diagonal line ran from the middle of the left slash down through the bottom of the right. Three dots hovered within. *Ma'yabesk.* Protection. The knowledge was bestowed upon Geoffrey, and upon Ruprecht observing from afar.

"Ma'yabesk," Geoffrey whispered in awe.

Geoffrey, with Ruprecht perched inside his mind, began drawing the rune with a shaking finger on the clammy floor in front of him. The cold was returning. He drew the rune madly, messily, and continued to repeat the word.

Miraculously, the first drawn rune began to glow golden yellow on the floor. The second illuminated next to it. Then the third, and as light poured out of the drawn contours, the first two runes connected to one another. Soon golden light spread to the third and fourth.

It was hard for Geoffrey to move. He was exhausted mentally and physically, and his right leg was numb from the knee down—if it was even still attached to him at all. But he forced himself to twist and rotate, until he had completed the runic circle all around him.

Geoffrey's left ankle was still on. He could see it now in the golden glow. But the flesh from his calf to his toes was black and cracked. There was not now—nor would there ever again be—life below his left knee.

The golden light warmed him, its love restored and calmed him somewhat. But the beast was nearby. He could feel it.

And Leopold could feel Geoffrey, too. Leopold could also feel a new and unwelcome presence lodged inside his prisoner's mind. He drifted over to investigate.

And Geoffrey saw Leopold by the golden light for the very first time. A floating wraith. A skeleton of black bones within rotted rags. Hate incarnate.

The new treacherous light was nearly blinding to Leopold. Infuriating. This man would have to be destroyed once and for all. Though it had been so deliciously gratifying to toy with him again.

Ignoring the repulsive brightness, Leopold forced himself closer to his prisoner. The prisoner was looking up at him. The prisoner had eyes behind his eyes. Weak eyes.

Leopold sucked on the vision of those secondary eyes. Probed them for memory. Leopold saw his precious book. He saw his missing black eyes.

And Leopold attacked. The wraith lunged down at Geoffrey to sink his bony maliciousness deep into the pathetic man's mortal flesh. He wanted nothing more than to rip into the host and menace the cowardly voyeur behind the mask—the voyeur in possession of Leopold's treasures.

Geoffrey cowered like an oft-struck mongrel dog. Ruprecht's presence was hastily expelled.

Shuddering convulsively, Ruprecht found himself again in the sparse Meriden field where Ohlen sat peacefully nearby, where Arden and Boudreaux were just emerging from their trip into the wood, and where tears and mucous were mixing liberally in Ruprecht's thick brown beard.

*White-gray and milk-yellow plates covered a massive
serpentine body that extended back into the tunnel.*

Chapter Thirty-Three
THE ROCK EATER

Gnome sprinted as best he could up the twisting tubular tunnel. Whatever stirred in the depths sounded enormous. In his great haste Gnome's feet slid on the highly polished surface, and he found himself scrabbling upward using his hands as well.

The mirror-smooth lip of the entrance curved outward in all directions like a bell. This made it particularly challenging to reengage with the coarse rock wall, since getting close to it with toes or fingers meant risking a plummet to the rock-strewn earth far below.

The clicking grew louder and preceded a roar that blasted so forcefully out of the tunnel, Gnome's ears would ring for over an hour afterward. Gnome flopped on his belly—face upturned toward the tunnel entrance, eyes scanning for whatever behemoth was coming—

and scooted himself backward so that his feet protruded out over the edge.

Just a little farther.

Massive snorting breaths and countless clicks emanated, ever closer, out of the dark tunnel.

Gnome splayed both hands flat, and pressed his palms and fingers to the sloping smoothness to maximize his contact points as he gingerly nudged down the slippery sloping edge.

Nearly there, Gnome thought desperately. He needed to get his hips to the edge so that his legs could bend, and his toes could locate a good hold.

The Rock Eater exploded into the daylight above him with another deafening roar. From Gnome's vantage point below, the parts that he could see appeared to be all armor—armor and legs. White-gray and milk-yellow plates covered a massive serpentine body that extended back into the tunnel. There must have been a hundred legs in Gnome's field of vision. Two exterior rows were long, and powerful-looking and ended in spear-like points. Hugging the body, however, were two sets of smaller rapidly twitching legs each of which had three independent finger-like digits that opened and closed maniacally.

The last Gnome saw—as his toe found purchase on the divoted rock wall, and he clambered hastily downward—the Rock Eater had arched its back, raising its massive front quarters and flailing limbs. It bellowed once more. As loud and incomprehensible as the noise was, there were distinct parts to it—syllables almost—as if the Rock Eater was *yelling something*, and not just howling like some wild beast.

Back on the ground Gnome fled the scene as fast as his legs would carry him. Even though—as far as he could tell—the Rock Eater had not exited its lair, Gnome ran at top speed back to the fallen trees, past the muddy grooves, and out into the barren field between the Meriden colonnade and the mountain peak. He did not slow his pace until he recognized his friends walking toward him around the left side of of the colonnade.

"What're you running from?" Boudreaux shouted merrily through cupped hands, as they neared each other.

"I saw it, you guys. I saw it!" Gnome panted breathlessly.

"Looks like you saw a ghost, to me!" Boudreaux jeered.

Gnome had reached them, and hunched over, hands on his knees, breathing hard.

"And I saw *her*," he said in his best level tone. "She's IN there!"

Ohlen drifted over to Gnome and placed a hand on his shoulder. "Recover, friend," he said soothingly, gently, eyes closed. A moment later Ohlen continued, "Tell us what happened."

Gnome's breathing slowed. He stood up straight, and studied for a long moment Ohlen's inscrutable expression.

"Thank you," Gnome said in wonderment. His panic and exhaustion had somehow bled from his body, through his shoulder, into Ohlen's warm and steady hand.

"The Rock Eater lives in a giant cave in the mountain. To get there I had to climb high up. The climbing is easy, but the entrance itself is sheer like ice, and slopes steeply. It's hard to keep your footing. Alzbeda is in there. She's in some weird state like she's been frozen or something. That's good because it looks like she's missing both hands."

Gnome's tale was met with astounded stares, especially from Arden and Ruprecht, but at this last bit of information there were gasps.

"Yeah, I know," Gnome continued. "But I don't think she's dead. It's like she's sleeping. I don't know if the Rock Eater is eating her or something, like piece by piece?"

"Maybe we should stop calling it 'Rock Eater,' then, you know?" Boudreaux looked around for smirks, but his was the only one.

"Anyway," Gnome was unphased. "The thing is huge. It woke up somewhere way down there and started coming up after me. I ran out, and as I was climbing down I saw it."

"What does it look like, Gnome?" Arden jumped in.

"Whew!" Gnome blew through his teeth. "Actually I only saw the bottom of the front part of it. It's huge, first of all, and the bottom is all legs—tons of them! I think there are big legs it walks on," Gnome pointed his hands stiffly at the ground, elbows out, and swayed back and forth to mimic large outer walking legs. "But then it also has tons of little ones in the middle, with little fingers," and here he brought his hands in close to his chest and wriggled them wildly.

"Isn't, like, *everything* huge to you, Gnome?" Boudreaux joked.

Gnome scowled.

"I'm serious!" Boudreaux reacted defensively to the round of dirty looks he received. "I mean, how big is big? Like as big as me? As big as that column?" He pointed at the colonnade. "As big as that tree?" He pointed at a towering evergreen.

"Alright," Gnome conceded, "The underbelly I saw was as large as four of those tree trunks bundled together side by side. Maybe five. And that doesn't include the legs. I didn't see it all, but the part that stuck out of that tunnel was about four Boudreauxs long, stuck end to end. Does that help?"

There was a pause while everyone digested the description.

Boudreaux's mood in particular seemed to change. His hand crept to the hilt of his large dwarf broad sword, "Is it soft or hard underneath?" he asked in a low somber voice.

"Hard," Gnome replied. "It looks hard, Boudreaux."

"I don't believe we have been properly introduced," she continued amiably. "This is Brunka, and I am called Nezka."

Chapter Thirty-Four
MOONLIGHT

Following Gnome's revelations about the Rock Eater and Alzbeda, they headed back to Petric's to get X'andria and make a plan.

"Geoffrey's in deep trouble you guys." Ruprecht finally shared what had been weighing him down all afternoon.

"Who?" Boudreaux blurted.

Ruprecht winced. "Geoffrey! The selfless, brilliant man who saved my soul, Boudreaux? The one—as I understand it—who saved you all from being incinerated? The one who bought us time to flee from Rockmoor?" Ruprecht was clearly exasperated.

"Yeah, yeah, yeah, I get it," Boudreaux admitted grouchily. "I just didn't remember his name is all."

"What kind of trouble, Ruprecht?" Arden asked, concerned.

"It has him," Ruprecht's voice was small, despondent. And he proceeded to describe his vision of Geoffrey's abduction, his ankle, the cold, the runes, and the wraith.

Gnome rapped four times on Petric's column.

The afternoon was chilly and clear—the wind had picked up a bit. Ohlen gazed southward.

"Well, Ruprecht," Gnome started in as they waited for a response, "I think we finish up here by tomorrow, and head back to Rockmoor straight away. Geoffrey knows how to take care of himself. He'll just have to last until we can get to him. This whole thing," and here Gnome gestured at their environs, "has been a big giant waste of time anyhow."

"I think you may find, Gnome," Ohlen spoke into the cool rushing wind, "that Meriden has mysteries yet to be uncovered—that our path has led us here for a reason."

Petric's door whirred into action and slabs of concealed stone began sliding down into the ground.

"This place is so amazing," Arden said earnestly. "But I'm not at all sure I like it very much."

X'andria came up Petric's stairs followed by Petric himself, who moved slowly and looked more frail than ever. He wore the same sequined vest that they had seen on their first encounter, but it fit looser now, and the boyish exuberance was long gone from his eyes.

"Hey guys, how's it going?" X'andria said with a brightness that seemed a touch forced. "I'm sorry to be slow today, but I'm totally ready now. All rested up."

"Petric," Gnome beckoned their host down toward him. "Lean in here, I need to tell you some news."

Petric bent down and Gnome whispered in his ear. A moment later Petric was standing up straight again, and grinning broadly.

They had not seen him grin like that since he first served dinner the night of their arrival in Meriden.

"That, my friends, is welcome news," he announced. "So what will you do?"

"What news?" X'andria was confused.

"We need to get X'an's brain on it, make a plan, and then get her back for you," Gnome said conclusively, winking at X'andria.

"Please, please be careful, my friends," Petric exhorted them. "The Rock Eater is a cunning and fearful beast and," and here Petric lowered his voice to a whisper, "I am learning that not every Meriden wishes for our dear Alzbeda's return." He then concluded in a normal voice, "I must go to meet some of my brethren. But I will be back after sundown. May the wind guide you forth and the rock be firm beneath your feet."

With nowhere else to sit comfortably, the six friends walked to Meriden's center and sat next to one another at the base of Alzbeda's Altar To The Wind And Sky.

"Gnome I can't believe you did that!" X'andria seemed rattled by Gnome's story of the tunnel, the Rock Eater, and Alzbeda. "I mean, it's amazing you found her, but what if something had happened to you?"

Boudreaux chuckled darkly. "That's funny coming from Little Miss 'I'm gonna go off and do whatever I want by myself and not tell anyone'," he scoffed. X'andria shot him a dirty look.

"How are we going to fight this thing?" Arden stood up and began pacing back and forth in front of them. "It sounds huge, heavily armored, and weaponized with hundreds of stone-splitting legs."

Chapter Thirty-Four

It was several minutes before anyone spoke.

"Maybe we don't have to fight it," Ruprecht suggested quietly.

"Uh..." Boudreaux said loudly, feigning contemplation, "Like maybe we should try and be friends with it? Offer it a brew? And then ask if it'll return the nice lady it stole and ate the hands off of?"

"Actually," it was Arden again, pacing faster now, "when we've heard its cries, it's been at night. It must come out then. Maybe a few of us could distract it, lead it away, and then the others could race in and get her."

"Get who?" An airy voice floated across the darkening courtyard toward them.

Nezka, accompanied by a fit Meriden man, sauntered out from between two columns. The man wore flowing black pants, a high-collared white tunic, and a crimson cape fastened about his neck with a gold chain. Nezka bore a forest green fitted garment that crawled up her neck in organic scallops edged with black filigree. A belt swooped around her waist that appeared to be made of woven gold thread.

"I don't believe we have been properly introduced," she continued amiably. "This is Brunka, and I am called Nezka. We know you are guests of Petric, I am quite sorry we have not yet had the occasion to welcome you to our home."

An awkward silence followed Nezka's greeting, until X'andria stood and said with surprising assurance, "Well it's very nice to meet you both. Would you care to join us?"

"How kind you," this time it was Brunka talking. While Nezka spoke the common tongue effortlessly, Brunka's speech was clipped by a thick Meriden accent. Brunka's dark eyes lingered for a long time on X'andria's, as though to add emphasis to his sentiment. X'andria, smiling, held his gaze.

"Is that snake?" Nezka exclaimed emphatically, pointing at Arden's feet.

For a moment it seemed as though Arden had forgotten how to speak. He looked nervously between Nezka and Brunka, before collecting himself to reply. "Y-yes, actually." He slid his left foot forward to better expose the green snakeskin boots he had procured back in Bridgeton.

Brunka chuckled, "Much wear, no? That troll?" He was pointing at Arden's soles. Only X'andria noticed the briefest of sideways glares from Nezka before she added smoothly, "The craftsmanship is sublime, I have always adored square-toe boots on men, and troll hide is simply the best."

Arden was blushing, indeed his gorgeous boots were very worn-looking. The sole of his left boot had a hole eaten through beneath the big toe where it had come in contact with Elias' tattooed warrior turned seeping-acid-pus-monster in the Rockmoor sewer.

Even so, he was really starting to enjoy the conversation. "You know, I've always heard troll hide lasts a lifetime. I was actually pretty disappointed when this little problem developed," he lifted and turned inward his left foot, pointing and frowning at the small hole. "But it's seen, you might say, extreme wearing conditions. I would definitely get another pair."

"And that is a *very* large sword," Nezka turned to Boudreaux.

"A big man needs a big sword," Boudreaux flashed his toothy grin and stood up jauntily.

"Dwarf, no?" Brunka added shrewdly. "Dwarf ore is best."

"I'm curious," Gnome chimed in icily, "why the hell we're not talking about Alzbeda and the huge rock monster over there?" He jumped to his feet, standing atop the first shelf of Alzbeda's altar—which was turning steadily darker in color to match the fading light

273

of the sky above.

"Oh Gnome," X'andria burst in with a short laugh. "We're having a *conversation* with these nice people." She shot Gnome her best reassuring smile. "Brunka, Nezka, I'm X'andria. And this is Boudreaux, Arden, Gnome, Ohlen, and Ruprecht. It's nice to meet you two."

"Gnome?" Nezka replied. "Of course we are all very concerned about Alzbeda. Her disappearance is quite troubling indeed. Petric is especially concerned—of course he would be—but sometimes bad things happen, do they not? We are all on edge, to be honest."

Ohlen and Ruprecht exchanged cryptic glances. Nezka's statement sounded more rehearsed than honest.

"And are you referring to our Rock Eater?" Nezka laughed lightly. "She's harmless really. She makes a lot of noise sometimes, but then again she also made all of this." Nezka gestured to the columns all around them.

What followed, as the moon rose in the dark sky above them, was a pleasant but somewhat awkward conversation centering mostly around clothing and design and the mechanics of the Meriden rockwork city. Both Nezka and Brunka seemed keen to hear about anything special or unusual, and took great interest in X'andria's jade necklace, and Gnome's deep-sea eel-skin slippers, and the silver bracers protecting his forearms that he had picked up from the dwarves beneath the Westoveran Mountains.

Ohlen and Ruprecht sat side by side, still as statues, and contributed nothing to the conversation. Boudreaux was transfixed with Nezka, who seemed to enjoy the attention and frequently let her eyes roam over him appraisingly from head to toe. Gnome warmed, Arden chattered, and X'andria gently pried.

"We came here in a really nice carriage from Rockmoor," X'andria stated matter-of-factly. "Who was the driver?"

"It could be anyone," Nezka replied. "We have many drivers."

"I see…" X'andria pretended to ponder the response. "So, who are they? I mean the people down there at the foot of the mountain? They're not Meridens, are they?"

Brunka snorted but it was Nezka who continued to speak, "No, no, not Meridens. You must be talking about the people of Woodmont."

"I *must*," X'andria encouraged, her tone making it clear that she was not yet satisfied by the answer.

"Oh they are a simple people, X'andria. We have a business relationship with them going back many years. They trade some of our wares, everyone benefits. Simple, you know?"

"Sounds simple to me!" X'andria agreed brightly. "I've met a few of them coming and going, they seem really nice, actually." X'andria's eyes bore into Nezka's. Ruprecht and Ohlen both seemed to wake up—they looked in unison in X'andria's direction. Nezka looked suddenly alarmed, as if she had been slapped.

Boudreaux, oblivious, piped up, "Which one is yours Nilka?" He gestured at the columns around them.

Nezka turned to Boudreaux, and her frozen scowl slowly thawed into a smile. "Let me show you, Boudreaux. Brunka, entertain our guests for a few minutes would you?"

Nezka wheeled about and offered her hand to Boudreaux, which he readily took into his own. "I am called Nez-ka," she said slowly as if teaching a child.

They crossed the courtyard, and as they stepped between the first row of columns Nezka asked entreatingly, "I noticed you and your friends this morning down by the forest. Did you find anything interesting?"

Boudreaux's heart was hammering in his chest.
He could smell her hair—it was intoxicating.

Chapter Thirty-Five
EXTRUSION

She was perfect in every way.

Her slender fingers, chill from the cool evening air, fit easily inside Boudreaux's large, calloused hand. The drape of her long, straight, black hair alternately obscured and revealed her chiseled features with the sway of each step.

Boudreaux was smitten. And Nezka was interested in him, too! She asked him questions. She complimented him. She admired his physique with her eyes and her words.

So Boudreaux babbled.

"Oh, not much down in the forest. Just a path leading somewhere," he offered absently, "Arden's really good at paths."

Her eyes were like little universes, reflecting the stars in oceans of black oblivion.

Chapter Thirty-Five

"Why? Oh, it's strange. Ohlen and Ruprecht can sense things, you know? I don't pay much attention, but Ohlen thinks there's something bad in there. He's got these black marbles that get inside you and take you over. Anyway, he thinks there's some connection."

And she was so elegant. From the moment he saw her, Boudreaux knew Nezka was a classy woman. Her clothes, the body inside those clothes, her words and her enthralling faint accent—she had this way of halting mid-step and turning slightly toward him when he was saying something interesting.

"X'an? She's harmless. Super smart is all." More steps, more gentle questions. "Me? No, not at all. I mean, she's alright I guess. But strange, too, you know?" They reached the perimeter. "That's the first I heard about her talking to anyone up here. I don't know who she talked to, really."

She was turning toward him. Getting closer. Looking up into his eyes. She felt for his other hand. Boudreaux's heart was hammering in his chest. He could smell her hair—it was intoxicating.

"Gnome says he found her." Boudreaux answered another soft, innocent question. "He said that rock monster's got her. We're supposed to go get her. Might even go tonight."

She was so close now. Her leg brushed his. Her body was pressing up against him. She released his hand and began running her fingers up his torso, pausing over each ridge of defined muscle.

"Stop talking, Boudreaux," she breathed. "Kiss me now."

And so he did.

Their mouths locked together. Her lips were cold. Surprisingly cold. And dry.

The first prick was in the soft palette in the back of the roof of his mouth. It hurt pretty bad, like someone was inserting a needle up into his nasal cavity. But then there was another prick inside his upper lip by his gum. Then there was another in his tongue. Then another, and another. Then five more, ten more, fifty more.

Boudreaux felt like his head was being split apart. His eyes flew open, but they were the only part of him he could move.

She was backing away from him. But it wasn't her any more. Her body was the same, more or less, but her mouth was wide open, and thousands of hair-like tendrils had exploded out of it, and were snaking their way into his inert body.

He could not move, but he could see, and he could feel.

More filaments burst out of her hands and swam through the air toward him as if each had a mind and will of its own. They searched for bare bits of his skin. They crawled into his hands, his arms. They inserted themselves into his cheeks. They found his eyeballs.

Boudreaux screamed and screamed but no sound came out. Every part of him felt like it was burning from the inside out. It was a new level of pain.

Where the hell did that idiot go? X'andria stalked angrily out of the courtyard just as soon as she found an opportunity to excuse herself.

I don't know what these people are up to, but it's bad, and she's the worst, and Boudreaux is just so daft! She was fuming.

In the distance, The Rock Eater let out its first tortured wail of the evening.

This place is so confusing! X'andria turned this way and that, peering down one moonlit columnar corridor after another.

She started to run. Guessing, she turned and sprinted toward the west. Some part of her felt silly, felt like she might come breathlessly upon a gross intimate moment between Boudreaux and Nezka and have to explain why she was running around Meriden like a scared child.

But X'andria didn't care. She had a feeling.

She wheeled around a corner and found them.

Boudreaux was frozen, eyes open and wild, lying on the ground. Nezka, or whatever this thing was, hovered a few feet away, suspended by thousands of hairs that had exploded from her mouth and hands—that had penetrated into poor catatonic Boudreaux.

The hairs were moving with a slow wavy undulation. And something was leaving X'andria's friend, Boudreaux. A faint glow seemed to be traveling out of his perforated body and into the monster's.

It was horrifying.

Before she even knew what she was doing, X'andria plunged her hand inside her robes and found her scroll-wrapped dart.

Anger consumed her as she imagined the dart slicing through every filament, arcing through the air, dragging deeply back across Nezka's stupid face and neck.

Shra'muhrjnik. Wound. The word tore out of her throat like a shriek.

The violence of her thought-made-manifest, caused X'andria to stumble and fall to her knees.

The night filled with a blood-curdling screech.

Nezka shrank backward, blood pouring from a huge gash in her face and neck. The severed tendrils extending out of her mouth and hands flailed wildly, and sprayed a bloody mist of red-gold luminescence.

Nezka's hands came up to the wounds on her face. Her

screaming continued to bubble through clumps of the bloody siphon filaments filling her mouth. She spun wildly in the air, blubbering and dripping.

Boudreaux was nonresponsive. His body was covered with teeny squirming wormy tendrils. Each was leaking blood. Desperately, X'andria began grasping at the droopy filaments. They came away easily enough, leaving red smears behind.

People were coming. X'andria heard shouts over Nezka's continued sucking sobs.

With her right hand closed tightly around her scroll-covered dart—she thought she could manage one more spell tonight—X'andria madly scraped away all the blood-soaked mats of fine strands still inserted into her friend's skin, eyes, nose, and mouth.

As Brunka tore around the corner, X'andria realized in horror that the hair on Boudreaux's head, Boudreaux's own hair, had all turned to grey.

This left Arden, Boudreaux, and Ruprecht stunned, in a sort-of otherworldly stand-off, staring into the ghastly face of a monstrous creature who had just snatched their friend Ohlen before their very eyes.

Chapter Thirty-Six
EXTRACTION

What followed was a blur for X'andria.

Arden had banged into view right behind Brunka, swords dancing in both hands. Brunka had started yelling in his choppy language and fell to Nezka's side. Others came. Meridens emerged from columns all around, and collective sounds of alarm issued from the group.

Soon the Meridens had surrounded Nezka and obscured her from view. Arden hoisted Boudreaux into the air with a worried grimace. Ohlen was at X'andria's side. They began melting back away from the crush of Meriden bodies. Angry accusatory looks found their way between folds of clothing and the increasingly animated chatter.

Petric did not answer their knocks. Everyone wanted X'andria to tell them what happened. They all seemed angry. At her. X'andria was so flustered. Gnome—it must have been Gnome—suggested they retreat to the woods.

So they did.

"It was EATING him!" X'andria screamed. "The damn thing was eating him from the inside out!" Tears leaked from her eyes, and she hastily wiped snot from her nose with the back of her sleeve.

Ohlen was talking. He was reaching for her, but X'andria pulled away. *No one was getting it. Something horrible had happened to Boudreaux. She had to do something. Didn't they understand?*

"X'andria," it was Ruprecht. "X'andria, HEAR me," he said. It was definitely Ruprecht, but his voice was different, bigger. It shut out all the other sounds, it even seemed to dampen the madness.

"I BELIEVE in you, X'andria." Ruprecht was smiling at her. "You are good. You have done your best. This I know."

X'andria's breath began to slow.

They had hurried into the woods. It was very dark.

"But I need to see him!" Arden was pleading, rustling around on the ground next to Boudreaux. "I don't care if they find us."

"I'm out of bugs, used my last one earlier." Gnome admitted.

"X'an?" Arden pressed.

"I can't, Arden," X'andria was telling the truth. What she had done to Nezka had cost her significantly.

But light came—a dome of clear bright light. In the middle of the dome Ruprecht sat crosslegged, eyes closed, murmuring beneath his breath.

Boudreaux had changed. He had aged. Arden slowly, lovingly,

cleaned the blood from his face and neck. Ohlen descended to the ground and placed his hands on each side of Boudreaux's head.

Gnome shifted from side to side, unsure what to do. X'andria, though calmed, continued to cry.

"Boudreaux lives," Ohlen said softly. "His spirit is diminished, but he lives."

"X'an," Gnome grasped his oldest friend's hand, "Can you help me look for a beetle or two? Something tells me they might come in handy before all of this is over."

Grateful for the distraction, X'andria joined Gnome scraping and digging in the dark forest soil.

Boudreaux sputtered and coughed. An entire mouthful of blood and flaccid saturated tendrils erupted onto his chin. Arden, muttering soft reassurances, set about cleaning his friend's face anew.

Several minutes passed. The Rock Eater's distant roar broke the stern silence.

"So what happened, X'an?" Arden finally asked.

"You saw it, Arden." She replied from her spot on the ground a few feet away, fingers methodically probing the soil. "That monster was sucking Boudreaux's life out of him through those hair-things." X'andria shuddered. "They came out of her mouth and hands," it seemed like an important detail to add.

"So I cut them off," she added flatly, "I didn't know what else to do."

"You saved his life, X'andria," Ohlen said sincerely. To X'andria it sounded almost like a compliment.

"Found one!" Gnome exclaimed with muted excitement. He tucked the wriggling beetle into one of his beetle-sized pockets.

"Now we know what's been happening to the missing children," Ruprecht added mournfully, eyes still closed in concentration.

Chapter Thirty-Six

"What children?" X'andria asked. And Arden, placing a hand on Boudreaux's chest, explained about the desiccated corpse they had found in the woods.

"It's just so awful," X'andria reacted. Then a moment later she continued, "So that must be how they operate those doors. When everyone was out, I got really close and examined the spot on the wall Petric touches when he opens his door. There are these teeny holes. You'd never see them, but they're there."

"X'an, were you telling the truth when you told Nezka you had spoken to some of the folks from Woodmont?" Gnome was standing and brushing the dirt off his hands.

X'andria looked at the ground. Everyone waited.

"I know some things. I did some sneaking around." She blew out a heavy breath, as if coming to a difficult decision. "Look, I don't want to talk about how I know this stuff, so don't ask me. But here's what I know: The Meridens use the people of Woodmont to trade their Abgoa Leaf and whatever else. Twice a day, a pair from Woodmont comes up here with coin and then they get locked up in a jail cell. Two others, who have been in the cell, get released, and take bales of Abgoa back down the mountain."

X'andria concluded bitterly, "The people of Woodmont are slaves to the Meridens, it's not 'beneficial to all' like Nezka would have us believe."

Boudreaux sputtered again, and struggled to sit up. The best he managed, though, was to put his hand on his forehead and groan.

"How're you feeling man?" Arden asked softly. "Take it easy, alright?"

"Oh," Boudreaux exhaled, bloody spittle splatting out onto his lips. "Oh," he said again, "That was bad."

"What do you remember?" Ohlen asked, his hands were still

placed on Boudreaux's temples.

"Worst..." Boudreaux had to breathe between words, "...Kiss. Ever."

And Boudreaux began to cough. But it wasn't just a cough, it was a laugh. And then Gnome, and X'andria started to laugh too. And then Arden, and Ruprecht, and then even Ohlen.

There in the desolate, dark forest, in a golden dome of light, with Boudreaux recovering on his back, the friends laughed. It felt good.

"Let's just get her," it was Boudreaux. Several quiet hours had passed.

They had dozed in shifts, Ohlen and Arden traded off ministrating over Boudreaux, until he finally sat up and brushed them away.

"But how do you feel, Boudreaux?" Gnome asked earnestly. "We're gonna need you if we come up against that thing."

"I feel terrible," Boudreaux replied honestly. "Weird actually. But I'm starting to like Ruprecht's plan. Maybe we can distract it and get her while it's out. Clearly it goes out at night."

"Someone explain to me why we don't just leave right now," Gnome queried, ever practical. "Petric lied to us. These people are soul-sucking monsters that eat children—and adults too, apparently—what do we care if their leader gets eaten piece by piece by a rock monster?"

"That," Arden concurred, "is an excellent question, Gnome."

"Because she keeps them together somehow." X'andria replied

evenly. "Because the Sorcerer saw her in Elias' demon book. If we don't get her back, then the thing Boudreaux just went through will start happening to more and more people all over the place. This is bigger than Petric and Alzbeda and Nezka. It's bigger than us."

They hugged the tree line, and headed north. The moonlight was adequate. The wind had picked up even more, and whistled through bending treetops. Boudreaux stumbled a bit, but managed to keep up.

Another wail echoed through the night, accompanied by an earsplitting crack of rock breaking onto rock. The Rock Eater was near.

The plan called for X'andria and Gnome to enter the tunnel and extract Alzbeda. The others would set up camp in the trees, after sparking a fire in plain view. They would lob rocks and branches at the fire to make noise and, hopefully, attract the attention of the Rock Eater, without having to face it directly.

"It's pretty easy climbing until the top, X'an," Gnome whispered, as the two of them silently approached the base of the Rock Eater's cliff. "Once we're up there, I'll go in, get a secure hold, and drop Arden's rope down for you to grab onto. You can handle lifting Alzbeda and getting her down?"

"I can," X'andria replied stonily. The rest had done her some good.

They hovered at the base of the rock wall. Waiting for Arden's fire to light across the open expanse.

Arden could hear it. It was somewhere above them in the dark, up the mountainside. Ruprecht had helped to gather kindling while Ohlen and Boudreaux scouted for a good protected place under the cover of the trees. Now it was up to Arden to light the fire.

Arden pulled out his short sword and placed the tip on the earth, holding the hilt so that the blade angled up and over his dry kindling. He pulled his flint stone out of the pouch hanging at his waist and glanced it lightly and swiftly with the blade by shoving the hilt rapidly forward and away from him.

Never had striking a spark seemed so loud. Never had the sparks looked so bright. It felt to Arden that the whole of the mountainside must have heard and seen the spark, and it seemed as though the noises from above had ceased.

But the fire had not yet caught.

Sweating, he struck the flint again. And again. And then a fourth time. The fourth spark landed on his kindling and winked up at him. Years of making fires in just this manner told Arden the job was done. He hastily sheathed his sword, and raced to join the others.

"That's it," Gnome breathed. The fire was lit. "It's straight up from here, X'an, just follow me." They scaled the wall in silence.

Gnome reached up and ran his hand along the polished tunnel entrance. Using the sweat on his palms, he maximized the contact of his skin on the sloping surface as he carefully maneuvered his toes to higher holds that would allow him to securely push up and over the edge.

The Rock Eater tore down the mountainside. Everything about it was loud, the clicking of its many legs—its breathing like a bellows for the world's largest fireplace. It reached the fire and roared a burst of incoherent but clearly articulated cries.

Gnome was in. He dropped the end of Arden's rope down to X'andria, hastened around the first bend in the tunnel, and gave the rope a tug.

Ruprecht, Arden, Ohlen, and Boudreaux watched as the behemoth Rock Eater advanced toward the flames. The body extended behind it was just a giant shadow in the night, but its face was clearly illuminated.

Supported by a series of powerful, pointed forelegs—just as Gnome had described—it's massive scaly face narrowed somewhat to a set of jaws so densely compact that it looked like they could obliterate anything placed inside of them. Above its bone-chilling maw a series of glistening smushed-in orifices, hidden in deep folds of scaly tissue, probably served the functions of eyes and nose. It was an exceedingly ugly beast.

Its jaws flew open revealing lines of flat, hammer-like teeth, and it bellowed with such force, its breath nearly put out the fire entirely.

X'andria's weight had caused Gnome to slip and slide along the tunnel as she ascended. But she reached the top and steadied herself long before he was near the edge.

Grabbing his newly acquired beetle, Gnome imagined illumination once more. *Mjargi'lig,* he hissed. Light. And so it was.

"Careful now," Gnome said. "There's quite a drop at the end." They trotted down the twisting tunnel, with another wail from the Rock Eater filling the air at their heels. X'andria fumbled in one of her inside pockets for her gold loop.

Snuffling noisily and grunting like a pig with its nose in a feed trough, the Rock Eater trampled over Arden's fire. The fire went out quickly and completely beneath the multitude of legs.

With the extinguishing of the flames, several awarenesses bloomed at once.

Arden noticed the glow emanating from the Rock Eater's tunnel high up on the cliff across the field. The Rock Eater noticed it, too, and made a wild braying sound. And Ohlen, who had reached out to the beast through the ether murmured in surprise, "It cares."

"She's just around this corner, X'an," Gnome called in a mock whisper. They had reached the end of the twisting and tubular entrance to the Rock Eater's lair. As before, Gnome was struck by the sheer enormity of the space, and the unexpected precipice.

Chapter Thirty-Six

"I've got her," X'andria grunted, holding her gold loop before her. She seized the air around Alzbeda and lifted her from the rock. Alzbeda's legs, and handless arms dangled as she rose upward—as if hoisted by an invisible string attached to her sternum. Maintaining concentration was X'andria's biggest challenge now. She needed to ignore Alzbeda's bloody stumps, and the misty film covering her still body. X'andria would need to maintain focus even while climbing down the rock wall at the other end of the tunnel.

The Rock Eater turned its long serpentine body around and started heading toward the light emanating from its tunnel. Not knowing what else to do, Arden yelled as loud as he could and raced out into the open, pulling his bow from its shoulder mount. He released three arrows in rapid succession, before the others caught up with him. He fired off three more, still shouting—imagining what would happen to Gnome and X'andria if the Rock Eater discovered them stealing Alzbeda. The massive beast turned around once more and scuttled like a huge millipede back toward the source of the sound and the annoying pinpricks.

It was on them. There was nowhere to go. No way to outrun it. They had to take a stand. Breathing heavy, noisy breaths, the Rock Eater lowered its huge smushed-in face to the ground before them.

Arden and Boudreaux both drew swords. But it was Ohlen who advanced, weaponless, palms facing outward.

Fear is what Ohlen sensed. *But fear of what?* Certainly the Rock Eater did not fear these four puny strangers.

Quick as lightning, the beast's head lifted to reveal a network of scuttling interior arms that grabbed Ohlen and hauled him underneath and down the length of its body. This left Arden, Boudreaux, and Ruprecht stunned, in a sort-of otherworldly stand-off, staring into the ghastly face of a monstrous creature who had just snatched their friend Ohlen before their very eyes.

"Take this end of the rope, alright, X'an? Be careful." Gnome stopped and braced himself in the same twist of the tunnel he had used for support when helping X'andria up over the edge minutes before.

X'andria said nothing. Rope in her left hand, gold loop in her right, Alzbeda dangling like a grotesque marionette in the air behind her, X'andria stepped slowly and deliberately toward the edge of the Rock Eater's lair.

She sat down. She breathed slowly. She scooted forward on her bottom. She slipped right off the edge.

Gnome felt the rope go suddenly taut. It pulled with such force it slipped through his fingers. It took both hands to stop it from sliding, but then—with no hand on the wall for traction—he started sliding along the tunnel floor as well.

X'andria gripped tight to the rope. She could not support herself for long with just one hand, but the tension of the rope was enough to slam her, shoulder first, into the exterior wall. She had just managed to get a toehold—left shoulder screaming from the trauma and stretch—when she realized she had dropped Alzbeda.

But where?

A moment later Alzbeda's still body slipped off the bell-like tunnel entrance above X'andria's head. Hugging the wall, and squeezing her gold loop, X'andria brought all her focus to catching and holding the body falling above her.

It's so gentle! Ohlen marveled. Supported by hundreds of hand-like appendages, he was ushered smoothly along the underside of the Rock Eater. *Connect*, he asked. He reached out ever so slightly to try and place a hand on one of the whirring arms. It responded instantly, and the movement stopped.

I'm here, was all Ohlen hoped to communicate. He reached out with his consciousness into the huge, armored body and felt for its essence. Seconds later he began sailing forward, back toward the beast's head. He was deposited on the ground—placed perfectly onto his feet. And Ohlen found himself face to face with the Rock Eater once more. Behind him Boudreaux, Arden, and Ruprecht looked on, bewildered.

Ohlen reached out and put his hand firmly on the Rock Eater's face.

The energy Ohlen encountered was in turmoil. Trembling fear fueled confusion and worry. This being had experienced loss. Ohlen sensed a great desire to communicate, and a frustrated inability to do so. *I'm here*, he projected once more.

They were down. Her hands were stinging from rope burns, X'andria's shoulder was most definitely injured, and her brain ached from the intense sustained concentration of carrying Alzbeda—just hours after cutting into Nezka with her mind.

She managed to follow Gnome down the rocky slope and into the trees, before she collapsed on the ground and allowed Alzbeda's body to thump down beside her.

The wind was blowing crazily now, howling and gusting around them.

Gnome rushed over to arrange Alzbeda's body in what seemed like a more comfortable position. She had fallen to the earth with her left leg bent back beneath her right at an odd angle, and her right arm pinned behind her back.

As he got near to her, he realized the film surrounding her was more like a swirling mist than ice. When he grasped her left ankle to free and straighten it, the mist puffed around his hand like grey smoke.

Gnome had just finished placing her right forearm across her chest when Alzbeda's eyes blinked open.

"MY HANDS!" she cried, lifting her bloody stumps up in front of her face in horror.

Then, with a tortured grimace she looked imploringly at Gnome and moaned, "Oh Bodomek," before her eyes clicked shut and she lay still once more.

She floated on a thick cloud of billowing air.

Chapter Thirty-Seven
ALZBEDA

Many years ago...

Alzbeda's earliest memories were of smiles and sunlight. She loved the sky. Before she could walk her mom and dad would lay her on the grass outside, and she would look up at the vast blueness and bask in the love of their glowing faces as they smiled down at her.

Her dad traveled a lot. As she grew up she spent most of her time learning from her mom, walking in nature and reading books. Occasionally she played with the other children, but even from an early age Alzbeda's soul seemed older than the rest, she had a rare wisdom about her for one so young.

And on those wondrous occasions when her dad came home from his travels, she would squeal in delighted anticipation, and bound out to meet him. He brought gifts of course, and she cherished each and every exotic item he gave to her. What she loved even more was hearing his stories and his vivid descriptions of each object, its makers, its significance, why he chose it, and how he came to acquire it.

Sometimes her young friends would leave and Alzbeda would never see them again. Her mom brushed off these departures, explaining that some people had relatives in other parts of the world, and others left on trips to see new things, or learn about other people. "Like your father does," her mom had said.

They moved frequently—all of them. Her friends, their parents, her parents, everyone she knew would pick up stakes from time to time and go someplace new. This was never a fun experience for Alzbeda because it never seemed to be a fun experience for anyone else—especially for her mom. There was urgency about each move. *Did they have everything? Were they forgetting anyone? Were they moving fast enough?*

There was quite an emphasis on speed during the moves, and often they would leave in the middle of the night. Alzbeda did not like getting up in the middle of the night, she did not like being rushed, and the combination of the two was particularly unpleasant.

They also rarely had proper homes. This was not strange to the young Alzbeda, because she had never known anything else. But around her tenth year, they took up residence on a wooded mountainside near a town filled with people in tidy homes. That fall it grew cold at night in their collection of lean-to forest dwellings, and she learned from her father that the smoke on the wind at night was from the people in the village who heated their sturdy walled homes with fire.

Through the trees she had spied some of the town's children playing during the daytimes—she never interacted with them, of course, that was forbidden. She also saw odd sickly-looking people with wrinkled faces and grey hair hunched and ambling slowly. She asked her mom about the sick people—she had never seen anyone with grey hair or wrinkled skin. It was one of the rare times Alzbeda's mom scolded her, and did not answer her question.

One particularly cold night, Alzbeda wrapped her fur blanket around herself like a robe and ventured from their lean-to toward the town. It was pure curiosity—she wanted to see what smoke looked like coming out of a chimney.

But on the way to the village she came upon an odd scene. Two of her parents' friends, Nezka and Brunka, were holding a squirming village child roughly by the arm. The child was whining, and trying to pull away.

What happened next was horrifying, but it would be some time before Alzbeda fully understood what it was—what it meant to be Meriden.

All she knew was that the village child died at the hands of her parents' friends. It died scared and alone and in intense pain, and the very next day they all hastily packed their belongings and fled the wood, heading further up the mountain just as fast as they could go.

No other people lived further up the mountain. It was desolate. The only fun thing Alzbeda enjoyed up there was going with her friend Anica to explore tunnels created by rock protruding out of, or fallen down onto, the earth. The girls called them *castles*.

One crisp, clear morning about three weeks after their ascent up the mountain, Alzbeda ventured out early to find Anica in the fur-lined crevice where she slept with her parents each night. But when Alzbeda arrived Anica was nowhere to be found. Instead Alzbeda came upon Anica's mom crying, with puffy red-rimmed eyes, pounding feebly on Anica's dad's chest while he mumbled incoherent

Chapter Thirty-Seven

consolations.

And Alzbeda knew exactly what had happened—what had been happening. And the weight of her realization was crushing.

She raced back to her own parents' rocky shelter, and snuggled, trembling, in between them. Alzbeda knew she would run away soon.

That night she dreamt of Anica. She imagined Nezka and Brunka doing to Anica what she had seen them doing to that village boy. But as the dream morphed Anica became Alzbeda, and Nezka and Brunka became her own mom and dad. She awoke in the frozen pre-dawn sweating profusely beneath her furs. Now was the time.

Alzbeda quietly wrapped herself in as many layers of clothing as she could fit. She folded her fur blanket over her arm for later use. And she stole out of her rocky shelter and headed toward the sunrise.

But she was seen. She was followed.

At first Alzbeda wasn't sure if her ears were deceiving her. She quickened her little steps, and glanced over her shoulder from time to time. But before long her pursuers were out in the open. She started running, and so did they. There were at least ten of them, adults, gaining on her quickly. Someone was yelling behind them.

Tears streaked and froze on Alzbeda's cheeks as she stumbled blindly across the rock-strewn plateau. There was never really hope of outrunning them, but any stubborn sense she had of fleeing was dashed when she came upon the cliff.

They closed in like a pack of wolves. Surrounding her. She could see their siphon filaments beginning to extend from their hands, to lick the air around their mouths like many fine tongues. The yelling was closer, too. It was her mom, crying and shrieking, "It's not her time! It's not her time!"

Through her fear Alzbeda realized suddenly that it was her youth that would keep them young. It was the youth of the other children—villagers and Meridens alike—that sustained her people's lives. That the "sick" people she had seen in the village were not sick at all. They were just old.

In a final act of desperate defiance, Alzbeda turned and leapt off the cliff.

But she never hit the bottom.

Instead she floated. She floated on a thick cloud of billowing air.

"What is it you desire?" the wind asked her in a series of wordless gusts.

Mystified, Alzbeda looked all around for the source of the voice, but she saw only undulating cloud.

"I-I want to give them what they need," she stammered, "I want to make it, so they stop hurting people."

"And so you shall," the Sylph of the Wind and Sky replied.

Alzbeda was returned to the rock-strewn mountain clearing where her friend Anica had perished. The Sylph of the Wind and Sky placed her gently, like a precious baby, atop a swirling sweeping altar fashioned out of the sky itself.

In that place she could feel their pressing need. Not only for youth, but other things, too, like loneliness and sadness and confusion and especially guilt. Alzbeda's own siphon filaments extended for the first time out of her hands into the air like a thousand antennae and with them she discovered she could stir the wind and sky. There was so much grief. It was as big as the mountain peak looming above them. She stirred and stirred.

A silver mist began leaking out of her own mouth—through the siphon filaments inside her—cool and thick it passed her teeth and lips and dribbled heavily like cold liquid ore down her chin and chest and onto the altar at her feet.

The altar's swirls formed channels and the mist filled the channels and flowed down toward the ground in wavy streams.

The savages returned, wiping their mouths and brows. She could feel their shock and surprise at seeing the altar—at seeing her. They gathered around, drawn to the thick mist, and one by one they knelt before her and drank of its essence.

The last to arrive—stumbling, devastated, and alone—was Alzbeda's father, Petric.

Months passed.

Each night Alzbeda ascended her altar, and called forth the wind and sky. Each night her tears mixed with the mist as she recalled the many victims she had known, as she experienced through the ether the remorse of those responsible, as she thought of her mom smiling down at her in the innocent sunlight of her childhood.

Sometimes the mist attracted other things. It fell to the earth and rolled slowly outward or seeped downward, and Alzbeda felt the simple spirits of the animals, and the occasional troubled needs of a lost and wandering human being.

About half a year passed and things began looking up for the Meridens. Never in Alzbeda's lifetime had they lingered in any one place for this long. Her mist was healing for both the mind and body, and without the need to prey on humans—or each other—the community began to thrive and build.

But Alzbeda herself became increasingly depressed. She stopped speaking to anyone. Her rituals not only drew her into the vastness of her people's needs over and over again, but she began sensing a deeper isolation.

It was ancient, intractable, hopeless.

Her mist was seeping into the mountain itself. And for several weeks, as she trudged slowly and heavily up to the top of her altar, she began thinking that maybe, just maybe, she was communing with the loneliness of the mountain itself.

Until one night the earth exploded.

Terrified Meridens flew in all directions. Alzbeda, stirring and crying as always, stopped what she was doing.

Before her very eyes a beast rose into the night. A beast of such profound sadness, she nearly fainted from the weight of its grief.

The beast scuttled to her, its massive and terrible head rushing up her altar at a dizzying speed. It stopped before her, opened its terrible jaws, and begged for help with the loudest sound Alzbeda ever heard before or since. She was terrified and trembling. But she stood tall and began her dance with wind. *What is it you need?* She wondered. *What could something so great and terrible possibly want from the wind and sky?*

And the mist began flowing out of her once more. Siphon filaments extended out of her mouth through the air like long fingers, and delivered the gift directly into the Rock Eater's gaping jaws.

And in that moment she felt its crushing isolation. In that moment the Rock Eater experienced Alzbeda's grief and wisdom and kindness.

The wind and sky had given the gift of communication. And their long, unlikely friendship began.

They closed around him. Knowing what to expect only worsened the agony of the experience itself.

Chapter Thirty-Eight
BELOW GROUND

———————

All the torches were lit. Dancing light spilled from each of the narrow pointed alcoves lining the long central Meriden meeting hall.

The soft grating of smooth stone on smooth stone signaled the opening of yet another door—another council member arriving through one of a hundred private passageways the Rock Eater had made for them so many years ago.

"You know the rules, Petric," the interrogator pressed.

The newest arrival silently joined the line of dark-shrouded council members standing along the wall.

"No one did anything!" Petric protested. "None of you did anything!" He tried to look around, but the bonds restraining him to the heavy oak chair did not allow for much movement.

"I'll ask again, Petric," the interrogator sighed. "Why did you bring the outsiders?"

"To find her, of course! To find Alzbeda!" And as he spoke his daughter's name Petric lost control and began sobbing convulsively.

"But they intercepted two of our workers, Petric. The workers are fearful now, and did not come today. This is costly."

"Nezka and Brunka are FEEDING again!" Petric shouted wildly. "What are you even talking about? How can you ask about workers when we're FEEDING again!"

"Nezka and Brunka are not brought before this council, Petric. You are. You are accused of treason, Petric, and you know the seriousness of that charge."

"I just got them to help find her, to bring her back..." Petric's voice got swallowed in mucousy sputters.

"He's not answering." A cold voice floated over from the wall. "Perhaps it is time to drain."

"NO!" Petric squirmed, "Answer what? I'll answer anything. What do you want to know?"

"Have they?" The interrogator continued, "Have they found her?"

"Yes," Petric said in a small voice. "The Rock Eater has her."

This was met with considerable murmuring along the walls.

"What do they know about Meriden?" The interrogator continued.

"Nothing," Petric said quickly. "Nothing important."

"He LIES!" Someone yelled shrilly.

"NO, I'm not lying! I mean, I showed them my home, they know about the Rock Eater, the columns, that's all they know."

Another door ground open, and there was a sound of rushing feet.

"Look what they've DONE to her!" It was Brunka, hysterical.

He raced to the long table and laid the bloody, ruined Nezka upon it. Severed dying siphon filaments still lolled out of her mouth, and she emitted strangled noises as she attempted to breathe around them.

"YOU did this Petric!" Brunka roared, advancing on the prisoner.

Petric shouted accusations back at Brunka, but the room had already erupted in chaos.

They closed around him. Knowing what to expect only worsened the agony of the experience itself.

My Alzbeda, was all he kept saying to himself, as his life was pulled from him through a thousand tiny straws.

And the last thing Petric heard before all his thoughts ceased forever was Brunka shouting maniacally, "NO, NOT NEZKA, NOT NEZKA!"

The wailing and raging went long into the night.

Chapter Thirty-Nine
ABOVE GROUND

——————

"You actually got her!" Arden exclaimed breathlessly as he, Ohlen, Ruprecht and Boudreaux came upon Gnome, X'andria, and the inanimate Alzbeda.

"We need to move now," Ohlen said tersely.

"What's up Ohlen?" Gnome asked. But the answer came in the form of an earsplitting wail from the mountainside.

"Bring her," Ohlen told Arden who was standing next to him, and uncharacteristically Ohlen took the lead plunging forward into the forest.

The noises behind them were of violent destruction. Roaring and rampaging, the Rock Eater must have been tearing up the field and trees hunting for them—for her.

On they stumbled, branches whipping their faces, tripping over unseen obstacles on the forest floor, fighting through brambles—anything to put as much distance as possible between them and the fearsome Rock Eater.

The wailing and raging went long into the night. But eventually they decided their forest cover was deep enough to slow and rest.

"What is that swirling around her?" Ruprecht was the first to speak the following morning.

They all looked, but no one knew.

"How are you feeling Boudreaux?" X'andria asked. Boudreaux looked like he'd aged about fifteen years.

"It was good to sleep," Boudreaux replied somberly. "My mouth is killing me," he mumbled, "it's like I tried to chew a bunch of Arden's arrowheads."

"How about you, X'an?" Gnome spoke up. "She was amazing last night, guys. Carried Alzbeda and climbed down the cliff at the same time."

"An' saved my life." Boudreaux grimaced.

"It was a group effort, folks." X'andria tried to deflect the attention. "Are we ready to get going?"

"Just about," Arden chimed in. "But Ohlen needs to tell us what happened with the rock monster?"

"Yeah!" Gnome agreed. "What happened out there last night?"

Ohlen appeared lost in thought. This, though, was not unusual.

"The Rock Eater is a complicated being," Ohlen began. "I believe we have not understood it properly." He looked around at his beleaguered friends. "While I certainly do not know all there is to know, I learned three things. I learned it can be gentle. I learned it can be merciful. And I learned that it cares deeply for this Meriden here."

"I wish you two could have seen it," Ruprecht added enthusiastically. "The Rock Eater was heading back toward you when Arden raced out and got its attention. Then there we all were, out there, facing it, ready to fight or something. And Ohlen just walked right up to it," Ruprecht shook his head. "It grabbed him and he disappeared for a while, and when he came back out it was like they were friends, and it let us just walk away."

"Given Alzbeda's disappearance, I doubt very much it would let us walk away again," Ohlen said gravely.

"What's a bud muck?" Gnome asked. They all looked at him.

"A what?" Arden queried.

"A bud muck. Alzbeda woke up for a second last night and said 'bud muck.'" Gnome explained.

X'andria laughed. "I know," she said teasingly. "Does anyone else?"

No one knew.

"Well first of all, she didn't say 'bud muck,'" X'andria explained patiently, "Alzbeda said 'Bodomek.'"

"Loverboy!" Boudreaux exclaimed, but immediately winced and brought his right hand up to his lips as if he had just bit his tongue.

"Boudreaux!" X'andria was clearly surprised and impressed, "That's exactly right. Bodomek was the boy Petric told us about who loved Alzbeda and couldn't have her and was so upset about it that he threw himself off the bridge."

"Did she say anything else?" Ruprecht asked.

"She just held up her arms and cried 'my hands' and then said "Bo-do-mek' and then went back to sleep," Gnome explained, holding his own arms up in front of his face.

Chapter Thirty-Nine

"There is only one place he could be," Ruprecht replied darkly, massaging his chest through his brown robes with the fingers of his left hand. "X'andria," he asked, "Do you have a spare bit of parchment I might use?"

There were two eyes, but only one of them opened.

Chapter Forty
THE CAVE

"Someone needs to stay here with Alzbeda," Gnome suggested.

"I'll stay," Boudreaux offered, looking at the ground.

X'andria piped up, "You know what? I'll stay too. I'm sure you four can handle Bodomek, and Boudreaux and I will hold things down here with Alzbeda." She seemed reflective looking down at Boudreaux's hulking but somewhat deflated form.

"Done." Gnome agreed. "We'll find the Bodomek—if that's really what Ruprecht and Ohlen were feeling with their special feelings— see if it's got Alzbeda's hands, and meet you back here."

"What are we supposed to do with the hands?" Arden asked.

"She will know," Ohlen—looking down at Alzbeda's mist-encased body—sounded confident.

Chapter Forty

With Gnome out front, Arden, Ohlen and Ruprecht crept through the thick eastern forest toward the main path between the bridge and the Meriden colonnade. They would need to cross the path and head west under the cover of the trees to pick up the scrappy trail south of Meriden that Arden had found the afternoon before—the faithless place to which Ruprecht had been drawn, and where Ohlen had recognized the emanations of darkness.

Just before they arrived at the main path, however, they heard whispers and the crackling swishing of foot traffic.

Gnome's fist shot into the air and the foursome stopped instantly.

Creeping along the path toward Meriden was a motley gaggle of farmers. Ohlen recognized scythe man—scythe in hand. There were also several townspeople in grey robes, one of whom had been the driver of their carriage.

Arden made a rash decision, and whistled. It was a short, sharp, piercing sound.

The procession stopped clumsily—some faster than others. A strained silence fell.

"Friends," Arden whispered audibly, and walked forward past Gnome, who was staring at him with an expression somewhere between irritation and admiration.

The farmers and villagers turned and squinted into the trees, gripping their field implements and family weapons tightly.

"You've discovered who has been stealing your children," he proclaimed in a normal but softened voice as he emerged from the wood. Vague recognition flashed across the driver's stoic face.

"Who're you?" scythe man asked aggressively.

"His name is Arden," Ohlen strode out of the wood as well. "And I am Ohlen. We met on the road and you asked about your dear missing children. Do you remember?"

"Course I 'member," scythe man spat. "An' you tol' me you didn't know, an' we foun' out they're up here, an' now here YOU are." The gaggle flexed collectively.

Gnome and Ruprecht stepped tentatively into the open as well.

"We did not take your children," Ohlen said calmly. "But we now know who did."

"Have you seen 'em?" a woman asked shrilly.

"We have," Arden spoke again, his voice sounded defeated and he did not meet her eyes.

"They're gone ain't they?" scythe man muttered, already knowing the answer.

Arden nodded, looking up slowly to meet the old man's sun-wrinkled eyes.

"Monsters," this time it was the carriage driver who spoke.

"Myrtle and Gru, here, came down the mountain the other night pretty upset," the carriage driver indicated a man and woman to his left. The woman, Myrtle, had a nasty gash on her forearm.

"And Nerl," the carriage driver gestured at scythe man, "had visited us in Woodmont earlier that afternoon asking after the farm children, and we just put things together."

"Enough is enough." Myrtle added savagely.

"Do you know what they do?" Ruprecht asked darkly.

They all turned to face him.

"Do you know what the Meridens do?" Ruprecht asked again. "If you are seeking revenge, you best be prepared for what you will be dealing with."

"We've heard stories from our parents and grandparents," Gru replied.

"*We* 'aven't!" Nerl called.

Chapter Forty

And so Arden described—in the best detail he could—all that he had witnessed between Nezka and Boudreaux the night before. Several of the farmers began to cry.

The villagers and farmers wanted to know what the four friends were doing here—if they would join with them in their effort to halt the Meriden tyranny.

"We cannot join you this day, for we have been summoned here on a spiritual quest to face an ancient evil that has taken up residence in this very mountain," Ohlen explained. "It is a dark force we have battled in the earth, in the forest, and by the sea. It has upset the fragile balance of Meriden, and it has played its part in the terrible tragedies you have endured. Face it now, we must, as you seek justice for the wrongs committed against your people."

No one understood anything Ohlen said.

Had it not been Ohlen saying it, the explanation would not have been sufficient. But it was Ohlen, and the steadiness of his words, and the kindness of his presence, convinced them that they were hearing the truth.

So the farmers and villagers snuck forward toward Meriden with new information and greater resolve, and Gnome, Arden, Ohlen and Ruprecht entered the forest on the south side of the path.

"Hang on a minute," Ruprecht asked.

He was feeling increasingly uncomfortable. His head felt foggy and pressurized and his chest was throbbing.

Seating himself on the ground—while Gnome, Arden and Ohlen looked on—Ruprecht fished out of his pocket the corner of yellowed parchment X'andria had given to him.

He spit on the dark soil. He spit again, and again. Gnome's hands were on his hips, Arden was squinting, and Ohlen looked serene with his eyes closed.

Ruprecht stirred his saliva with a little bit of soil using his forefinger and made a dark slurry. Then, using his muddy finger, he painted a symbol on the parchment with three vertical slashes, a few connecting lines, and some dots. *Ma'yabesk.* Protection. It was the knowledge he had gained from The Great One while perched inside Geoffrey's mind.

Satisfied with his rune, Ruprecht stood up—a little unsteadily—and said, "Alright, let's go."

They pressed on through the forest for about an hour. Ohlen felt increasing weariness and dread in the atmosphere. Ruprecht stumbled a few times.

"Here it is," Arden exclaimed suddenly. They had come upon a faint winding footpath.

No sooner had they started down the path than they heard through the trees behind them the now-familiar tormented wail of the Rock Eater.

"That's bizarre," remarked Arden. "We've never heard it during the daytime before."

"Bizarre indeed," Ohlen concurred.

The path meandered on for several minutes before depositing them at the southern border of the forest—it was also the edge of the chasm they had crossed by bridge on the day of their arrival in

Chapter Forty

Meriden.

"Well that's unexpected," Arden exclaimed, backpedaling away from the sheer cliff.

"It is not far now," Ohlen intoned.

Ruprecht nodded once, and looked like he might be ill.

"What's that?" Gnome asked, and scampered left along the rim.

The others followed slowly.

Gnome stood up after examining something small on the ground. He turned with a sour expression on his face and put his finger to his lips in a *be quiet* gesture.

The thing on the ground had been a squirrel. But all that was left was a squirrel-shaped, dried and shriveled husk. Gnome indicated the chasm edge behind it with his head. There was a worn groove where something had clearly traveled up and down with regularity.

The distant Rock Eater's roar sailed over the treetops once more.

Gnome was the first over the edge. The worn dirt path was steep and had slick muddy pockets here and there. Knotted roots were exposed and offered firm footing, but also a chance to catch a toe and go sailing off the cliff.

A short way down the chasm wall, they came upon a small crevice—little more than a crack in the wall. Strewn around the opening were many more desiccated bodies, mostly birds, and several rodents.

Gnome looked back over his shoulder and arched his eyebrow as if to ask, "Are we ready?" He pulled his dagger from its sheath on his thigh and clamped the blade between his teeth.

Gnome slipped inside and was followed quickly by Ohlen and Ruprecht. The smell was noxious. As his eyes adjusted Gnome realized he was standing on more depleted corpses.

Something black, and bony, and shiny slumbered against the far side of the cramped angular cave. The walls themselves were covered with scratched images and symbols.

"BODOMEK!" the call came from behind them outside the cave entrance, just as Arden was trying to squeeze through. "BODOMEK!"

And the slumbering mound stirred. Gnome, Ruprecht, and Ohlen froze. Arden reversed course to prepare for whoever or whatever was coming from behind them.

Glistening slabs of reddish black flesh flailed in a rapid flurry as the creature called Bodomek hoisted and propped itself upright. It lunged on four pole-like bony appendages with thin-stretched sinew snapping taut between them. It shambled toward them, nearly falling from one jaunty step to the next. There were two eyes, but only one of them opened. It was blood red.

Gnome was aghast. It was hard to feel anything but pity for this pathetic creature. Ruprecht, mind burning, lifted his parchment. Ohlen stepped out from behind his friends and unsheathed his sword.

Outside Arden hefted his family weapon in his left hand—best to leave one hand free for balance in this precarious situation. Sliding down the path came Brunka, "We have to GO, Bodomek! Mom's gone. Let's GO!" he yelled.

But then he saw Arden. Brunka stopped abruptly. He stood straight up on the ledge, and hairy wisps began extending out just beyond his fingertips.

Chapter Forty

Bodomek was most concerned with the brown-robed, parchment-holding bearded one. A sword and a dagger were of little concern, after all he'd been through. Siphon filaments belched from his crooked mouth. But these were not the fine hair-like tendrils of his youth. These were matted together in a blood-black rope-like cord that snapped like a giant frog's tongue into the bearded one's stomach, punching him to the ground.

The blades fell upon Bodomek as he knew they would. The short one stuck all the way through a wall of his flesh, the other cleaved off a bone he used for walking. No matter. Bodomek had more flesh, more bones, and he was long past feeling pain.

Brunka advanced slowly and cautiously. It was a long time since he had been in any kind of fight. He preferred his victims to be either children, or to be thoroughly restrained. This human looked to be adept with a sword, but all Brunka needed was to land one siphon filament in his opponent's flesh, and he would be paralyzed and ready for feeding.

Brunka released his right side like a whip, retracted it as fast as possible, and then attacked with his left.

THE CAVE

It was the same foe. Ohlen felt it deep in his soul. The orbs and demon statue beneath the mountain, Elias' book and conjured abomination, and now this rambling sack of skin, bones, and malice, they were all strains of the same terrible disease.

Bodomek turned jerkily, like a bat trying to walk upright, and vomited his ropelike appendage toward Ohlen. Missing the bone-leg Ohlen had cut off, Bodomek fell forward onto what would have been his chin, but he still managed to hit Ohlen's thigh with tremendous force. Ohlen stumbled backward toward the wall.

Bodomek was dimly aware of the dagger sinking repeatedly into more of his other parts.

Arden was not fooled. Perhaps the amateurish fake-with-the-right-side-and-then-go-with-the-left routine would have worked—on a child—but Arden was difficult to fool even by the best of fighters.

Arden swung his left hand deftly across his body, generating just enough power by a right foot plant and pivot to slice through the approaching filaments without committing overmuch. The grotesque flailing threads were severed and spewed a bloody mist into the air, but Arden did not stop to watch them. The assault from the right came quickly after, as he knew it would. Any desperate fighter wounded on the left would follow immediately with an undisciplined strike from the other side.

Arden ducked low, following the weight of his sword forward and then extended fully off his bent right leg exploding up and out to the left. He spun his blade in his hand just before striking Brunka's right arm above the wrist, to ensure a clean cut. Brunka's severed right hand sailed out into the chasm like a comet with its tail arcing behind.

Brunka's last weapon, his oral filaments, might have been a problem had Arden not already seen Nezka's the night before. As if in slow motion, Arden followed the arc and weight of his weapon onward, tucked into a crouch, and extended his left leg as his stroke carried him around in a complete circle. His leg swept Brunka's feet out from under him, and the Meriden fell sideways out into the chasm trailing long hair-like siphons and bloody mist behind him.

Ohlen was down. Gnome took a bony kick to the ribs. Ruprecht, wobbly from having the wind knocked out of him—and from the blood pounding in his head—steadied himself on his knees.

The creature Bodomek lumbered back around to face him—slurping back in it's glistening knotted filament weapon. Ruprecht lunged forward. He landed awkwardly on Bodomek's near side. The creature grunted and cursed, its bony protrusions struggled under the weight of another. Ruprecht reached past the open slurry-red eye for Bodomek's mouth, and stuffed in his piece of parchment while yelling *Ma'yabesk*! Protection.

The rune, crumpled around Ruprecht's fingers, glowed inside of Bodomek's crooked mouth.

Bodomek's body convulsed once and then became rigid and still.

And Ruprecht began to see.

He saw Bodomek the Meriden boy, child of Brunka and Nezka. He felt the forbidden urge to feed. He looked up into Alzbeda's disapproval atop her Altar To The Wind And Sky. He hid his need. He fed in secret. But eventually they found out. It was more than he could bear. Consumed by confusion and guilt, he flung himself from the Meriden Bridge.

But that was not the end for Bodomek. He was given new life and new purpose. It was injected into him by a dark silhouette. And while for years he would not even be able to move, the black oil of his benefactor would slowly pull his splattered pieces back together on the canyon floor. The oil trapped and consumed bugs at first, and later small rodents, and with time converted them into joints and sinew and flesh.

And when at last Bodomek could move, he knew he had but one task. Destroy Alzbeda. And with his parents help he nearly succeeded. The look of horror on her face when she saw him on the altar was delicious. Alzbeda's screams when he cut off her hands—her connections to the wind and sky—exceeded his blackest hopes. But then the rock beast came and took her away before he could finish the job. And it was all Bodomek could do to escape back to his cave clutching his two trophies.

The bearded one was tearing him apart. The black oil that held him together was being expelled—separated from his Meriden flesh. Golden light was scalding him from the inside out.

And then Ruprecht clattered to the floor of the cave atop Bodomek's shriveling remains. Dark fluid retreated into the stone and dirt, and all that remained were splintered bones.

"Hey!" said Gnome, picking himself up off the ground, "Look at this."

Near the wall of the filthy cave, lying amongst cracked bones and rocky debris, were two small hands, deposited several feet apart, each covered in slowly swirling silvery mist.

The wind whipped and tumbled around them.

Chapter Forty-One
THE ALTAR

"I just hate that they've made those people in Woodmont their slaves all these years," X'andria explained to Boudreaux. "They keep two of them locked up at all times just to keep them in line. And for what? So they can get rich and stay up here on their little mountain with their exotic treasures and fancy doors. It's repulsive."

"Yeah," Boudreaux said glumly, staring straight ahead.

X'andria had managed to work herself up. Boudreaux did not seem to share her outrage, however, and she was just beginning to regret the conversation when he continued, "My master used to make me kill the hogs."

X'andria's mind slowed a bit, and she waited.

"He'd just give me a knife and a number. 'Thirteen,' he'd say. Then I'd walk in the pen and start killin' 'em." Boudreaux sighed. "I was skinny and terrible at killin' hogs. And they didn't want to be killed. So you can imagine the racket it made."

X'andria almost said something, but hesitated just long enough for him to keep going. "But he'd whip me no matter what I did, good or bad. I think he just liked whippin' me."

"Oh Boudreaux," X'andria said in a small voice. "I don't think I had any idea about any of this."

"Yeah," he mumbled, "I don't talk about it much."

"How'd you get away?" she asked.

"Funny thing, really. I've never told anyone, but I'll tell you," he looked up and caught X'andria's eye. "I ran away one day. And my master found out and started chasing me. I came onto a lake I'd never seen before, and in it there was this lady. She asked me what I wanted, and the only thing I could think of was *strong*. So she made me strong. When my master caught up to me he was in for a surprise." Boudreaux smiled wryly.

"We found Alzbeda's hands!" Gnome shouted as he, Ruprecht, Ohlen and Arden burst into the little makeshift camp.

"Incredible!" X'andria called back with enthusiasm forced past her visceral personal resonance with Boudreaux's tale of enslavement, and her overwhelming curiosity about his mysterious Lady Of The Lake

Even so, the others had arrived, and so X'andria called brightly, "What happened?"

Over Arden's protestations, Boudreaux elected to carry Alzbeda. Gnome kept the severed hands wrapped up in a length of Arden's

field dressing.

Ohlen's plan was to bring Alzbeda to her altar and let her take it from there.

They were walking briskly down Meriden's main path, figuring ease and speed was more important than secrecy—since they were heading directly to the center of the colonnade in broad daylight anyhow.

"The Rock Eater sure has been active," X'andria remarked after Gnome and Arden finished filling in the details of their encounter with Bodomek and Brunka.

"It really has!" Arden agreed, "And that's pretty unusual for daylight hours."

"It is looking for her," Ohlen offered sagely.

"Oh, we met some villagers from Woodmont and a few of those farmers who had missing children earlier," Gnome mentioned casually. "They looked ready for a fight."

"This could be an interesting day," Boudreaux panted between steps.

A chill remorse rolled over X'andria.

They heard the destruction before they saw it.

Meriden was being obliterated column by column, compartment by compartment, by the Rock Eater. The rear of the beast, which they could now see for the first time, was an enormous stinger that spiked downward like a hammer to crack through the thick Meriden plaza. Broken stone, pieces of columns, furniture, and terrified Meridens were then hauled out by the Rock Eater's many hands and tossed indiscriminately in all directions.

The farmers and villagers they had encountered were cowering in the tree line, mesmerized and horrified by the spectacle.

"It is time," Ohlen assured his friends. "Let us bring her to the altar."

Boudreaux marched forward with Alzbeda in his arms. Jogging to keep up, Gnome followed unwrapping the gruesome pair of hands.

Arden, Ruprecht, Ohlen and X'andria were close behind.

"YOU!" the screech came from the tree line.

It was hard to hear anything because the Rock Eater was still raging through the colonnade, and the air was filled with crashes and screams.

"YOU'RE THE ONE!" Myrtle, the villager with the gash on her forearm, had left the cover of the trees and was running after them.

Boudreaux stepped onto the devastated Meriden plaza. Broken columns and people were littered in all directions. One of the few things left untouched was Alzbeda's Altar To The Wind And Sky. Gnome was right beside him, but the others seemed distracted and had fallen back.

The Rock Eater saw them coming. Two of its many spiked outer legs had impaled unfortunate Meridens. Countless bits of the intricate subterranean city were held along its interior arms. The massive hammer-stinger was poised to crack through another quadrant of the plaza.

But the beast froze for a split second. Then it dropped everything it was holding. Then it roared—bits of crushed column falling from its jaws—and it rushed toward Gnome and Boudreaux at an insane speed.

"YOU did this!" Myrtle finally caught up to them, and grabbed X'andria by the arm.

X'andria spun around, heart pounding, but she had no words.

Ruprecht, Arden, and Ohlen stopped and turned as well.

"There must be some kind of misunderstanding," Arden began.

"Oh no!" Myrtle insisted. "She's the one, Gru!" she screamed, pointing.

Gru arrived. The other villagers were not far behind. X'andria just shook her head and backed slowly away.

"She did THIS to me," Myrtle pressed on, "And she lifted Gru up and held him upside down over the edge of the bridge." Myrtle turned directly to X'andria, "You're a monster!" she cried.

"Is this true, X'andria?"

Ohlen was watching her closely.

Gnome lifted up Alzbeda's hands to the oncoming behemoth. It seemed like the only thing to do.

"We got the HANDS!" he shouted, gesticulating wildly. "Alzbeda's hands! We got them!"

Boudreaux just kept walking toward the altar.

The Rock Eater brought its massive face within feet of them. It seemed determined to watch their every step.

"We're going to the ALTAR!" Gnome yelled, scrambling in front of Boudreaux onto the lowest folds of the sky-blue structure.

The wind began to howl.

It was so unfair. X'andria saw the outrage in the villagers' faces. She saw Arden's and Ruprecht's confusion. She felt Ohlen's concern.

If they had just done what she asked!

She was just trying to help.

X'andria took another step backward. The villagers, still lusting for blood—any blood to avenge their loss—looked on with angry accusation in their wrinkled eyes.

She had worked so hard. She deciphered the scroll. She saved Boudreaux's life!

"Just tell us what happened, X'andria." Ohlen's patient voice was nothing more than a rehearsed mask for his disapproval. She knew it.

Fumbling in her pack, X'andria took a few more steps backward.

"Oh no you don't!" Myrtle cried, and she began to run—followed by Gru, and Nerl with his scythe.

Arden was running, too, swords drawn, shouting them down.

X'andria pulled free Elias' invisibility cloak and threw it over herself. She disappeared from view. She vanished from their sight— no longer an object for their derision.

And she ran away.

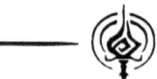

Boudreaux laid Alzbeda gently at the top of the altar. Gnome placed her severed hands on her stomach. They backed slowly away.

The wind whipped and tumbled around them.

Apparently satisfied, the Rock Eater retreated a short distance and watched carefully, ignoring the many moans and cries coming from shocked and wounded Meridens above ground and below.

With a sucking gasp Alzbeda woke up. The shielding mist surrounding her melted away into the atmosphere. She cried out in pain, and both Gnome and Boudreaux could see that her wounds had begun to bleed afresh.

Even so, she stood. It was hard to watch, as she had to use her forearms for support to get up. The severed hands rolled off her and landed on the altar.

Wind frenzied. And even as unsteady as she appeared to be, Alzbeda started to sway. She lifted her arms before her and began dancing slowly, rhythmically.

The altar began to glow. It was as if a bit of the sunlight in the sky was shining up from beneath them.

Alzbeda painted symbols in the air. Golden sparkling streaks flowed behind her motions like shooting stars. Her severed hands lifted into space before her, and the gold flowed around them, guiding them back to their places on her body.

Alzbeda's wrists fused back together, and the seams shone with thin lines of vibrant electric blue.

It was so spectacular, so otherworldly, that Gnome and Boudreaux did not even notice the shouts and anguished pleas coming from their friends in the field to the south.

The hardest part was yet to come.

EPILOGUE

X'andria had an idea.

About two weeks had passed since she last saw her friends in the Meriden fields. For days and days she had heard their shouts as they looked for her. Boudreaux ranged the farthest and yelled the loudest, but it was the occasional mournful entreaties from Gnome that pulled hardest on her heartstrings.

But, ruby rolling compulsively back and forth between her forefinger and thumb, X'andria had sunk deeper and deeper into her inner sanctuary of conviction.

Throughout her life she had only ever truly been able to count on one person. Herself. Her mother had not been able to protect her from the fat slaver. The Alchemist had sought to own her accomplishments and claim them as his own. Elias had betrayed her. Even her friends, her dear Gnome, were well meaning but did not seem to understand and truly support her need for freedom. Ohlen, it seemed to X'andria, had come to despise her ascent to mastery—or perhaps he was just jealous.

No. It was time for X'andria to strike out on her own. To free herself from the restrictions holding her away from knowledge, keeping her from possession of the power that would ensure she would never be subservient to anyone ever again.

Eventually the voices cracked and faded, and this gave X'andria room to think less about being discovered and more about her own development.

And now she had an idea.

X'andria was good at lifting and moving objects, at spontaneously making fire, and even causing wounds with her mind. These exertions of concentration and will were extreme, to be sure, but she was getting better at it. She was gaining capacity.

What she wanted now was to be able to switch quickly or even combine her skills. Fumbling between her gold loop, and her little silk bag of flint, parchment and ash, or the rune scroll and dart with Myrtle's blood and tears, was unwieldy at best. Most costly was the focus sapped from her mind as she put away one component and selected another.

The branch would have to be perfectly straight. When held, it would have to fit her hand precisely. It would need to be hard but resilient, perhaps recent growth from an ancient tree.

An ancient host for ancient wisdom, X'andria thought as she wandered further into the mountain forest looking for the oldest tree.

Massive roots arced serpentine out of the rich, black soil before plunging back into the earth. The base of the poplar formed its own ecosystem with shelves of earth and wood. It was surrounded by a winding network of bark-armored roots, and hanging, spongy, parasitic striations of moss, vines, and mushrooms all fighting and feeding one another in the cool, damp, sheltered darkness of the prehistoric giant.

X'andria spent several hours picking her way around and through the many nooks and crannies. She dirtied her fingers as she grasped and squished the moist growth she encountered along the way.

On the far side of the tree, the trunk formed a deep fold that— upon closer examination—X'andria realized she could squeeze between. The space within was cramped indeed, but it provided X'andria her first secure shelter since her desperate departure from Meriden.

Feeling determined and excited for the day to come, X'andria hugged her knees to her chest and allowed herself to doze off encircled by the ancient and curving woody walls.

Morning light filtered through the thick high canopy and roused X'andria from what had become a long and deep slumber. Pushing awkwardly down and out into the boundaries of her tightly confined chamber, X'andria managed a standing position and stepped creakily out into the forest stillness.

Hands on her hips, X'andria squinted up at the countless limbs extending in every direction high above her.

So many choices, she thought, *and how am I supposed to know which one, unless I bring them all down here?*

It was midday when, neck aching, X'andria struck on a new idea.

A root, she pondered, *maybe a root is better than a branch, deeper, more connecting.*

And so she set about scanning the network of massive undulating roots beneath and around her feet. She followed each one until its final dive into the earth. Seating herself upon narrowest and furthest-ranging candidate, X'andria located her gold loop and endeavored to pull it out of the ground.

She was not successful.

Brain searing from effort and concentration, X'andria collapsed after her fifth and final attempt to lift the leviathan from its resting place. Due to all the recovery time needed between each effort, darkness was now beginning to fall.

Frustrated, X'andria returned to her hiding place and slept once more. It was a fitful, dream-addled slumber this time, filled with snaking vines and suffocating earth.

The next two days she spent excavating, gold loop in her left hand, ruby rolling ceaselessly in her right. All day, whenever she had the strength to do so, X'andria would send dirt flying in all directions as though small explosions were detonating along the diving, snaking, dividing root system.

Finally, on the fourth day, she spotted it. Deep in the hole she had created, the root branched yet again and produced precisely what she had been looking for.

Long past caring about cleanliness, X'andria jumped into the damp dirty hole and started sawing at the root with her hunting knife. Minutes later she held a perfectly straight section of root, it was about as long as her forearm, about half as wide, slightly bigger around at one end, and narrowing toward the other.

X'andria placed her prize on the floor of her muddy crater. Standing, and leaning back against the dirt, she extracted her silk bag containing flint, parchment and ash.

Just a little to dry and seal, she thought, as she willed the wooden rod into flames.

The wet, and until-recently living tissue whistled and popped in the flames. Its thin brown skin peeled and shrank away leaving only the white core. Gently but firmly X'andria rolled the burning rod in the wet dirt and doused the flames into hissing smoke.

That night she went to sleep feeling triumphant, clutching her dried and clean rod tight. Her dreams, however, were even more turbulent than the night before.

On the fifth day, X'andria worked feverishly with her hunting knife and one of her clean darts, to hollow out the thick end of her prize. Twice she slipped and gouged the fingers of her left hand, but she ignored the pain and the mess. She also kind of liked the blotchy stains her blood left on the shaft.

Once she was satisfied with the hollowed cavity, she sank her hunting knife hard into the trunk of the ancient tree. Golden, sticky, piney, sap seeped out of the wound. X'andria collected it on her blade and mixed it with the tiny shavings from her rod to make a grainy pulp. She then pulled her small silk bag out of her grimy robe, carefully removed her three fire components, and gingerly inserted each—the tiny piece of flint, the small square of parchment, and the bit of ash—into the hollow end of her rod. This she sealed with the sticky, sappy, pulp.

On the sixth day X'andria awoke in a sweat feeling nearly as tired as she had when she went to sleep the night before. To the vines and suffocating earth of her dreams had been added blood, and fire.

Undeterred, however, X'andria spent the entire day making a shallow and precise groove traveling along the length of her rod. The groove made a tight turnaround before the tip, and then ran in parallel back to the base to link up with its beginning. Into this groove she molded and inserted her gold loop. She then stabbed the enormous tree once more and filled the space around her loop with sticky sap. With this accomplished, X'andria gripped the base of her rod, and willed the sap to ignite into flame, cauterizing the seal.

EPILOGUE

X'andria awoke on the seventh day in an anxiety-ridden terror. Her mind had been assaulted all night long with visceral experiences of burying and stabbing and burning.

But she had work to do. The hardest part was yet to come.

With the same dart she had used to hollow out the thick end of the rod. She now began drilling into the thinner tip. This was slow, painstaking work, and she hunched at it without ceasing into the early afternoon hours. Once the thin hole was finally deep enough, X'andria removed the drilling dart.

Next she produced the dart dipped in Myrtle's blood and tears. Holding this dart's tear-drop shaped shaft down with her foot against a particularly large exposed root, X'andria sawed on the base of the metal tip with her hunting knife. After much grunting, slipping, cursing, and aching, the awkward job was finished.

It was dusk and X'andria had not even eaten yet today. But she did not stop.

With all her care and focus, X'andria inserted the vicious Myrtle-stained dart tip into the tiny hole at the narrow end of her rod. Ever so gently she tapped on the end with the handle of her hunting knife, until the metal shaft disappeared flush into the tip of its root host.

Almost there, X'andria thought wearily.

Drilling dart in hand once more, she drew its point across her own forearm. If there was any pain, she was hardly aware. X'andria then dipped the point of the dart into her own welling blood and began to draw a series of tiny crimson slashes and points on her precious root. *Shra'muhrjnik*, wound, she thought with a fevered smirk.

Last thing, she thought, heart racing.

She raised her hunting knife to stab the giant tree one last time.

Then stalled.

She dropped the knife carelessly to the ground.

Then X'andria lifted her rod instead.

Shra'muhrjnik. Wound. She rasped out, drawing the decorated white rod through the air before her.

A huge gash appeared on the side of the tree trunk. Bark bits scattered into the air around her. Immediately the tree's sap blood began to flow.

With a flick of her rod, X'andria lifted the hunting knife, handle first, into to her outstretched hand. Turning the knifepoint against the thick handle of her rod she made a small, round indention. Into the indention she inserted her precious red ruby.

Finally, X'andria bathed her rod, her ruby, her bloody rune, her gold loop, her Myrtle dart, and her fire components in the free flowing life blood of the ancient poplar. She sealed them all together with a short burst of searing blue-hot flame.

And it was from this place of blood, dirt, exhaustion and obsession, that X'andria noticed the silver mist. At first it seemed like just a bit of fog. But this fog moved strangely, heavily, purposefully. The mist rolled toward her. It tumbled into the blasted-out hole she had excavated, and emerged on the other side.

X'andria turned and realized it was all around.

And coming soon

DORMARION

BOOK FOUR OF TINDER & FLINT

By
Matthew Hinsley

Art by
Billy Garretsen

A special preview...

The knight would survey the scene slowly, before lifting the head of some unfortunate victim for all to see—a new trophy for the line of spikes surrounding the castle wall.

Chapter One
SHADOWLAND

For some reason the milky white, yellow-veined nocturnal grubs tasted slightly better than the black ones that scoured the drying blistering earth during the heat of day. More meat and less leg, he supposed. Young Olssen had discovered the white ones on accident. Venturing a single step gingerly in the dead of night, his toes had squished through the drenched mud onto the back of a fat wriggling albino blob. He'd been starving, and without a second thought his hand stabbed through the muck, grasped the slippery foot-sized scavenger, and brought it—mud and all—directly up to his lips and teeth.

Before dawn—if that's what you could call the oven-hot fire-red sun-baked madness that erupted across the sky each morning—Young Olssen worked himself deep into the muddy earth. This way he could pass the daytime less exposed to the scorching heat, and remain undiscovered by the black winged lizards littering the red sky searching and shrieking, and the hunched slobbering pig men who whipped the living and carried off the dead.

I sure showed them, Young Olssen often caught himself thinking. He replayed the scenes in his mind over and over again, his dad looking embarrassed, his friends making jokes, as he insisted red-faced and shaking, that he had seen a pig monster in the woods outside of Westover.

They're probably all dead, now, he assumed. A few more slaves had arrived in this dreadful place after his group, but then—for whatever reason—they stopped coming.

His group had come through the portal under the mountain into the heat of day. Hannah and Peter in front of him were crying and stumbling. The pigs pulled and prodded them forward, up and out of a hot crater of cracked mud, before urging them across the ugly and barren terrain. They had scarcely begun their march along level ground when roiling grey clouds appeared on the distant horizon. As darkness fell, and huge drops of ice-cold water began pounding down from above, Young Olssen noticed that the clasp on the single shackle binding his left wrist to the chain of prisoners was not securely closed.

The march lasted two brutally hot days and two frozen wet nights. Sometime in the middle of that second night—fingernails bent and bleeding—Young Olssen managed to crack open the tenuous clasp. He wasted no time, and dashed sideways, slipping and sliding into darkness and a kind of bizarre ironic freedom.

The castle might have been beautiful. It was certainly enormous and sprawling with elements of stone and metal and wood. But there were no trees or grasses or shrubs. Those, Young Olssen had realized, were nowhere to be found in this awful place. And most striking about the castle was that its behemoth angular foundation jutted outward and upward beyond the soil. Each night the torrential rains washed huge volumes of bake-dried dirt from beneath the giant stone platform. Parts of the foundation itself had cracked off in the absence of earthen support.

And he supposed that's why they needed the slaves.

All day, every day, the slaves—chained by one ankle to huge stone blocks placed at regular intervals around the perimeter—shoveled earth back up the steep slopes in a futile attempt to replenish the soil shrinking away from the castle.

Covered in his hole a safe distance away Young Olssen saw the flying sentinels bring more stone from afar for retaining walls, he saw slaves pass out and perish from stress, and starvation and heat, he saw the pigs alternately whipping, feeding, and barking orders at the slaves and each other, and once in a while, he'd seen a knight in black armor appear stoically on the edge of the crumbling foundation. The knight would survey the scene slowly, before lifting the head of some unfortunate victim for all to see—a new trophy for the line of spikes surrounding the castle wall.

Several hellish weeks had passed. Young Olssen had come to understand the rhythm of the castle's brutal operations. He had seen terrible suffering. And one word had come to dominate his waking moments.

Enough.

ABOUT THE AUTHOR

Matthew Hinsley loves a story you can crawl right into, one that grabs hold and won't let go until the ride is over. He likes heroes you can root for, who do things you might do. He doesn't like villains at all...

He and his wife Glenda live in Austin, Texas.

ABOUT THE ARTIST

Billy Garretsen is an established video game designer and artist with over 100 game credits for mobile, console and PC. He loves to make art, music, and creating exciting worlds and characters. He has a terrible soft spot for '80s cartoons and fantasy.

CPSIA information can be obtained
at www.ICGtesting.com
Printed in the USA
LVHW111709041218
599236LV00003B/472/P